Horace G. Hutchinson

The Golfing Pilgrim on Many Links

Horace G. Hutchinson

The Golfing Pilgrim on Many Links

ISBN/EAN: 9783337288181

Printed in Europe, USA, Canada, Australia, Japan

Cover: Foto ©Andreas Hilbeck / pixelio.de

More available books at **www.hansebooks.com**

THE GOLFING PILGRIM

THE
GOLFING PILGRIM

ON MANY LINKS

BY

HORACE G. HUTCHINSON

METHUEN & CO.
36 ESSEX STREET W.C.
LONDON
1898

PREFATORY NOTE

PORTIONS of this Pilgrimage have been published before in *Golf*, the *Golfing Annual*, *Harper*, *Blackwood*, and *Murray*, and two incidents are borrowed from *Macmillan* and the *Cornhill*. For the leave to use all these the writer's thanks are due and gratefully given.

CONTENTS

THE PROLOGUE

FELLOW-PILGRIMS

IF any golfer ever reads the " Pilgrim's Progress," it is scarcely possible for him to help regretting that John Bunyan was not a golfer. There, at hand, or beneath his feet, would have been found such a wealth of allegory. Even the poor ordinary golfer, who has given names to the features of links, has seemed inspired with some small measure of his genius. At the " long hole going out," do we not struggle on to the blessed " Elysian Fields " after cruel peril of " that parlously named bunker Hell," in which lurk monsters of many shapes, from Giant Despair to Apollyon the Destroyer ? But the imagery has not been half exhausted. That very company to which John Bunyan intro-duces us, do we not meet them all, and recognise them as old friends upon the links ? Who does not know, only too well, Mr Talkative—talkative in season and out of season, on the stroke, and in the club ? Who has not laughed in cruel triumph, with Mr Faint-heart as his opponent ? And who has not cursed him, by all the gods of Golf, when mated with him as a partner. And Feeble-mind, and Presumption and Simple, do we not know them all? We only wish we could catch the last-named a little more often. And there is Mr Obstinate and Mr Pliable, and the "man with the muck-rake" or putter, who goes crawling round all the bunkers when he might win a splendid crown—or at least half-a-crown—by boldly flying over them. And Mr Despondency is always with us, and all his family, namely, Mr Never-up, Mr Bad-lie, Mr Hard-luck, and Mr "I can't hole it." And besides all these there is Mr Heel and Mr Toe, Mr Pull and Mr Slice, Mr Top and Mr Sclaff, and Mr Baff, to say nothing of Mr Miss-the-Globe, whom we all know. They are a noble company to go golfing with, and all our friends. And amongst them we may now and then find a Mr Great-heart, a Mr Far-and-sure, and Mr Lay-them-dead, with whom we may struggle on through all the valleys of humiliation, and win the match at last. There are also Mr Filthy-lucre, Mr Match-maker, and Mr Cannot-count, but these we need not reckon in the rank of friends. We may pass them by, if we cannot redeem them, and leave them to some giant or monster or Slough-of-Despond. Mr Facing-both-ways we meet on every putting green. "Oh, I'm so sorry," he says, as he lays you a stimy.

"Serve him jolly well right" you know is what his true face is expressing. "He's had all the luck so far; time I had some." This Mr Facing-both-ways has a less courteous brother (his is a very large family), who says in like circumstances, "Oh, it isn't a stimy,—there's lots of room—you can't miss it." You believe him just as much as you believe the dentist, who tells you that "it won't hurt." As soon as you have played and missed it, you will very likely hear him say to his partner, "Oh, I knew he couldn't hole it; I don't think it was on." Then he comes up to you with all the sympathy of the crocodile and says, "It's great rubbish, you know; stimies ought to be abolished; don't you think so?" After that it is a thousand to one you miss your tee-shot. There is a great deal to be done in little ways of this sort, and it is thus that Mr Golfer Wiseman lays up his inheritance.

John Bunyan was a tinker, so he ought to have been able to strike the ball a good blow. At all events he would have made the sparks fly out of a good many golfers we know of. Mr Facing-both-ways is an interesting study when he gets a very vain golfer into his toils, and what golfer is not very vain? He beats you, and then he says, "Well, you know, you ought to have won that match. You did win it really, you know; you'd be certain to win it another time. Morally speaking you did win it, but, yes, you owe me half-a-crown." So you go out and play him a second round, with the result that you soon owe him another. See him again with a very long driver opposed to him. He comes up to the long driver as they approach the tee, and says to him, indifferently, "By Jove, I saw young Jehu"—our long-driving friend's especial rival in length of carry—" drive a tremendous ball here yesterday. It went right on and on over that far hill yonder "—he points to one about a quarter of a mile off. As a matter of fact, young Jehu was not playing Golf yesterday, so of course Mr Facing-both-ways never saw him, nor could any human Jehu drive as far as the said hill, but our long driver does not realise this, and grunts and puffs and presses to show Mr Facing-both-ways how much further he can drive than young Jehu's "boasted force," and of course misses the ball almost altogether, and Mr Facing-both-ways is happy.

There is also another dreadful bad character at Golf, whom John Bunyan does not mention, Mr For-ever Scribbling-about-it. We wish to goodness we could hear rather less of him, but he goes all the journey with us.

"A POTTERING, old man's game, that golf!" says, in scorn, the cricketer.

"I like St Andrews," a lady told me lately. "I like it for the children; golf's such a nice game for children!"

Now, do you, O golfing pilgrim, under stress of such criticism, endure it with that equanimity which is so essential a quality if you would become worthy of the great name you bear—nay, rather accept it as the highest, though involuntary, testimony to the merits of the pursuit you love, to that Royal and Ancient Game which, as these would-be carpers testify, you may play even from the cradle to the grave. And as to whether it is a game with any claims on youth and strength, I will appeal to you, O Cricketer, to mark the enthusiasm with which it is pursued by many highly graced with these good gifts. I will beg you to look at the exhibition of them, as every muscle of the human frame is strained to smite that ridiculously elusive little lump of gutta-percha, the potent source of so many joys and sorrows, which we call "golf ball."

Whenever you ask a professional teacher of this

wonderful game for all ages and all seasons how his latest novice is progressing, the stereotyped answer upon these occasions is a laconic "most surprisin'!"—a formula which, while it sounds most flattering, may be construed much according to your fancy. There can, however, be no possible doubt about the construction of this expression as applied to the progress in England, during recent years, of the Royal and Ancient Game of Scotland. It is probable that twenty years ago there were not as many Englishmen with any adequate idea of the game as there now are Golf Clubs well established in England. It is true that the annals of the Blackheath Club go farther back than those of any other Golf Club in England or Scotland; but in England, Blackheath stood alone. Blackheathens of to-day will perhaps pardon the suggestions that this may in some measure account for the slow progress of the game in England, for, at Blackheath, golf is pleasure under difficulties, such as flintstones, nursery-maids, lamp-posts, and perambulators. Yet, when golf was inaugurated at Westward Ho! where the new life of English golf started, the old Club came nobly forward to foster the youngling, presenting to the Westward Ho! Club one of its earliest challenge prizes— yclept the "Blackheath Badge," whence he who wins it earns, *ipso facto*, the proud title of "Black-

heath Badger" for the ensuing year. Then followed the institution of the Royal Liverpool Club
at Hoylake, and, in their turn, a host of others.

Yet, in spite of all competition, and the fact
that it is far from faultless as a golf links, there is,
still, no place to the golfer like St Andrews. Be
driven in desperation, by the hard lies and bumps
which insult your ball, to take refuge at Carnoustie, more accessible now that the Tay Bridge
is built than in the days when, as an old golfer
said on that troublous journey, "You need to be
awful sober to travel in this country;" go, I say,
to Carnoustie, one of the best golfing greens on
the east of Scotland; go to Hoylake, where the
greens, when in condition, are so true and glassy
that the ball of the skilful "putter" seems to steer
its way towards the hole by motive intelligence of
its own, like those ships of the Phæacians which
Homer tells us of; go to Sandwich, where are
mighty "carries" that appal the heart—go even to
Westward Ho! whereof it is but my duty, seeing
it is my native heath, to put on record my conviction that it is the finest green in the whole wide
world;—go where you will, the soul of the golfer
that is in you will hanker to be back among the
rubs and hardships of the royal and ancient links.

What is it in the place? Who can say?

Well, partly it is that Nature has so laid down

the bunkers that the holes can conveniently be placed at such distances apart that they can be just reached by two—or three, as the case may be —good shots by a fairly skilful player. But there is a far subtler influence than this at work. The breath of the *genius loci* is upon you and around you ; and as you draw near St Andrews, whether in the train, whence you look forth upon the golfers on the links beside you, or on the drive from Leuchars, in course of which the grey old towers of the historical University town show themselves in their best aspect, there steals upon you the indefinable spell of this all-pervading *genius loci*, who is the patron saint of golf.

What "Lord's" is to cricket, St Andrews is to golf. On his first visit to St Andrews the young golfer feels as if he were setting his foot on Olympus, with all the demigods holding holiday in their high places. There he meets the heroes whose names have been to him words to conjure with ; meets them in the flesh, those great ones of the generations before him. There he may chance to find that golfer who took out all the professionals of a past day, and beat them, one by one ; announcing, as the final and great result of this ever-famous achievement, that "the way to beat a professional is *never to let him get a hole up.*" He will meet men renowned in theology, in letters, in

arms; will meet them upon the terms of friendship, if not always of equality, on which men meet
in the rivalry of golf.

How absorbing is the interest there taken in the
royal and ancient game! The question of the day
is not how the Eastern question has been settled,
not what are the latest amenities that have passed
in "the first legislative assembly in the world," but
who has won such and such a match? It is not confined to sex, to age, or to station. Youth and beauty,
grey hairs and fustian jackets jumble forward to witness the final putt, while eager eyes look forth from
the Club window and from every window round.

"What sort of man is So-and-so?" the stranger
will ask, coming to St Andrews; and will be
sorely puzzled when, instead of information anent
the social qualities of the So-and-so indicated, he
hears in reply: "Oh, I can give him about a half."

Yes, it is that—the absorbing interest that is
taken in it — that makes golf what it is at St
Andrews; makes it what it is nowhere else.
There is a deal of human nature in the golfer.
Indeed, there is no pursuit, perhaps, which brings
human weaknesses so readily to the surface, none
which so imperatively demands coolness and
command of temper.

The safety valves which the golfer has invented
for getting rid of excess of this latter combustible

are numerous and ingenious. Some break their
clubs over their knee, others throw them in pursuit
of the ball.   There was one gentleman [1] whose
caddie used to carry amongst his set of clubs an
old umbrella, and when his master got into a
"bunker" would hand him his "niblick," as he
descended into the Avernus, and placing the old
gamp in a corner of the bunker, would retire to
watch the course of events. Events, under these
circumstances, might shape themselves into either
of two courses. If the gentleman got his ball out
of the bunker with the first stroke, the caddie
came forward, gathered up the umbrella, and the
game proceeded. But if the ball did not come
forth on the first intent, then, by perilously ac-
quired experience, the caddie knew his master's
disposition to tend towards destruction with the
niblick of the first object that his attention
favoured. This, under due precautions, taken as
described, would be the umbrella; after the de-
molition of which the rage would have come out
of the golfer without injury to any sentient thing.

Then, besides the golfer irascible, you will find
the golfer despondent ; he of whom you will be
told "he cannot play a losing game ; you have
only to win the first two holes and you are bound

[1] For information in this regard, see the section on "Early
Pilgrims in the West."

to beat him." Win the first two holes and keep them is always a good rule at golf.

Then there is the golfer excuseful—he who takes it as a personal matter that a lark should sing in the firmament while he misses his putt. As many types, in fact, as there are in human nature, and possibly a few more, are brought into salient prominence in course of playing this most royal and ancient game of golf; it would tax the analytical genius of an Aristotle to even name them all.

Nor less diverse or noteworthy are the physical styles in which the golfer makes his addresses to the little ball which is so hard to hit. From the Club window you look forth upon a whole forest of golf clubs, weirdly gesticulating in response to cataleptic movements of the human frame. In the accompanying diagram the figure R. H. U. is not hurling the heavy hammer, as might be supposed, but is at precisely the same crisis of the golfing swing as the figure J. H. J. Figures A. F. M. and J. E. L. do but illustrate a slight difference in opinion among the very *élite* of the golfing faculty as to the ideal attitude for the putt. Even the figure H. S. C. E. is not an illustration of the creature known to naturalists as the Praying Mantis, nor of the Leaf Insect, but an accurate representation of the human form divine as contorted by one of our most excellent and consistent golfers in the agonies

of addressing himself to a driving stroke. There
is, indeed, a golfer who has met with some share of
success, and whose figure I should indicate by the
letters H. G. H., to whose contortions, if what one
hears be true, those here portrayed are not a circumstance : yet as I have never seen him play a
stroke, I am compelled to acknowledge myself
unable to do him justice.

Then, besides its styles and its tempers, St
Andrews has its seasons. About midsummer the
"boy" season is at its height. St Andrews is a
great place for education (did not that famous lady
who was in a class by herself at a certain Cambridge Tripos, acquire some, at least, of her erudition at St Andrews?), and in the summer
weather the name of boy at St Andrews is legion
—boy light-heartedly scalping divots from the turf
with a profusion that no links of more truly golfing
—i.e. of more sandy—quality could withstand.
From among these boys will arise the medal
winners of the future. Do they not even now
rate all and sundry in strict accordance with their
altitude on the golfing scale? How well I can
remember, as a boy, at Westward Ho ! the awe and
reverence with which I and my contemporaries used
to look upon the medal winner even in that corner
of the golfing world ! How proud we would be
for days did he but shake hands with us or speak

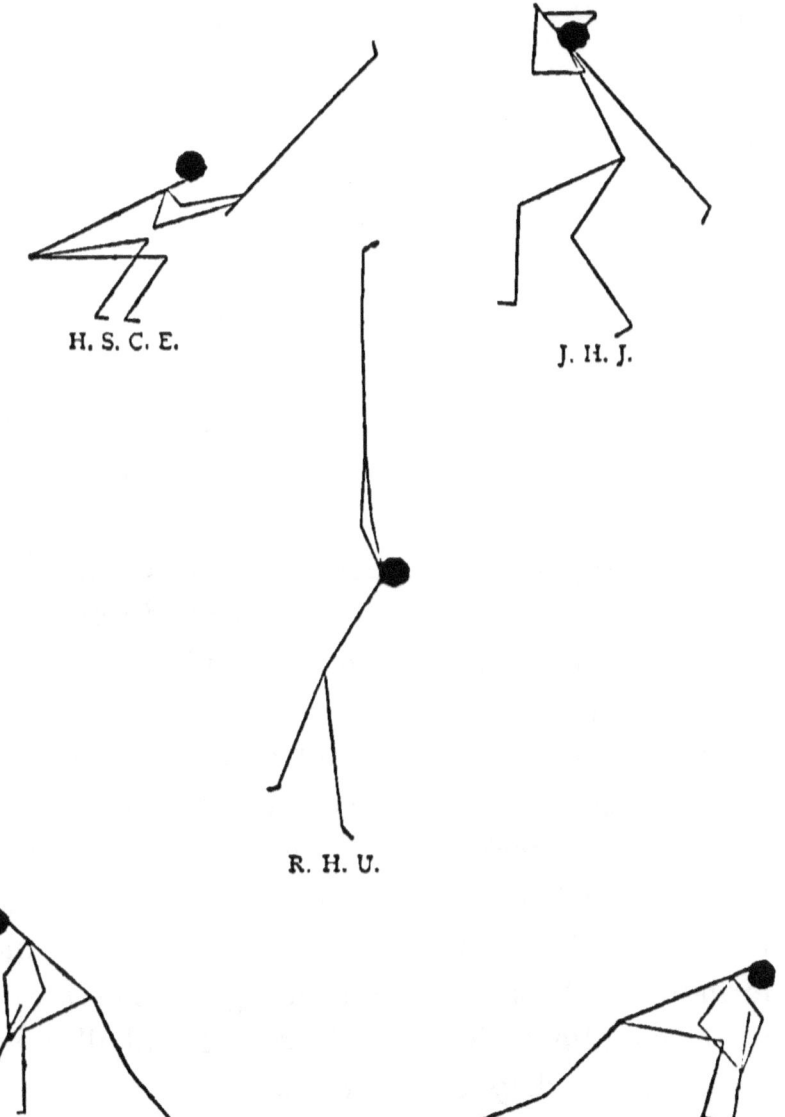

H. S. C. E.

J. H. J.

R. H. U.

A. F. M

J. E. L.

to us ; and if he deigned to praise our stroke, our cup was indeed full to overflowing!   Possibly we were specially gifted as hero-worshippers ; but I rather fancy the quality is common to most boys —and happy that it is so.

Then, after a time, the boys go home, to enliven the family circle, and the " visitor " season sets in, the season *par excellence*.   Then it is, in August and September, that there is congestion on the links—parties waiting in large coveys at the High Hole, sitting on those seats which a beneficent committee set up for us in the year of Jubilee ; for golfers from every links in Scotland and England have come to the golfing Mecca to do homage to St Andrew's shrine.   In and out between the parties, with no recognised existence—no number, that is to say, on the starter's list—dodge occasional survivals of the " boy " season, carrying their lives in their hands, together with the two decrepit clubs which form their stock-in-trade, in hot pursuit of a care-worn ball almost invisible from age and ill-usage. Forcibly do they bring to mind that system of " running a wild cat " which is in vogue on American railways, and consists in driving a train which dodges from station to station, without recognised hours of arrival and departure, whenever the line is unoccupied.

Among the visitors there is distinguishable a strong legal element, dignitaries of the Scottish bench and bar giving gratuitous judgment and counsel on the subject of a ticklish putt.

Indifferent to most things on earth, or elsewhere, the keenness of the caddies in the game of golf is marvellous. On summer evenings at St Andrews you may see them congregated about the short holes in front of the Club, following, with absorbed interest, a putting match between two, or four, of their number, until it is too dark to see ball or hole. As you dress yourself in the morning you see them driving practice shots down towards the burn. But the great lounge of the caddies is the corner by the Golf Hotel, where the road turns down from Golf Place—how the very names proclaim the all-importance of the royal and ancient game ! There the caddies analyse the comparative failings of their respective masters, with a keen partisanship which does not preclude the utmost freedom of discussion. The golf caddie has probably unequalled opportunities as a student of human nature, yet it is perhaps less from the use he makes of these than from his very unusual facility of graphic description that his conversation, if not from every point of view strictly edifying, is full of entertainment of a certain sort.

Wishing to identify, on the links, a certain gentleman who was known to him only by name, a golfer once enquired of his caddie what manner of looking man Mr So-and-so was. " Eh, weel, he's jest a bull-neckit, hog-backit, bandy-leggit chiel, and shapes fine for a gowfer," was the answer; and for terseness and vigour it is inimitable.

A caddie once testified to his master's merits in these terms : " He's a fine free-spoken gentleman ; but, whiles, blasphemious ; " and inasmuch as the remark in the mouth of this particular critic trans-gressed so flagrantly the spirit of the proverb about glass houses and the throwing of stones, a further question was put with the view of eliciting the caddie's views upon the moral heinousness of profane swearing.

" Sweerin' ? " said he, " ou aye, it's awfu' wucked ; but," said he, suddenly abandoning the position of the stern moralist, for a more æsthetic standpoint of criticism—" but it's a gran' set-off to the con-vairsation."

Other recorded answers afford amusement from the insight they give of the caddie's theory of social custom and professional etiquette.   Thus one, when asked who such and such a person was, replied : " I no rightly ken his name, but he's a Major something—at least he's no a real major, but he married a major's widow and took the title."

Perhaps we are no more accurately informed of the value of distinctions in their social level, for when a caddie was asked if such and such, another fellow caddie, had no other profession but that of club carrying, he briskly replied: "Ou aye, he has that—he breaks stones."

The "visitor" season is the caddie's harvest time. He then makes money rapidly and spends it royally—with the result that in the winter, when the golf languishes, he is often in sore straits. Besides the wage for carrying and for playing, if he be anything of a player, the professional golfer makes money in job work in the club-makers' shops. Moreover, as he starts upon the round of instruction with a Tiro, he will often brandish a club attractively before his victim.

"That looks a nice club you've got," remarks the latter, affably falling into the snare.

"Aye, it's a gran' club," says the other indifferently.

Tiro takes it and waggles it, knowingly. In truth it is a good weapon, with a fine steely shaft, thorough-bred looking head, and good balance—such an one as the professional knows well how to make for himself, and how to use, when made.

"What will you take for it?" says Tiro at length, hardening his heart.

"'Deed, and I'm no' thinkin' o' sellin' it, for I can drive with it fine; but," as with an afterthought, "if ye like to gie me a sovereign for it, ye shall have it."

The deal is concluded.

After a few struggles with the new purchase

Tiro begins to suspect that it does not suit his
style as well as that of his mentor. A few more
efforts, and he gives expression to a conviction
that it is the worst club that man was ever called
upon to play with.

Mentor, with virtuous indignation, gives substantial proof of its excellence by offering to buy
it back for five shillings—with which offer Tiro
incontinently closes, and is at peace.

But after a few more "tee-shots"—two hundred
yards on part of Mentor, distance quite inconsider-
able on part of Tiro—the latter commences again
to cast longing eyes upon this magic wand of Jehu.
Another sovereign passes into the possession of
Mentor, and the club again into that of Tiro—
only, as before, to be exchanged for a crown after
a few more howls of exasperation. A club has
been known thus to change hands three times in
the course of one round, to the mutual advantage
of the novice and the professor : for to the latter
it represents facilities for much prospective whisky,
while the former has purchased the invaluable conviction that it is not the club that makes the golfer.

The visitor season and the harvest season of the
caddie culminate together, in the Autumn Medal
Day. The last Wednesday in the month of September has, from time almost immemorial, been
the date of the autumnal meeting of the Royal

and Ancient Golf Club of St Andrews. It is on
that day that the members of this, the premier,
club compete for the medal given them by King
William IV.— a challenge trophy which goes to
him who makes the lowest score in a single round
of the links. It is on that day, too, that the
captain - elect of the club plays himself into *de
facto* captaincy by striking off a ball from the tee
in front of the club-house; and it is on the evening of that day that the dinner is held in the club-
house, with quaint ceremonies that recall old days.
It is in this latter feature, rather than in the importance of the actual medal competition, that the
meeting - day of the Royal and Ancient Club is
notable. Championships, both open and amateur,
no doubt redound with greater glory to their
winners, but there hovers over this St Andrews
meeting the spirit of a vanished past, when men
moved and golfed and had their being after a more
stately wise, before our modern fuss and flurry and
irreverence had pervaded the world. As the hour
approaches at which the captain shall drive off, a
crowd begins to gather in front of the club-house
to witness the annual event. Small boys collect
at a certain distance from the tee; for the captain
will at first drive off a single shot only, thus formally "playing over the links and winning Queen
Adelaide's medal," as the secretary will ceremoni-

ously announce at the dinner in the evening ; and
the ball thus formally driven off is a prize to these
youngsters—a prize which the captain himself will
very probably redeem from the youngster who has
possessed himself of it in the scrimmage, to hand
it down, under a glass case, to his posterity, as the
ball with which he won the captaincy of the Royal
and Ancient Club.   Now, at this proud moment,
while the captain is awaiting the stroke of the
clock to drive off, and the municipal officer, in
a singular uniform, is holding on to the cord
attached to the cannon which he will fire at the
instant of the captain's stroke—this moment is one
in which the captain may find occasion for self-
examination, and possibly for a rebuke on his
fondest vanities.   For it may be that he may
imagine himself a fine golfer and a far driver,
whereas these little caddies, expectant of his ball,
have grouped themselves at a very moderate distance from the tee, implying that they expect but
little of him in the way of length of drive.   But
he may well comfort himself with the thought that
they are calculating on a natural nervousness to
spoil his stroke : for it must need a man of iron
nerve to hit his best with all the highest golfing
talent and criticism regarding him, to say nothing
of the imminent roar of a cannon, the soundness
of whose metal is not above suspicion.

But the stroke, for better or worse, is struck; the cannon roars; the boys scrimmage; the crowd applauds. Then the captain tees up another ball, and strikes off again, partnered by the late captain whom his previous stroke has just deposed, to try to win King William IV.'s medal as well as Queen Adelaide's. It seldom happens, however, that the captain is chosen for great prowess in golf. Commonly, he is a territorial magnate, or, at least, a Fife laird; and these terms are not necessarily synonyms for first - class golfer. Therefore the crowd of spectators will seldom follow him out on his round. They will hang about the club-house until the first couple that includes a probable medal-winner starts from the tee, according to his number in the ballot. Him they will pay the compliment of following, intent on his every stroke, even all the way round the course until the finish, if he continne to play well. But if, on the other hand, he fare evilly, they begin dropping off from him, as rats desert the sinking ship, until he who set out with a great following returns, like Goldsmith's traveller, "unfriended, melancholy, slow," shorn of his retinue. All the day long knots of spectators will be seen following their favourites, and as the last couple holes out the last hole, the gun roars again to tell the world that the meeting is finished.

Somebody has won the medal. Everybody is explaining how, but for such and such a piece of unparalleled ill-fortune, he might have been the "somebody"; but it is hard to get a hearing. Somebody has won, though; that is the great thing, after all. Somebody who will find himself in a great bunker in the evening, when he has to return thanks, at the dinner, before the assembled captains, supported by the silver club and insignia of office and champagne. "He begs to assure —— of his appreciation of the honour. Feels he has been extraordinarily lucky."—("No! no!") "Sure no one is more surprised than himself." ("Question!")—and that is the end of the medal-day and of the "visitor" season.

Last year the winner of the proud distinction, King William IV.'s medal, was Mr Leslie Balfour-Melville. It is encouraging to all of us who are approaching the middle term of life to find the medal won by a player whose years are between forty and fifty. But it is to be said that Mr Balfour-Melville's middle age, if so it may be called, is more athletic than the youth of most of us, and probably he plays golf rather better to-day than he ever played it. His winning score was 82, a good though not a remarkable score. Mr Laidlay was a stroke more, and there were many between those figures and ninety. So in the evening, at the dinner, it fell to Mr Balfour-Melville's lot, as it had often fallen before, to hear his name called out by the secretary as winner of the medal, and to be summoned to the captain's chair to have the medal slung by a fair blue ribbon about his neck. Following him went Mr Laidlay, to be invested similarly with the order of the second medal. Then came the ordinary drinking of patriotic toasts and the good health of "golf and golfing societies," and, thereafter, observance of a singular custom. Among the insignia of the Royal and Ancient Club is a silver club, very massive. It is hung about with silver golf balls, and the custom is for each captain to hang to it a ball with his name engraved thereon. And if there be any new members at the dinner who have not performed the ceremony before, it is their duty to advance to the captain's chair, and there, beneath the benediction of the reverend A. K. H. B., honorary chaplain to the Royal and Ancient Club, to kiss the silver ball which the captain has hung upon the club, in token of loyalty to the club's traditions and homage to the authority of the captain.

So, after the visitors have departed, like locusts at a change of wind, then there sets in what you may call the "fisherman" season. Gentlemen gaily encircled in blue jerseys, crimson braces and an atmosphere strongly flavoured by brine and

herring, whack along a thing that does duty for a
ball, with tortuous shafted things that do duty,
and not badly either, for clubs, in a jovial, breezy
manner that contrasts strongly with the atrabilious
methods of the golfers of the medal week.   Such,
and a few residents, have the royal and ancient
links virtually to themselves, and St Andrew
mourns — possibly less than we think — the pilgrims who have been offering their labour of love at
his shrine.   Yes, for even as we take our pleasurable
part in the golf at St Andrews, we cannot but
realise, if we reflect at all, which, mercifully, we do
but seldom, that it cannot be now what once it was.

In days of old a select society from the Kingdom of Fife, who not only all knew each other,
but whose families had been bound in friendship's,
if not in kinship's, bands, for years, used to meet
in the Union Parlour—and how is it now?   A
modern Club, "replete with every modern con-
venience," and differing from an hotel only in the
fact that you pay for your attendance and your
writing-paper by the year instead of by the piece,
is filled with Tom, Dick, and Harry from every
part of the United Kingdom.   This is indeed the
golden age of Toms and Dicks and Harrys; and
let us who are of the nicknamed crew, while we
gratefully recognise the blessings that are ours,
yet fail not to appreciate that our gain is drawn

from the loss of those whom, by distinction, we will call Thomases, Richards, and Henrys. Only on my last visit to St Andrews a local magnate told me, with conscious pathos, that there were "seventy folk in the new hotel, and only twa gowfers!"

Great Stephenson!—or whoever was the inventor of railways—have we come to this! Cannot even the ancient University city, where the golfer holds high holiday, escape?—spite Firth of Forth and Firth of Tay and North British Railway Company, all in combination to make it hard of access. True it is, they have now bridged over these Firths? true they have a new station at St Andrews, far more inconvenient than the last—but yet we might have hoped that the shrine of St Andrew might have been invaded, if by the foreigner at all, then only by the devotee of golf.

Let us, at all events, as our sacrilegious niblicks cleave his hallowed soil, endeavour to fasten such fitting reverence in our hearts as shall not scare the *genius loci* utterly away from the shade of the grey towers of the city and the pleasant places of the links—let us draw near to St Andrews, with its historical and venerable associations, in a somewhat different spirit from that in which we go down to the sea to listen to the nigger minstrels and the German bands of our Margates and our Ramsgates.

OF the very many golfers who make an occasional pious pilgrimage to the great golfing
Mecca, comparatively few are at all acquainted with
its aspects in the winter months. The majority
would as soon think of Labrador as the East Coast
of Fife between November and May, but should
any venture so far from a south country fireside,
he will find himself in a St Andrews which he
will scarcely recognise as the St Andrews of the
medal week. Even when stranded at Leuchars
Junction to await indefinitely the caprice of the
train from Dundee, he will be sensible of a subtle
difference. Suggestions of the golf links strike
him as so conspicuously absent. He does not see
the inevitable men armed with shooting boots and
golf clubs—all is unfriendly. He betakes himself
to the waiting-room, wherein among fellow-sufferers,
who sit around the fire with the sad patience characteristic of the Scot, he strives to bear his wrongs
in silence. The train at length comes—and with
it the first flavour of the St Andrews of the untimely pilgrim's dreams—in the familiar face of

the guard, who must know so well the course
between St Andrews and Leuchars. The pilgrim
gets a first glimpse of the sand-hills of the links as
the train reaches Guard Bridge, so called one may
naturally suppose because no one but the guard
gets out there. He only gets out to wonder why
they are stopping, then in and off again. The
train goes leisurely beside the links, and the pilgrim
has ample opportunity to feast his longing eyes on
the hallowed land. He often has cursed, by all the
gods of Golf, this very train as it has passed him
putting at that " corner o' the Dyke " and whistled
with real Scottish accent, peculiarly incensing—
has even ventured an exasperated remonstrance to
the engine-driver, who replies with mechanical insult, turning on a little whistle of his engine to say
a steamy " Pooh "! In the haste of a missed putt,
many a golfer has sworn that St Andrews has
more trains than Clapham Junction. But at the
moment, to the travel-worn, untimely pilgrim, it
seems otherwise. Nor, though his train puffs and
whistles, is there a golfer to put off. It is all
deserted. Occasional couples, a wretched flotsam
of that great " Golf Stream," which on his last visit
flowed over all, straggle upon a high and dry
waste of links and bunkers. Where is the great
Golf stream? It is gone with the swallows, nor
till the May medal meeting will again be seen.

The pilgrim fares on.   In the abysmal depths of the new station he encounters a hungry crowd of clamorous caddies, " a mass meeting of the unemployed."   He leaves his clubs as a hostage in the hands of one of the banditti, and is fain to escape with his life and his portmanteau to the shelter of the Cross-key omnibus, which will convey him to the club and the house of his pilgrimage.   The club is in the hands of the painter and the decorator, and the pilgrim's first exploit is to transfer a moist portion of the decorations to his own new ulster.   The air is biting and eager.   The provident pilgrim is swathed in many layers of cardigan jacket and Shetland wool.   He feels as if he had several new inches of fat between himself and the familiar golfing coat.   The joyous freedom of the ideal swing is hard to realise.   Other troubles vex his soul.   The holes are stuck away in odd corners, to rest the " proper greens," as they are well called in contrast, the present greens being most improper, most bumpy, most vexatious.   Sometimes they are not on the green at all.   But, however remote, the professional adviser who carries his clubs will always direct him to play on the old lines.   His conceptions are based on previous conditions, and do not move with the holes (as migratory birds go over the sea on the paths they knew when it was land).   The caddie is himself a bird, mostly of ill

omen, whose conversation one at times might wish
more parrot-like—less tainted by the evidence of
original observation. Candour is its most particular
charm, and when his candour busies itself with the
pilgrim's achievement, the latter grows doubtful of
the absolute merit of truth. " That was a good
one, Jock ? " you will perhaps suggest in desperation, after waiting in vain for the more grateful
unsolicited praise. " Ah—het's the first shot ye've
struck at a' these three days." And the pilgrim's
retrospect darkens as he realises that in the truth
of the answer lies its sting. His master's perform-
ances are the test by which the candid caddie
gauges merit. " Him a gowfer ! He canna play a
dom—he's no muckle better than yoursel'." And
yet that caddie has, maybe, passed his standards,
and often written in his copy-book that " comparisons are odious." So thinks the pilgrim, reflecting
further on the observation of a golfing scribe,
" that part of a caddie's duty is to conceal his just
contempt of your game." Yet there are compensations, for though the links be nearly deserted
and gray as the very sea itself, at least there is no
congestion—no sitting to the number of six couples
together at the high hole, while parties in front
play out the short hole, a very weariness of the
flesh—as often happened in the golden summer.
There is no need to put down one's name over-

night, on a doubtful chance of getting started at
noon. The pilgrim has free and unimpeded field
for the drives he will talk about, and can retire
unobserved to a solitary bunker, with his niblick
and his caddie, to have explanations with his ball,
of which no one will hear him boast.

The east wind, too, is neither so bleak nor so
continuous as it has been painted. In this the
climate has suffered sad calumny. Even from of
old it was so, for from a fragment of a lost book
of Herodotus—dedicated to one of the graces—
discovered by Mr Andrew Lang in the library of
Trinity College, Dublin, it appears that the historian
visited St Andrews, of which he gives the following
among other particulars : " The wind blows so hard
from the east that ships are unable to leave the
harbour, except during the feast of the medal week,
at which time it blows so hard from the opposite
direction that ships are not able to enter the
harbour. Now some attribute this prevalence of
the east wind to the dryness of certain lectures.
But in this, as it seems to me, they say what is
unworthy of belief, for whereas these lectures are
most severe during but some few months in the
year, the wind blows from the east during the
whole year, except at the time called the feast of
the medal week." Herodotus, however, was im-
posed upon in this, as he was in other matters,

for the wind blows from the east about a third
part of the year, and that not continuously, but, as
the Americans say, " in samples." But he is right
in saying it often confines the ships in the harbour,
and then, when the easterly storm cone is nailed to
the mast, a ναυτικος ὄχλος fares forth upon the links,
with a rolling gait, as if making heavy weather of
it, and bulky with its whole available wardrobe
on its back. A fine free flavour of ozone and salt
water, with a little piquancy of fish, these mariners
exhale, and a fine free game of golf they play.
Some of them hit very hard and very crooked, but
they are handicapped by wearing a multitude of
clothes, over all of which pass their braces sup-
porting voluminous blue pants. They do not golf
well, but they know the game. They are courteous
and sympathetic to the pilgrim, and should the
professionals get up a big match among themselves, the fishermen will follow—a silent, eager
crowd. It will amaze the southern pilgrim. He
has been used to associate sailors with a " yeo,
heave ho," and a noise and commotion. But these
Scots roll on over the billowy links in silent appreciation of the play. They stand respectfully
motionless on the stroke. No better behaved
gallery could be. They are seen but little at
the time of the feast of the medal week, not so
much because the fury of the wind is so great, as

Herodotus says, as to prevent the ships from entering the harbour, but because if they do come in they are speedily away again after the herring —which pays better than the golf-ball. In a gallery of fifty fishermen who watch a golf match no two will have their hands out of their pockets, and the one who has is regretting the necessity of filling his pipe. Links and professionals are alike free and unoccupied in these winter months, yet it is not at this time that the good scores are made. Muscles are too stiff. Cold wrists will not work for the delicate approach strokes. It is the long summer evenings after the day's work of carrying clubs is over, and the wind has sunk to rest, as it usually does on the east coast of Fife at that hour, that the professionals go out in parties of two or three or four, and on a fine clear green do the good scores.

In winter the teeing-grounds are often advanced, and the holes thus shortened, but the queer catchy positions in which they are pitched more than makes up for this. And though the pilgrim will find a clear course over the links in general, yet, as he comes home again the last few holes will be black with schoolboys, released at twelve o'clock to cut divots from the links, an occasion of righteous wrath to the most pious pilgrim. The congestion strikes him more forcibly in contrast with the rapid circulation on the links far out. He feels like a Cunarder which has had a clear run over several thousand miles of ocean, and finds herself bothered by coasters as she approaches her haven. At these final holes boys are a frequent hazard. Death from Golf balls ought to be common with them, but there appears to be a special schoolboy's providence, and their numbers do not appreciably decrease. On a Saturday afternoon great is the mustering of townsmen and gownsmen, the scarlet gown for the time laid aside with the studies of divinity for the graver studies of the dynamics of the Golf-ball. For in the golfing Mecca, in the winter months, a deal of theology, scholarship, and the like trifles, mingle with the Golf. Even the conversation between the strokes is mixed— is not pure Golf. "The Elohist says,"—"There he's in the bunker"—"The text is very corrupt, Shilleto suggests as an emendation"—"Better try the niblick. They've been repairing the greens, and old Tom Morris says there's nothing like saund." Will not the gods of Golf take vengeance on such slipshod work as this, until the indignant caddie will remonstrate with, "Eh, ye're no givin' yer mind to it at all," and the pilgrim with shame confesses that he was wandering in the trivial bye-paths of Biblical and scholarly criticism. To make amends to him he takes his long-suffering caddie into his confidence, and tells him that once in the summer he went round in 99—to which the caddie, obviously incredulous, contents himself with replying with habitual candour, "Eh, ye'll never do that again." Such a response might almost drive the pilgrim to worse things than scholarship, maybe mathematics — of which we may observe by-the-bye that the science of arithmetic should be mastered before proceeding to the art of Golf.

Thus have we considered the winter pilgrim under the usual conditions of keen, dry, easterly wind. Shall we consider him under the conditions of a links submerged in snow, cooped in a club redolent and generous of wet paint ? or shall we not rather leave him unconsidered in those fearful aspects ?   But there are days, many of them, among the most easterly months of February and March when the sun will be shining, and it will be balmy as the land of the blessed. The snow will still show on the distant Grampians, so that " my father," that " frugal swain," would find poor feeding for his flock. Lochnagar—seventy miles distant — is visible in its white robe in a gap between the Sidlaws, but the skylarks are singing bravely overhead, and everything is full of the promise of spring. The few fellow golfers the pilgrim will find will be not of the old familiar types—the man who is always off his game, the man who, when he sits down to dinner, announces his intention of taking the next train away from St Andrews, having previously made a bonfire of his Golf clubs, but who by the time dessert comes on has backed himself to do the round in 90. These are not here—instead there are strange faces of men who do not appear in the fashionable season of Golf—men of a beautiful humility and self-depreciation, with whom therefore the pilgrim only makes a match on terms very advantageous to the stranger. "Who is he?" the exasperated pilgrim may ask his caddie, as for the fourth time in succession the stranger (is he perchance that mysterious stranger man of Waldo's, from the African Farm?) lays himself dead with his iron. But the caddie only murmurs : "I dinna ken wha' he is at a'. He says he's a beginner. He says he's a meenister. I think he's a leear."

Sweet saint, whose spirit haunts the course
And broods o'er every hole,
Who lends the driver vital force
And calms the putter's soul,

Thou giv'st me, to my life's last hour,
A golfer's fame divine ;
I boast thy gift, a driver's power,
If I can putt 'tis thine.

THERE is no doubt about this saint, nor about the home of his brooding. St Andrew, on the links to which he lends his name, is the gentleman referred to; and if he does not give a deal of fame to all to whom he lends the driver's vital force and the rest of it, he is, at all events, made very famous by the grand course of which he is the *genius loci*. During the recent boom of golf, golfers, and golf links, many new courses have been discovered and laid out; and now and again of some peculiarly excellent one, the phrase has been spoken, "As good as St Andrews, by Jove!"

It was the highest meed of praise that could be given, and in itself evidence to the surpassing quality of the classic green. And when these new courses, of which this great thing was said, were in process of making or had lately been completed, the golfing mind was for a while in a state of some perplexity. It was not quite sure, now and again, whether the phrase was not, perchance, a just criticism. It sat, as it were, in suspended judgment, as over the literary work of some contemporary or the achievements of a living statesman. It did not quite know how to class them. But now that our little Britain is fairly begirt with golf links, and that they have been for a while established, we are able to reckon up their qualities with a just and unimpassioned mind ; and the result of this mature criticism is to show that, though many of these newer links are indeed very good, the phrase was never quite justified of any of them. None of them, after all, is quite as good as St Andrews.

There is no doubt that much of its peculiar merit lies in the fact that its putting-greens are so very good when you get to them, and that they are so well guarded by hazards—that is to say, are so difficult to get at. This difficulty makes each stroke a stroke of interest. It is equally true of the strokes from the tee that, in most cases, you have a definite course to steer, a definite hazard to avoid.

The character of the Sandwich course is that it
is a course of magnificent "carries." Every shot
from the tee has to carry a great bunker. This
is very attractive, and we think St Andrews would
gain in interest if there were more "carries" there.
But, on the other hand, there can be no question
of the gain that Sandwich would reap if it had a
few of the dangerous side hazards of St Andrews.
Too often at the English green, so long as you
hit hard and high, the direction signifies little.
The lies through the green are none too good
either at St Andrews or at Sandwich, nor again
at Hoylake. At Prestwick they are good; but
for the best quality of golf in this particular, one
has to go to another English links—Westward
Ho! Westward Ho! is the first real links on which
golf was played in England. Previously, Scotsmen had played such golf as was possible on the
common at Blackheath, and in the neighbourhood
of Manchester, but the first sandy seaside links
laid out for golf in England was this common,
called the Northam Burrows, close by the water-
ing - place which took its name from Charles
Kingsley's jolly book. There the lies through
the green are so perfect that a man finds himself
with a perpetually teed ball, and has no need
whatever of a brassey. Both at Sandwich and
at Westward Ho! the greens are finely guarded

by hazards; but neither quite equals St Andrews
in this quality, and at neither of the English links
do the greens, when reached, compare with the
St Andrews ones.   A while ago one would have
claimed for an English green—namely, Hoylake
—the best greens in the golfing world; but their
glory, at the moment of writing, is rather under
eclipse.   Of course we trust it may be only a
temporary lapse; but in the meantime we know
none to vie with St Andrews.   The Prestwick
greens are fine, and the whole character of the
golf on this western course is of the highest
quality.   It has good, bold bunkers—a mighty
range of sand hills intersecting the course is well
worthy its awesome name of Himalayas;—its lies
are excellent, its greens are good, and the whole
surface freely undulating : but when all is said,
it does not charm the golfing fancy with the
attraction that St Andrews exercises.

These beautiful putting-greens of St Andrews
are a lesson to the golfing world.   About ten
years ago they were anything but good.   Then
the Green Committee sunk a well at each hole
and made them what they are—the biggest and
truest ever seen.

But St Andrews has now got two courses, and
that gives her a further advantage over her rivals;
for when the old course becomes too golf-worn,

she can close it for a while and make the world play on the new course. The new course is good : but golfers are conservative, and love to dig in the bunkers where their fathers swore and laboured.

It has been said often enough that it seems a necessary condition of a first-class golf course that it should be terribly difficult of access. St Andrews has been put much nearer the world by the Forth Bridge, which improves its access from Edinburgh, and by the Tay Bridge, which reduces one's sufferings in reaching it from the north. Formerly, one used to suffer terribly in those ferry-boats which plied across the great estuaries. But, nowadays, when we reach St Andrews our sufferings are worse. In the months of August and September, when we have to wait while six or seven couples play out the short hole, we greatly regret those ferry-boats, in which there was a chance of drowning golfers. Golf has become too popular to be pleasant at these great resorts.

For pleasure, one has to seek a medium. Macrihanish is said to be a very fine links; and "Old Tom" Morris came back from South Uist saying that there he had seen the best golf links in the world. It was perfectly safe saying, for the only three people who had ever

been to South Uist were not in St Andrews to
contradict him. But a golf links, however good,
is no use by itself, for you want some golfers to
play with, and you want a roof over your head
when you are not golfing. Now St Andrews
supplies you with a very good roof over your head,
for the club-house fulfils all its purposes; and,
moreover, the old university town is full of storied
interest. Its ruins are almost uniquely fine, while
as for golfers it errs in the opposite extreme to
South Uist and Macrihanish. At North Berwick
the course has lately been extended, with very good
results. It is now a course worthy of a championship meeting, whereas formerly, if we may say so
with abject apologies both to North Berwick and
to the ladies, it was rather worthy of a ladies'
championship. It was very short; but if it was
very short, it had the merit, in a very marked
degree, of well-guarded holes; and the consequence
was that every man who learned his golf at North
Berwick is a master of the pitching mashie. North
Berwick is a pleasant place to stay at, with less of
historical interest than St Andrews, but with a
prettier sea-scape. Its club is less satisfactory,
and its links are perhaps equally crowded; but
then there are compensations, like that which St
Andrews enjoys in its alternative course. There
is an alternative course at North Berwick, but it is

not greatly patronised. Within an easy drive or
bicycle-ride, however, there is a nice selection of
courses—Gullane, Muirfield, Luffness and Archerfield are all easily accessible, and a game on
any one of them makes a pleasant change. At
Prestwick, similarly, you may make a change by
playing on the neighbour links of Troon. It is
possible to play the first nine holes at Prestwick,
walk the half mile or so which separates the Troon
and Prestwick courses, then play the last nine
holes of Troon, lunch at the Troon Club House,
then play the first nine holes of Troon, walk the
intervening half-mile again, then play the Prestwick last half—and so you are at home again.
But Prestwick has not the good accommodation of
St Andrews and North Berwick. You will generally need to live in Ayr, and come out by the
train—a journey of a few minutes only.

In selecting a golf links for your pleasure this
question of accommodation is a large factor. At
St Andrews, and maybe at North Berwick, you
have golf at the doors of your hotel; occasionally
an errant ball will invade your area. At Carnoustie
you may lodge virtually on the first tee; and so,
too, at Hoylake. There are few of our English
links that are so favoured. Both at Westward Ho!
and Sandwich you have a little walk or (preferably)
drive to and from your work. But Littlestone is a

good links, though in an unbeautiful country,
namely the Weald of Kent, where an iron shot
from the last hole may break a window-pane.
Bembridge, in the Isle of Wight, has an excellent
little course, but from your hotel you have to cross
in a row-boat a small arm of the sea to reach it.
All these details of access are minor troubles, no
doubt, but they make a certain difference to your
comfort. In the Channel Islands and on the Continent you are always a little distance from your
golf, unless indeed you go and live in the Hôtel de
Panorama, which is fairly on the links of St Briac,
where the Dinard Golf Club plays. But from
Dinard itself you have to drive out several kilometres. The links, when you reach them, are
worth all the trouble, of the proper sandy sort,
erring a little on the side of being too sandy, but
giving you beautiful sea-scapes of the bold Brittany
coast. At Pau and Biarritiz you have a drive of
something like a mile from your hotel ; a little
over a mile maybe in the former case and a little
under in the latter. Both these are, from a golfing
point of view, inland courses, with a loamy or
clayey rather than a sandy soil. The soil of Pau
is actually the lighter of the two, though it is many
miles from the sea, whereas Biarritz is thundered
on by all the billows of the Atlantic. But the
golf course is high up above sea level ; certainly

no product of alluvial deposit. At Pau, on the other hand, there are evidences that the river Gave at one time overran all the plain of Billères on which men play golf to-day, and in times of flood it partially overspreads them even now. At Jersey a quarter of an hour in the train takes you from St Helier's to the club-house, and at Guernsey you reach the links by a service of tram-car and diligence. There is no mistake, however, about these two Channel Island courses; both are of the right sandy kind and give good golf, but all these considerations pertain more rightly to the scrip of the Pilgrim when he goes abroad.

Who that has tried the change does not know the delight of leaving an inland course, which bakes to a brick in the summer and becomes a morass in winter, for a seaside links, where the turf is always springy under the foot in the driest weather, and, no matter how it rains, you can go out in patent-leather boots and return dry-foot as soon as it stops? Your ball never gets clogged and coated with black mud; the green is never mountainous with worm casts; all is so clean that you might eat your dinner off it. A number of us are compelled to take most of our golf in the neighbourhood of London, inevitably on courses of the inland quality. We get good fun out of it, no doubt, and keep our hands in practice, but

know quite well all the time that it is not the real
thing. But how infinitely better than no golf at
all! And to what delightful places in the neighbourhood of our smoky metropolis are we thus
taken, which otherwise we probably should not
visit at all—Wimbledon Common, with its charming ravines and extended landscape; Chorley-
wood, undulating and breezy; Richmond Park,
with its sylvan and purely English loveliness; and
Mitcham Common, of less varied beauty, but
perhaps the best golf, and certainly the handiest
of them all! Or, further afield, there are the
courses of Woking and Byfleet and Guildford,
all in the midst of the loveliest surroundings, and
at each of these, even, it is easy to have two full
rounds, and more, between breakfast and dinner in
town. There are hosts of others, which it is perhaps invidious to leave unnamed ; but the name of
golf courses and golfers is legion.

We had almost forgotten to speak of Portrush
and Newcastle links and Dollymount, all in
Ireland. Certainly it would have been another
flagrant injustice to Ireland to have omitted them,
for they put themselves into the first class of golf
links by their own golfing merit, and one can
nowhere find golf in more beautiful surroundings.
At Portrush, sixty miles north of Belfast, you lodge
on the shores of the Irish Channel, and are close

beside your golf, which leads you out towards the enchanted land of the Giant's Causeway, and the Bushmills, where they make the whiskey.

The charm of visiting one of these golf-grounds where the soil is of the real sandy quality is greatly increased by finding the game so very much more easy. The grass of the links turf curls round into itself again in such a way that the ball is generally found lying *on* the grass—above it. On the pastoral ground of our inland courses we find our ball lying *in* the grass, among the blades, with many of them interposed between the ball and the club's face. It is quite obvious how much more difficult is the latter lie. And, again, nothing is so potent as a means of making one recognise the great part played by earthworms (as insisted on at length by Darwin) in modifying the surface of the ground as a course of golf on inland greens. The horrid little heaps of sticky earth that the worms throw up seem ubiquitous, and, insignificant as they look, can give you as bad a lie as you can find in the Sandwich "Hades," the Musselburgh "Pandy" (a euphonism for pandemonium), or the St Andrews bunker crudely and briefly named "Hell." There seems a virtual tautology in these infernal titles for the worst bunkers that the respective links can afford, but many golf links have their especial hazards.

Where will you find but at Westward Ho! those great clumps of rushes, like bundles of assegais, tall as a man's head? And, apart from their hazards, the difference that has been noted in the nature of soils means that a slightly different stroke has to be played, especially in the iron approaches, on the different courses. Where the ground is very hard, as often at Musselburgh and St Andrews, and always in summer on the inland greens, the iron will not go down into the turf as kindly as in the softer soils. It is necessary to hit the ball more cleanly, to avoid scrupulously taking even half an inch of turf behind the ball; and on visiting a strange green this is one of the first qualities of difference with which the stranger has to become familiar before he can hope to play on it what he is pleased to call his game. It is necessary for him to study, too, the way in which the ball runs when it pitches; for besides the very obvious fact that the ball runs further after a pitch on hard than on soft ground, there is a more subtle difference in the way in which different soils take the "cut" which every player—though the novice perhaps involuntarily rather than of conscious intent—puts on the ball when playing an approach stroke with the iron or mashie. And, finally, it is necessary for him "to get into the strength of the putting greens," as the phrase goes.

All these little differences add to one's pleasure, as they add to the variety of the game, in visiting different courses; and while there are some few golfers who seem to play equally well on every course, there are not a few who are comparatively useless when playing off their own green.

And there exist also differences more subtle, which no study of the soil can explain to us— differences in the golfing traditions, so to call them, of our various links, so that on one we are almost obliged, despite ourselves, to *play at*, rather than to *play*, golf, so gravely has the game fallen from its best estate, while at another the very atmosphere is charged with all the stately manner of the old Scottish school, and we take our part in the solemn pageant as if to the manner born. Unquestionably it is every golfer's duty to go once at least to St Andrews at the meeting-time, to hear the gun fired, while, before expectant multitudes, the captain hits off the first ball, formally opening the medal competition and gaining for himself the medal which was Queen Adelaide's gracious gift. It is all very royal; and then, in the evening, the ceremonial at the dinner, when the medal-winners are invested with their honours, is very ancient. You begin to see that you have in golf a link with a very remote past; that you are reviving manners and customs that are gone.

St Andrews presents golf to you in this aspect most perfectly of all, though others (and notably the famous old club at Blackheath) preserve something of the same spirit. The course that you should visit in order to make experiment of the opposite extreme—of that game which is to golf as "bumble-puppy" is to whist—had better be left unnamed. The selection would be invidious and tend to unpopularity; and the selection would be very difficult, for such courses are numerous. And you may please yourself as to which class of golfers you will stand in rank with. Of course, between the two extremes is an infinitely varying series of clubs which have more of the one spirit or of the other. As a rule, the ancient tradition is carried to the better links, and it is on those courses where one golfs with difficulty that the stately amenities are most disregarded, as well as the simple rules.

The best of golf is confined to the sea-side, but not necessarily the most beautiful. The pilgrim to the lake country, in the neighbourhood of Windermere, may find golf grounds that give as lovely views as Prestwick, which has all the beauties of the Clyde estuary for its surroundings, or Nairn, on the shores of the Moray Firth. The last-named, its latitude considered, has a winter climate of extraordinary mildness; and, indeed,

throughout Scotland, the actual winter is far less
abominable than it is represented. At Prestwick
and all the western greens the climate is mild
enough, and on the east its keenness is tempered
by its bracing dryness. But it is when the winter
is turning into spring, with cold boisterous winds,
and goodness only knows what visitations in the
shape of snow or sleet or hail, that you may well
wish yourself elsewhere—say on the milder shore
of Westward Ho! or the yet softer air of the Isle
of Wight or the Channel Islands. Pau, Biarritz,
or Cannes is perhaps preferable at these seasons;
but your Scottish autumn and summer are perfect,
with just that leaven of occasional evil days that
makes you appreciate your general blessedness,
and with a keen nip in the air that makes you
eager alike for your golf and for your dinner.
The golfing pilgrim may ring the changes pleasantly between the south of France and East
Neuk of Fife, and play perpetually the royal and
ancient game which knows no close season.

As a commentary, in lighter vein, on the above
general review of our golf links, I would add the
following account of a famous golfing pilgrimage,
confined, however, to the English greens, which
has been furnished to me, most kindly, by one of
the players who took part in it. The narrator takes
up his pleasant parable to the following effect :—

My friend and ˌfellow-pilgrim, James Macpherson, is one of the golfers known in the North
as "pawkie," that is to say, his game is characterised
by an unerring steadiness and unambitious length
of drive, combined with a putting style of great
deadliness. I, on the other hand, am a Jehu in
driving compared with my friend, but my shots are
apt to deviate disastrously from the true line in
my driving, and in putting to resemble the course
of true love in seldom running smooth. There
are thus compensations in our rival styles which
result in our making an excellent match. James's
appears to me a wretched unambitious style, while
he is ever ready with the formula to apply to my
play of "Eh, it's maybe a verra fine game that o'
yours, but ye'll acknowledge, am thinking, that
it's no the gowf." (I need hardly observe that
James is one of those Scotchmen who peculiarly
pride themselves on the purity of an English pro-
nunciation).

Of course James knows that I shall acknowledge
nothing of the sort, but yet it is not within the
power of either to get away from the other, so
that he should be able to claim for his own style a
definite superiority. Under these circumstances
we determined to take a holiday and make such a
pilgrimage to all the main golfing greens of
England as should put our comparative merits

once for all to a crucial test. Two rounds of
eighteen holes, or their equivalent, were to be
played at each locality, and he who was up at the
end of the tour was for ever after to be held the
better man, and the loser was to accept with such
resignation as he might any criticisms which the
victor, in the arrogance of his triumph, might
please to pass upon his style or execution.

Starting from north of the Tweed, our first
passage of arms was, naturally, to take place at
Hoylake. Blundellsands, Formby, Leasowe, Wal-
lasey—the links are many in the Liverpool district,
but none of them compete seriously with the
ancient fame of the Royal Liverpool Club's course
at Hoylake.

"No better potted shrimps did I ever taste!" I
exclaimed, as we stepped from our lodgings after
breakfast to commence the great contest.

"Eh, mon, and will ye be talking of shrimps at
such a time as this!" said James, in grave rebuke,
deeply impressed by the gravity of the occasion.

Maybe it was ill-timed levity, and its Nemesis
overtook me, for all that I put my hand to went
wrong at Hoylake. Stumps of old posts, the relics
of a disused racecourse, appeared in close prox-
imity to my ball as soon as it stopped rolling.
Corners of fields, which you may not play out of,
stretched themselves to supernatural proportions

to take my devious drives in their embrace. Hedges, rabbit holes, and ditches with black tenacious mud, which flanked the course—I made acquaintance with them all.

Meanwhile, James, trundling his ball in igno-minious security along the centre of the course, viewed all these hazards with a purely platonic and scarce sympathetic interest. He arrived at the putting green, as a rule, some two strokes before me. And oh, what putting greens they are—at their best they are the very best; so good indeed that one almost shrinks from setting down his nail-clad boot upon them; but then, as I had usually played two more, my interest in them was scarce less platonic than James' in the hedges, the ditches, and the fields. Seven up was James—no less—when we left our quarters at Hoylake for the long weary journey down to Westward Ho! Why are golf links so difficult to get to? After all, perhaps it is as well; and when you are waiting while five couples drive off before you, you are aware that there used to be com-pensations in the difficulties of ferry, of tramcar, and of railway—about an hour in all from Liverpool, I think—which used to beset the golfing pilgrim's progress to Hoylake.

"A pottering, old man's course, I call it, that Hoylake," I said to James.

"A real golfing course—a verra fine test of the real game of gowf," said he.   I knew he would say that.

It was in the train that I interrupted him to make this remark about the Hoylake course. He thought I was asleep, and was surreptitiously looking in the Stores List, which he brought out of his bag, to see on what he should spend the money he was going to win from me.   Wait a bit, Mr James!   Seven up, I thought to myself, is nothing with so many to play.

My word, it was a different pair of shoes at Westward Ho!   No old man's course that, I can tell you.   There are parts of it a man needs to be pretty active to walk over, much more to drive over.   It is in many respects like Prestwick.   In my opinion there is no such delightful place for golfing in the world as Westward Ho!   The course abounds in fine long sporting "carries," which are far more suited to my style of play than James's.   I succeeded in not only knocking off all the holes he had won at Hoylake, but even got two to the good on my own account.

"A fine sporting course, and the best lies through the green I ever did see," was my verdict upon Westward Ho!

"Ou, aye," said James, dourly.   "A fine green for a great slashing driver, but no a test of the real game of gowf." I should like to have a definition of that "real game of gowf," according to my friend, James Macpherson.

Now we were fairly beset by an *embarras de richesse* in knowing what green to select after leaving Westward Ho! We had already passed by Malvern and Minihinhampton, and, lower down, Burnham; and now we heard of golf in Cornwall, at Torquay, at Exmouth, at Bournemouth, at Portsmouth, at Hayling Island, and at Eastbourne; to say nothing of all the inland and metropolitan greens. We determined, however, as being, from all we heard, most worthy our attention, to pay a visit to Bembridge, in the Isle of Wight. I must say that James fairly caught me out on the way up. I felt so confident about the result of the match that I picked up his Stores List and began absently glancing at it, when I fancied him deep in the *Times*. I quite started when he quietly asked me,

"And what are ye needing?"

"Ah!" said I. "Oh, yes! I was just thinking of buying my wife a Westphalian ham."

"Ou, aye," said James. "And ye're a good thoughtful husband, but I'm thinking ye'll no likely find Westphalian hams among the silver candelabra." I must pay James the compliment of confessing that he is by no means so simple as his appearance would lead you to suppose.

James had a little the better of me at Bembridge. It is not a rough bit of common, as at most links, that you have to cross to get to the green from the hotel at Bembridge, but a rough bit of the harbour, in a boat. It was only about five minutes' row, but I arrived at the other side feeling queerish. Then I pulled my first tee shot very badly into the harbour. The tide was out, and, after a long search over some soft mud, we at length found the ball inside a dead and derelict dog. Dead, indeed, but faintly expresses him, he had been dead so long.

After this, I naturally lost a hole or two, but subsequently pulled myself together, and we left Bembridge with no appreciable advantage on either side in the great match.

Bembridge is very good golf indeed, what there is of it; but there is not enough. The space is so restricted that even to accommodate nine holes an arrangement something on the lines of the cat's cradle has to be resorted to, so that not only do you play the same hole very often, but you so often hear the same people calling " Fore ! " that you feel oppressed, when you get back, by an idea of the same thing happening to you all day long.

' A very good links when there is nobody on

it," was the verdict on which, for once, James and I were fairly agreed. And now for a drive inland to Wimbledon and to Blackheath, the time-honoured pleasure grounds of the golfers of the Metropolis. And herein I must plead guilty to an opinion which is a heresy and a paradox, for, in my judgment, Blackheath is a better golf links than Wimbledon. You have, perhaps, greater comfort at Wimbledon—a more commodious club-house. I am speaking of the club-house of the Royal Wimbledon, which is a secession from the London Scottish Club. Into the rights and wrongs of that secession one need not enter to recognise the present fact of the superiority, from the point of view of the golfer's comfort, of the Royal Wimbledon club-house. The London Scottish, however, are building themselves a new club-house, so perhaps the superiority will be all the other way soon. Then, as compared with Blackheath, you have eighteen holes at Wimbledon to Blackheath's seven. But then there are—goodness only knows how many!—more people playing the Wimbledon eighteen than the Blackheath seven; and twenty golfers will get more fun out of seven holes than a hundred golfers will out of eighteen, other things being equal. But other things are not equal, for the Blackheath seven are longer than any other

seven consecutive holes that ever were seen.
Moreover, the putting greens are well placed,
so as to make the roads available as good
hazards, and the lies through the green are as
good as those at Wimbledon.   At Wimbledon,
you can only play three days a week; but what
gives it its preponderance in popular estimation
over Blackheath is, doubtless, that it is available
for play on Saturday afternoons — the principal
London holiday; whereas Blackheath is on that
day delivered over to winter footballers and
summer cricketers.

The golfer, worthy of that great name, can
scarcely approach Blackheath without a rever-
ential feeling for its historical associations.   As
a golf club, its annals go further back than those
of any other club in the world—beyond those
even of the Royal and Ancient itself.   For years
it stood alone in England.   Some five-and-twenty
years ago, it lent a fostering hand, under the
direction of the late lamented Mr George Glennie,
to the then budding plant of golfing promise—
the Royal North Devon Club at Westward Ho!
It gave the Westward Ho! Club one of its first
challenge prizes, the Blackheath Badge.   Then,
golf being thus given an English start, the Royal
Liverpool Club at Hoylake soon came into existence—a club to which the golfing world owe

thanks for the initiative movement in founding the Amateur Championship meetings. Afterwards, the members of the London Scottish Rifle Volunteers Corps started to play golf round their Iron Hut at Wimbledon, and Wimbledon has now itself a mighty foster-child, in the links near Sandwich and the club called the St George's. Excuse this slight historical digression, and let us return to the great match.

Now, golfing readers, you will have noticed often, I am sure, that there are some days when all one's putts run bumpy. Well, it was like that with me when we played at Wimbledon. They are not by nature bumpy putting-greens, and I do not wish to be understood as implying that James's ball did not get just as much bumped as mine did; but all his bumps seemed to be towards the hole, while all mine seemed to be away from it, and that makes a good deal of difference. To make matters worse, there was one hole up a narrow ride between high whins —they call it the "racecourse," but when you come to drive at it, it hardly looks broad enough for "two shelties" abreast. Well, that hole, of course, I might have given James without playing it. Wimbledon is a wonderfully wild, breezy, natural place to be so near London, and it must do the metropolitans a power of good to carry back some of that air into the city with them. Still, that did not affect the score of the match— namely, four up to James—when we started to sample the soil, so sacred from its venerable associations, but so gravelly when you jerk your irons into it, of Blackheath.

At Blackheath you require to have a fore-caddie to run ahead with a red flag, as if you were a traction engine, and wave away nursemaids and perambulators, and such things; and you get lots of new experiences in the way of lamp-posts and benches, and iron railings. The caddies, too, are a species to themselves, clad in long frock coats originally made for men about a foot taller than the present owner—all except one, a worthy of some six feet three inches in an Eton jacket. They have no sense of the fitness of things. The putting greens are not at all bad, and there are two of the longest holes I ever saw. Poor James, I felt quite sorry for him. The longest hole of all was in the teeth of a strong wind, and when James at length arrived at it, he looked quite faint and pale, and said he felt as if he had been driving ever since he was a little boy. Superiority of driving is an overwhelming advantage at Black-heath, and I ought to have done even better than I did. As it was, however, I managed to pull down the four holes of James' advantage and to stand one up on the long match when we had finished at Blackheath. Sandwich was the next place set down on our programme, and I had promised myself a terrific massacre of poor James in this terrific course. We were comfortably housed at the " Bell," and a walk or drive of something less than a mile took us to the glorified farmhouse which does service as an excellent club-house. The course was in fine condition, and the carries were all that I could have wished them to be ; but that, cruelly enough, was the very thing that put me wrong. I was just a little off my driving, but, of course, I was bound to attempt the carries, and in many instances fell just short and made a most costly failure. The unenterprising James, on the other hand, went round each bunker, on the line indicated for short drivers by the blue flags, and the ultimate and most exasperating result of the day's golf on this long-driving course was that I, a long driver, had actually lost five holes to the short-driving James. I consider that it says great things for the impartiality of my judgment that I am able, nevertheless, to recognise the excellence of the Sandwich green.

The next scene in the drama was fixed to be laid at Felixstowe, and I warn all whom it may concern not to attempt, as we did, to get to Felixstowe on a Sunday. There were no direct trains that we could discover to Felixstowe, so we went by train to Harwich, which is on the other side of the river—so they told us. Well, that is quite true, but there are rivers *and* rivers, and this was an estuary some three miles wide. As the ferry boat was not going to run any more that day, we chartered a mariner to take us over in a row boat. He disembarked us and our kit on the pier head, which was quite deserted, on the other side, and we then asked him how far it was to the Bath Hotel.

"Two miles," he answered.

"Oh! And how can we get our bags and things up there?"

"I do not know," he said, and rowed away.

We sat there with our bags on the pier head, in the gathering twilight, till, to our joy, we heard the whistle of a belated yokel, with whose help we dragged our belongings over a causeway, through sloughs of despond, until we came to a small inn, where we chartered a cart to take us to our hotel. The green, as we discovered next morning, is a fairish one—not so good as Westward Ho! or Hoylake, but better than Wimbledon or Blackheath, or any of the inland greens. It has few features. It is rather

a characterless green, and our play thereon
partook of the neutral tint of the surroundings.
There was absolutely nothing between us at
Felixstowe, James was four up on the whole
contest, and we had but three stages left of the
great match, which was to determine for all
time to come our relative merits. It was an
exciting time, and gave neither of us much
ground for boasting. James had, indeed, doucely
observed as we left London: "Ye didna buy
your wife yon Westphalian ham, I'm thinking,"
but when I countered him with the observation
that "*Tu quoque*, you omitted your contemplated purchases at the stores," we relapsed
into a mutually respectful silence.

James had persuaded me to set down Yarmouth
as the next place on our programme. I had a
leaning, myself, to Cromer and Sherringham, but
James represented that these, though excellent
greens, were of an inland nature in their soil,
though well within view of the sea. Of Yarmouth we had reports which were unquestionable.
I do not think I was ever more surprised than on
my first view of the town of the bloater. I had
figured to myself a fishing village, its cottage
walls festooned with drying bloaters, exhaling an
odour of fish in decomposition, combined with the
briny flavour of ozone. Instead of which, we

beheld a noble city, a harbour in the centre of the town—Dutch fashion—concerts on the pier, and excellent hotels. A drive of a mile along a good road brought us to the links. There were few players, but the turf was real good golfing material, lots of sand—too much, James said—and eighteen holes of fair length. The club house is a fine building, amply sufficient for all purposes. Well, James and I fared forth, under the respectful admiration of some blue-jerseyed toilers of the deep, and what a time I had with him! For the links are sandy, as I have said, so that if you do not get good "carry" on your ball you do not go far. Now James's drives are mostly "run," so that they went very little way indeed, and you may picture my triumph when I found myself at the end of the day one hole to the good on the whole match.

One hole to the good and seventy-two to play is not a very substantial pull; but no one could have been more full of confidence than I when we started for the very last stage but one of our match over the Royal West Norfolk Club's links at Brancaster. There is an annoying drive of seven miles from Hunstanton before we reach the links; but we stayed at the most comfortable Dormy House in Brancaster itself, whence a half mile would take us to the club-house and the front tee. It is a cruelly punishing course—less dangerous for the tee shot than Sandwich, but the second shots and approaches to the hole infinitely more severe. I had the better of James on this severe green to the extent of four holes—I should have won many more—and started five up, altogether, for the last stage of the long match on the Northumbrian links of Alnmouth. Here, again, we were in the midst of a little nucleus of links—Ryton, Seaton-Carew, and several others claiming our attention. Yet, since Alnmouth appeared the chief golfing seat of the vicinity, it was here that we decided upon enacting the ultimate crisis of our great golfing drama. Excitement ran high. As I have said, I was full of confidence; yet, explain it how you will, I lost hole after hole of my advantage as we pursued our way over the grassy—too grassy—links of Alnmouth. There are only nine holes, but you can lodge with comfort beside the putting green of the last one, and, take it on the whole, it is golf of a quality not to be despised. Nevertheless, I made nothing of it. At lunch time, not only had I lost my holes of vantage, but James was actually one ahead upon the match. We conversed but little during lunch. The first round following saw no change in our position. Once I had James all even, but again he retrieved his one point to the good. As we descended for the last time of all the mighty hill which is the main feature of the links, he still led me, with two holes to the good, and the springy step of a victor. And then Nemesis, the Nemesis which waits upon pride, fell upon him. At the two succeeding holes he was unfortunate. I won them both. All even, and but one to play, upon our whole great match! If the eyes of Europe had been on us it had not been one whit more exciting.

I led off with a fair drive and James topped the shot. At last I held him in my clutch. No more shall he ever pass his strictures on my style of play! I have him.

On the putting green James lays a stealthy long one dead. Yet I have two to win it, and I am but ten yards from the hole. Only to hole in two, and the great match is mine. It is a gift.

I approach my ball to putt it. I am about to strike, when—what golfer does not know it?—a sense of the enormous responsibility overcomes me, a film comes across my eyes, I putt hurriedly, I am weak. Two yards at least are left for me to hole. I glance at James. He looks pale, but is composed, with tight-pressed lips. After careful study I address my ball. I strike it. "It's in, it's in—it's—no! That blade of grass!" On the very edge of the hole it has arrested it. The match is halved. "James, take home that blade of grass, enshrine it in a golden diamond-studded casket, for that blade of grass has saved you the great match."

Thus was the great match halved, and all the golfing and all the travelling were in vain. In vain, save for the enjoyment we had, for the cheery welcomes we met, for the store of health we laid in. And so, really, not in vain at all. If any should feel tempted to a golfing tour of like description, I have put on record this rough sketch of our experiences to aid them—a sort of golfing guide book—in knowing to what sort of land, from a golfing pilgrim's standpoint, their progress may be leading them.

THE PILGRIM ABROAD

Coelum non animam mutant

I T is surely fair to presume that no golfer góes abroad for the winter with any object other than to seek a climate for himself or some member of his household. A man of much experience told the writer that he knew no woman "whose health permitted her to live in the home which her husband provided for her." Be this as it may, it is certain that the British householder is occasionally driven to exchange the hardships of coal famines and London fogs for the sometimes greater severities of the winter of the South of France. We say "sometimes greater severities" advisedly, for fresh in our memory, at the moment of writing, is the winter of 1893-94, which saw 20° of frost, on the Fahrenheit thermometer, in such resorts of the British climate-hunter as Pau and Biarritz. The truth is, the weather of the Basses Pyrénées is not to be relied on. Now and again a winter is uninterruptedly delightful ; but these are exceptions occurring in a series of winters, of which each will comprise one or more

cold "snaps" of a week or two.   The merit of
the climate is that the cold "snaps" are brief, and
that when the sun shines the heavens delight you
with a more than British blueness.   While it lasts,
however, the cold is more severe than the cold of
an ordinary winter at home ;   it takes you more
by surprise, by reason of the suddenness of its
attack ;   it takes you at a disadvantage, because
coal-fires are hard to come by, and it is difficult
to heat the houses to the degree of British home-
warmth.   If it should catch you unawares without
warm winter clothing, it is more than likely to
search out weak joints in your harness.

No doubt the Riviera is better.   On the warm
days of the Basses Pyrénées the *habitués* will deny
it.   Gathering themselves together on the terrace
before the Gassion at Pau, and gazing at the snow-
clad Pic du Midi, or on the *plage* at Biarritz
admiring the tumbling breakers, they will fall to
congratulating one another as proudly as if the
glorious sunshine were the creation of their own
efforts.   "What the deuce does a fellow want to
go to the Riviera for, when he can get such
weather as this here ?"   But when the storm
cone is hoisted, and the scud comes racing up
over the lowering sky from the sea, with a falling
glass and falling thermometer, they will bethink
themselves in silent or in profane sorrow, accord-

ing to their manner, of the blue Mediterranean and the palm-trees of Cannes.

For there, too, they might be playing golf as well, in a sense, as at Pau or Biarritz. In a sense, far better, for at Cannes it is an easier game to play—a game with fewer difficulties; a shorter course, with fewer of "those horrid bunkers"; a very gentlemanly style of golf, in fact—so gentlemanly as to be almost ladylike. The ladies golf there, zealously, under the gracious patronage of the Russian Grand Duke; and since the train now stops to set down golfers at La Napoule, the course is easy of access. To the plain golfer of the east of Fife there may seem to be a little too much of grace and of high dignities about it; but, after all, golf levels non-golfing distinctions. There is no law of hereditary precedence about getting into the hole.

But at Cannes, no less than elsewhere on the Riviera, the golfer who is compelled to take thought about the temperature must be especially watchful in the sunset hours. From four to six is the time of danger, when the air strikes most chilly on the tender chest or lung. Later the temperature rises again. Moreover, when it is dark the golfer will naturally wrap his tweeds about him, whereas the sunset, in its gay beauty, insidiously invites him to go unprotected.

Nevertheless, when all is said, Cannes is a better wintering-place, regarding the winter months strictly, than the golf resorts of the Basses Pyrénées; and since there is golf there—of such quality as one may at least be grateful for on the Riviera—it may be said at once that the winter campaign of the climate-hunting golfer can nowhere else be as well begun. The accommodation, as everybody knows, is excellent, even if it be rather dear; but when it includes such a measure of warmth and sunshine, per-haps it is not excessive. So for December and January the golfer will do well at Cannes, and by early February he may be bethinking him-self of a change of quarters—not a change for the better, so far as the quarters go, but a change to better golf. About the first of February the climate of Pau is becoming trustworthy.

If a man is in a hurry, on leaving the Riviera, to arrive in the neighbourhood of the French Atlantic seaboard, the train service between Marseilles and Bordeaux is one of the best in France. It is more interesting, however, and in point of distance shorter, to crawl along from Toulouse, beside the upper waters of the Garonne, and to come down on Pau through the Hautes Pyrénées. Here you may pass by Luchon, may branch off to Bigorre, may find yourself in the neighbourhood of Lourdes, where they will perform any miracle upon you, even to the extent of curing you of missing short putts.

In Pau you will find a quality of softness in the atmosphere which even the greater warmth of Cannes did not supply. You will dwell, most probably, in one of those great and good hotels, the Gassion or the France, which stand on the high terrace from which you look out over the rushing Gave and away on over numberless billows of foothills, rising higher and higher till they lead the eye to the shining snow-peaks of the Pyrénées, culminating in the lofty isolation of the Pic du Midi. Or—there is always an alternative—for a week the whole landscape may be wrapped in haze, and you may have no visible evidence of a mountain within a thousand miles of you. By preference, however, let us take the more pleasing alternative. Then, after the "little breakfast," which you will supplement, if you are wise, with something certainly not less solid than an *œuf à la coque*, you will stroll along the terrace, westward, past the famous Chateau Henri IV., whose wonderful tapestries you will reserve for the consolation of your eyes on a weeping day, when the *vent du sud* has brought a curtain of rain to shroud from you the beauties of the Pyrénées. And

so you win your way into the wood on the
hillside, and along its winding footway, which
gives lovely peeps of the mountains between
the tree-stems, down to the links on the level
plain of Billères.   Here you find a club-house
more picturesque than most of the buildings
designed or adapted for such uses, with a
verandah, and a balcony opening from the
ladies' club-rooms above.   At a little distance
is Lloyd's club-making shop, surrounded by a
mass meeting of the unemployed caddies, who
will clamour in pleasant Béarnaise for your
custom.   Among these sabotted and berretted
oiseaux[1]—many of them sad rascals, it is too
likely, in the degeneracy inevitable in those of
the lower humanity who consort with the
golfer or the horse—are to be found some
sterling good players.   The plain of Billères lies
low, on a level almost with the river Gave.
South of the river the lower ranges of the
Pyrénées begin to rise immediately.   Doubtless
it is by reason of its situation that it is so
peculiarly windless.   The golfer, starting on his
round from the club-house, and playing out for
the first hole or two along the side of the
river—into it, if he pulls his ball—recognises at

---

[1] A plural of *oisif*, often in use in old provincial French =
"loafers."

once this peculiar quality. There is a peace in the atmosphere—a peace which is inexpressibly soothing to the irritated nerves (no man ought to lose his temper or to miss short putts at Pau), but a peace which is not altogether wholesome to one who comes direct from the golf links of our keen east coast. However, the judiciously spent interval at Cannes will have prepared the system for a grateful assimilation of the peace. The quality of the golf is in harmony with the soothing conditions of the climate. The lies are excellent, the turf more beautiful than we are accustomed to find it in links which do not skirt the sea,—wonderfully beautiful when we consider that we are out of our own country, which is the best turf producer in the world. Until we come to the four last holes, the absence of hazard assists the general suggestion of this all-pervading peace. The verdant plain is dotted with occasional thorny bushes, at which, when our ball gets into them, we should swear in any other climate. There are some bluff escarped faces, with the holes perched on plateaux above them; there is a hole among apple-trees; and, having accomplished these, we drive over, or into, the plot, valuable from its gutta-percha deposits, of a peasant of the country; and so, over another field, fenced by high hedges, back again to the smiling plain and the glancing river. Despite the comparative absence of hazard in these first fourteen holes, they are not to be done in a very low score, for they are long, though there is a certain sameness in their features or lack of feature. The last four holes amply atone for this—they are full of expression. For the first of them you may go straight, if you please, over Lloyd's shop, over several other outhouses, over the mass meeting of the *oiseaux*, over a branch of the Gave—but you will need to be a greater than Douglas Rolland to carry them all. Nevertheless, over this branch of the Gave you must go, or give up the hole and all the honours pertaining to it. If you face at right angles to the direct, heroic line to the hole, you may cross the river with a half iron shot ; but the bolder and nearer you drive to the straight line the shorter will be your approach stroke. For the last hole of all you again cross this limb of the Gave, with a full iron shot—a distance much the same as that of the St Andrews short hole going out. The two holes, intermediate, the sixteenth and seventeenth, bristle with brambles, while the latter, in addition, presents peculiar facilities for a visit to the river.

By all which efforts you have well earned your *déjeûner*, well cooked and served in the club-house, and thereafter, a smoke in the shade of the verandah, with the unequalled panorama of the Pyrénées before you. Here you will discuss the bad luck which attended you on your round, and when your friends are weary of this theme, you will be told the story of the foundation of the club — how, with the immortal exception of Blackheath, it is the most ancient golf club south of the Tweed, in all the world as known to the moderns. The writer having claimed an uncle as one of the original founders of the club at Pau, a waggish friend informed him that it was rare to meet a man whose uncle had not founded the Pau Golf Club. The truth is, that a little colony of Scottish and English gentle-men finding themselves at Pau, sorely in need of occupation, and with the plain of Billères be-fore their eyes, betook themselves to golf as naturally as ducks to water, and established the club which now flourishes so pleasantly. In the club parlour hangs a picture of three surviving founders — Archdeacon Sapte, Colonel Hutchin-son and Major Pontifex — to whose likenesses the golfer will turn grateful eyes.

Inured by the training of Cannes to the atmo-sphere of peace, and invigorated by the *déjeûner*, the golfer may again tempt fortune among the *buissons*, the escarpments, the apple - trees, the hedges and the ramifying Gave. Only, on his return from this afternoon round, let him beware, for here too, as on the Riviera, the sunset hours are the most treacherous. He may walk homeward again through the grove, or, more likely, may prefer to drive in one of the closed hack-carriages which he will find in attendance. For the homeward walk is up - hill, and this is not the "caller" air of the kingdom of Fife. In the English Club he may find whist or games of greater hazard, or billiards, either French or English, or literature equally polyglot. He will find multitudes of his compatriots—always a consideration to the English innocent abroad—and many fellow-countrymen of the original immortal "Innocents."

The climate throughout February is nearly sure to be a joy to him. If he please, he may vary his golf by hunting with the Pau hounds, who probably show the best sport of any pack out of England. He may make expeditions into the Pyrénées, with the object of shooting *izards*—the Pyrenean chamois—who are an elusive quarry. If he be exceptionally fortunate, he may even achieve the glory of shooting a bear. But by the end of February it is likely that he will

begin to find the peace rather too much for
him. A disinclination to a second round, which
he had never known in the keen air of Scotland,
will be beginning to warn him that the too kindly
climate is relaxing his energies. He will sigh for
a keen breeze to revive his vigour, and will listen,
with the ear of longing, to the frequent dictum
of the *habitué* of Pau, that "it always blows a
gale at Biarritz." He bethinks him that it
would be good for his lungs, good for his
muscles, good for his appetite, good, finally, for
his golf, to taste once more the flavour of a
gale — and the final consideration decides him.
The journey is not a great one. Three hours
or so, according to the caprices of the train
service, should take him to Bayonne, whence a
further train voyage, or a drive of something
over three miles, will land him at Biarritz and
the caves of Æolus. In the Æolian qualities he
may chance to be disappointed—the bags of all
the winds are not always opened at Biarritz, as
the reports which he heard at Pau had seemed
to indicate—but he is not likely to fail to notice
a salutary ozone-laden breath off the sea, which
is refreshment after the great peace of the plain
of Billères. He may even comment on this to
a *habitué* of Biarritz, and in that case will be answered by an "Oh, Pau! My dear fellow, one

cannot breathe there," which should induce reflection on human nature and on the inestimable
blessing of contentment with one's lot. At
Biarritz he will find hotels as good as those
at Pau, and somewhat cheaper. Indeed, he will
recognise that his expenses — other things, such
as his thirst, being equal—have been in a de-
creasing scale with each move, — Pau cheaper
than Cannes, Biarritz cheaper again than Pau.
There is satisfaction in this, as in the more
generous, more free air that he inhales gratis.
He will repair to the club of his compatriots,
which he will find similar to that of Pau, though
smaller ; and again, in its designation, he may
note a suggestion of greater liberality. At Pau,
it was the "English" Club—here, with appreciation of the delicate susceptibilities of an island
adjacent to England, it is yclept the "British"
Club ; in which name the Scotsman too may
have enough Caledonian patriotism to rejoice.
In place of the snow-clad Pyrénées, his view
shows him a tumbling race of white - crested
billows—as fine a sea as any on the Atlantic
coast. He will mount an open fly—with the
mental observation that the flies of Pau were
like the plain of Billères itself, shut in—and be
driven a short mile, up-hill, to the golf links.
He will reverse the order of the going which

was his habit at Pau. There he habitually
walked *to* the links, and drove *from* them, because they were down-hill from the town. Here
he will by preference drive *to* them, and walk
down—always choosing to walk in the direction
of the less resistance. Moreover, in the more
vigorous air he will find the walking less fatigu-
ing. At the same time, he will reflect, if he
be wise, that the climate of Biarritz, which he
may trust now that it is March, was scarcely
to be depended on, equally with that of Pau, in
February.

From the high ground, if the day be clear,
he may still see the Pyrénées and the Pic du
Midi, but at so great a distance that his driver,
who would preferably talk Basque, tells him in
French, which he has a difficulty in understanding, that it would promise better for the weather
if the snow-clad peaks were not visible. The
club-house he will find to be a building of less
glory, beauty and comfort than that of Pau,
though answering its purpose adequately.

The links of Biarritz and of Pau do not
compare well; they are too dissimilar. While
the features of the latter are their length,
their flatness, the excellence of their lies and
their comparative immunity from hazards —
the links of Biarritz are remarkable for their

boldness, their undulations and their numerous difficulties, which are not always avoided
when the ball lies on what ought to be the
good green of the course. The putting-greens
themselves are good enough; it is the green between the holes which might be better. In com-
pensation, as it were, for its greater difficulty, the
Biarritz course is considerably shorter than that of
Pau, and, in consequence, it is an easier course to
the good golfer—a course which the good golfer
will accomplish in fewer strokes than he would
require at Pau. On the other hand, for the weak
or erratic golfer it will be found more difficult, by
reason of the vileness of the lies on parts of the
course, and by reason of the ubiquity of hazard.
Wherefore Biarritz may be said to be the better
school for golf—a school in which the golfer must
learn, perforce, to play all his clubs; whereas at
Pau, in a way of speaking, he might play all
round with his putter, always, however, excepting
from this statement the last four holes. The
golfer whose ball cleaves, like the serpent, to the
earth will make no way at Biarritz. The drives
must be good, carrying shots, the iron approaches
must pitch well up to the hole. Consider, for
example, the second hole, and tremble. The well-
struck tee-shot will put you within ironing range
of the hole. Others have ironed there before

F

you, so your troubles may be complicated by an evil lie. Without that complication they are sufficient. First there is a hedge, then a road, and then another hedge, and the hole is just beyond the second hedge. These troubles do not face you fairly, but slant away from you, running up close beside the hole, so that you have to pitch the ball "like a poached egg," as Mr Alfred Lyttelton puts it, to get at all near the hole. And you dare not harden your heart and resolve to be past, for if you are much past—five-and-twenty yards past—you are over the edge of a tremendous sea-cliff hundreds of feet high, and both ball and hole are irretrievable. When you have putted out this hole successfully, you tee off on the edge of the chasm which used to be a famous feature of Biarritz links. The sea thunders away at the chasm's floor, and across it, from brink to brink, you had to go, for disaster was fatal, and there was no way round—no way, at least, that was worth the going. But, after all, the chasm should have appalled only to the very faint-hearted, or the very feeble. A stout half-iron shot would have sent the ball across. It was only the frowning aspect of the sheer cliffs that made it terrible, and in point of difficulty it was not a circumstance to the approach to the old second hole.

In the inception of golf at Biarritz, nine holes

were the extent of the course.   Latterly it has
been enlarged to eighteen, and there remain some
which are still a little "in the rough."   These are
those holes of which the Pau golfer asked, aghast,
"What! d'you call this a golf links?   I call it a
grouse-moor!"

The covert is being worn away; there is
scarcely heather enough now to give a very good
screen for a covey, but there is enough to give a
very bad lie for a golf-ball.   Still, what is education but a series of adversities?   In the keener
air of Biarritz the golfer is equal to "howking" a
ball out of a lie before which he would have sat
down and wept in the midst of the great peace of
the plain of Billères.   The grouse-moorish holes
are full of interest; indeed, of the entire course
of the Biarritz links one may say that there is not
a stroke which is without its special interest; and
that is a deal to say—more than one can say of
Pau, though there the lies are so much better.
On the older half of the course the turf is as good
as is to be found on any links which are not of
the real seaside sort.   The principal hazards are
hedges, ditches, roads, bunkers in which there is
real sand, as if the links were of the seaside
quality, and deep holes which the golfer calls
punch-bowls, and which, one is told, were gravel-
pits in their original purpose.   There is no

symptom of gravel in them now. When it is said that these links are not of the real seaside kind there appears need of a word of explanation, since the Atlantic thunders beside them, and often swallows an erratic golf-ball. These links are truly enough beside the sea, but they are not seaside links in the golfer's sense — not seaside links in the sense in which the links of St Andrews, Prestwick, Westward Ho! Sandwich, and the rest of them are so called. All these famous links occur near the estuary of some river, and undoubtedly are the work of what geologists call alluvial deposit, aided by the action of the wind in blowing up sand-dunes; so that all their turf is short and springy, with its roots in sand. Biarritz links are not like these. Their turf is of the consistency of down turf,—very similar in soil, only without the chalk, to the Eastbourne links, which also are close beside the sea, and yet are not seaside links according to the golfer's phrase. Nevertheless, they are sufficiently good for the golfer to disport himself thereon with pleasure and with profit—profit primarily to his golf, and secondarily to his health, which, after all, is a consideration.

For, though he will not find himself in so un-redeemed a cave of Æolus as his friends at Pau would have had him believe, he will yet meet with

plenty of bracing breezes to freshen his energies
after the relaxation of the climate of Pau. He
will find a refreshing *déjeûner* quite good enough
for the hungry golfer, if he be careful in the
ordering of it beforehand, in the club-house; he
will find in Willie Dunn a very obliging and fairly
efficient club-maker; and, unless he be a dweller
on the highest branches of the golfing tree, he will
find more than his match in one or two of the
bigger caddies. The quickness with which even
the least of these little urchins picks up the duties
incidental to the honourable profession of club-
carrying is strong testimony to the alert intelligence of their nation, and they show an aptitude
for playing the game which is characteristic of so
athletic and game-loving a race as the Basques.
Sunday is their great practising day. Though
the liberal-minded golfer will sometimes so far
forget his insular scruples as to play on the
Sabbath, yet the majority willingly take this
one holiday out of seven. The flags are not set
out, so that a fore-caddie is a necessity. The
club-house, however, is open, and a few indefatigable spirits pursue the game. Nevertheless the
links are for the most part vacant, and the caddies,
sometimes with their female relatives in attendance, emulate the week-day example of their
masters. Many will be playing with clubs of their

own manufacture—a springy shaft thrust into a block of wood for the head ; and even with these rude weapons they make better practice than is often achieved by the masters. They have begun at the right age, and it may be that a future champion is studying, in sabots and berret, on the links of Biarritz.

Both at Pau and Biarritz the golfer will find fairly good short links for ladies. At Pau, after the first of April—*absit* any kind of suspicion of *omen* from the inauspicious date—ladies are allowed to play on the long links after four o'clock, but at Biarritz this high privilege is only accorded by special leave of the committee. At Biarritz, as at Pau, the golfer may vary his regular occupation by hunting. It is not the hunting of Leicestershire, for the country presents an alternative of very small fields and immense sandy-floored pine forests, but it may serve as a change. The month of March is rather late for any sport in the way of shooting ; but fair trout fishing may be obtained by a little "roughing it" in the way of sleeping in rude hostelries in the neighbourhood of Irun. But always there are interesting expeditions to be made into the beautiful Pyrenean country—to Cambo, or, across the Spanish border, to Fontarabia, or San Sebastian ; and if the golfer have a turn for military history, he may study on the spot the scene of much of Wellington's masterly strategy in the Peninsular war.   He may play tennis, if it pleases him, in the oldest tennis court in the world—the model of all our tennis courts—the *trinquet* court, as it is called, at Bayonne.   But, above all, he will not fail to visit St Jean de Luz, and to take his golf clubs with him, for there too is a golf links.   It is only of nine holes, of later inception than the Biarritz links, and not equal to these in excellence; nevertheless, it makes an amusing change in the middle of a month's golf.   There is no club-house on the links, so the golfer who has come over by road or train will do wisely to take *déjeûner* at the Hôtel d'Angleterre, which is all on his way from the station to the links. He will find caddies who stand in need of much instruction in the game, and their education is rendered the more troublesome by the circumstance that their language is the undiluted Basque.   The St Jean de Luz links, though they are small, are by no means of the sort which a man can play over with a putter.   The tee-shots require to be driven with a good length of carry, for the ground undulates steeply, and there is no run on the ball.   One tee-shot presents features like those of the Biarritz chasm. The chasm, in fact, embraces a far wider arc of sea, if one drive at all straight for the hole, but affords a better chance of circumnavigation by the inland route.

Towards the end of March the golfer will find days at Biarritz in which a solar topee is a grateful style of head-dress, though the sun's rays strike with less power than in the frying-pan of the plain of Billères.   Nevertheless, they will scorch him sufficiently to make him think with some regret, tempered by a wholesome memory of certain days when the British March is lion-like, of the keener breezes of the East Neuk of Fife. The wholesome memory, however, will give him pause before he takes passage for London in the *Peregrine* or *Hirondelle* from Bordeaux, or purchases a through ticket *via* Paris.   Then a friend will not do him a bad turn if he suggest to him that there is such a place as Dinard, and within three or four miles of it the links named St Briac, which are better than any he has yet tried in France.   The sea-coast of Brittany is surely a good half-way house for the golfer about April, between the ardent sun of the Basses Pyrénées and the east winds of Great Britain.   The course to Dinard, however, is not too clearly marked, unless the golfer be fortunate enough to hit on a good fore-caddie in the person of someone who has already made the journey from Biarritz.   The *indicateur* points to Bordeaux inflexibly as the first stage. After that there is a puzzling choice between going by way of Paris, by way of Tours, or by way of Nantes. Other things being equal, and Paris possessing no pressing attractions, the last line—*viâ* Nantes—is certainly the best. It is also the cheapest. It is a safe rule to travel with in France, that you save money whenever you avoid Paris.

A second safe rule is to avoid, if possible, night travelling on any except the great arterial lines of France. Bordeaux to Nantes scarcely falls within this category, though the train service is good, and the golfer will do wisely to accomplish the journey by daylight. With this view he will spend a night at Bordeaux, where an excellent opera-house will perhaps have attractions for him. We may indicate to the golfer that he will find an excellent restaurant attached to the Hôtel de Bayonne ; but as for his lodging we are at a loss to give him counsel, for a hotel which will meet his British requirements is hard to come by. However, it is but for a night, and that a short one, for he must be in the train by 8.25 the next morning, to get through, with any comfort, to Nantes. This hour means an earlier start than would appear, for the French railway companies have a masterly way of setting down their station where it best suits the main purposes of the line, without any very studious regard for landing the traveller conveniently near his hotel. Thus, at Biarritz he will have driven more than two miles to the station, and again the same fate will overtake him at Bordeaux, with the aggravation of cobble-stoned streets to drive over. Nantes is but little better. He will arrive a few minutes past five, after a journey through a flat and uninteresting country, gradually exchanging the land of the vineyard for the land of the apple orchard. At Nantes, the Hôtel de France is good. They understand the arts of cooking, of comfort, and of charging. There are those who prefer the Hôtel des Voyageurs, where the last art is not practised in so great perfection, though still they are adepts at the minor ones. Certainly the rattle of the carriages, which seems almost night long, on the cobbles of the great square at Nantes, before the Hôtel de France, is a trial to the wearied nerves of the traveller.

The next morning the start, sufficiently early still, is not so intolerable as from Bordeaux. The 9.20 train, going by way of Redon, will bring the golfer to Dinard in the course of the day— late for dinner certainly ; too late for dinner probably, but the exact hour depends on the varying arrangements of the local train services. There is a merit, which the golfer will now begin to recognise, if he did not so before, in these trains of France; they are not rapid, but they arrive with a wonderful exactness. The great loco-motives resemble the "mills of God," in the slowness and the exceeding sureness of their grinding. The distance from Nantes to Dinard is roughly about half that between Nantes and Bordeaux, yet the journey, as will be seen, takes longer. In truth, on this, the last day of his pilgrimage, the golfer will spend as much time out of the train as in it. At Redon he will have an hour or so in which to breakfast. At Rennes he will have yet longer, and may in-spect the big town, and see multitudes of soldiery. At Dol he will spend an unprofitable half-hour; and at Dinan, where, probably, he will dine, he may be interested in seeing the quaint nooks of what is perhaps the most typical and pictur-esque town of old Brittany.

The links on which the men of Dinard play golf are not precisely at Dinard. They are nearer the town of St Briac, and are more strictly, though still not exactly, known as the St Briac links. In point of fact they are be-tween St Briac and St Lunaire. If, in Dinard, you ask a cab-driver how far it is to *le golf*, he will tell you "eight kilometres." This, after

deduction for cab-driver's measurement and con-
version into English, means about four miles.
In the season your cab-driver will charge you
some six francs for taking you there and back,
by which is meant that he will not do it for less;
if you were to pay him on the scale of his first
demand, without *marchander*-ing with him, you
would not do the journey without the expense
of gold. In winter he will take you there and
back for three francs. Even this moderate expense is unnecessary thrice in the week, for a
diligence runs on alternate week days, starting
soon after one. Thus it will be seen that the
ordinary golfer of Dinard is a one round man;
it is possible, however, to stir him up to a
better sense of his duty in grasping golfing
opportunity.

The golfer need not stay in Dinard. There
is a hotel almost at the first tee—within a
quarter iron-shot of the golf club-house. Commonly it is closed in winter, but, for a party of
golfers, no doubt they would open it for a month.
Or again, there is a better hotel nearer St Lunaire,
about a mile—a short mile—from the club-house.
This latter hotel is absolutely on the ladies'
links, so the members of the golfer's family
ought to be well satisfied, if they too play
golf. In Dinard there are more varied delights

—a nice, social club, very good gravelled lawn tennis courts, a certain society, and shops. There is boating, too, in the mouth of the river. But it is possible to boat at St Lunaire; and, after all, a small party, sufficient unto itself for its society, might find in the unrestraint of the out-of-town hotels charms which would more than compensate for the dear delights of Dinard. The golfer would find himself installed among the sand hills, with golf links all around him, with an unimpeded view of a bluer than British sea and a bolder than British coast, with just a stretch of dunes for his children to run over before they come to the pleasant sea sands—dunes inadequately clad with the bent grass out of which the skylarks will arise, and wind their way up to heaven to sing a song of thankfulness for Brittany. It is not without purpose that we call these sand hills *inadequately* clad with the bent grass. In a heavy gale of late 1893, the sand was torn off them and strewed in a thick bunkery mattress over all the ladies' links. Previously, these ladies' links had been the best of all such places reserved for ladies which the writer has seen. Since the storm, parts of them are ruined, temporarily—and it is difficult to say what chance there is of their recovery. The remainder, which was protected by sand-hills, clad with a closer garment, has escaped, and is as good as ever.

If the golfer stay in Dinard his first drive to the links will charm him by the views it unfolds to him of the sea, studded with the many islets which make this coast so hard of navigation. Stretching to Cape Frehel he will see all the arc of the beautiful bay with its infinite indentations. His golfing soul will receive the peculiar inspiration, which Pau and Biarritz alike had failed to give, of approaching his golfing business over land which is real links, real sand hills, real bunkers. Quite unexpectedly he will find himself beside the club-house, for it lies cunningly sheltered from the east by a rising bank of ground, and all the way from Dinard the east wind has been at the golfer's back.

He will find the accommodation of the club-house ample, if not luxurious; for though no luncheon can be obtained without previous orders, he may make up for this at the hotel close by—if it be open. He can always get tea, however, after the afternoon round; and for the most part he will fall in with the native manner, and content himself with one after-*déjeûner* round. A balcony outside the first floor

club-room is a good look-out place whence he
can watch the incoming couples and the trials
and sorrows of most of the round.

And, let it be said at once, this course on
which he looks out is something altogether different from Pau or Biarritz. It has claims to be
considered a first-class links. It *is* links—really
sandy ground, too sandy since the storm of last
year, which has visited parts of it with only a
little less severity than that with which it visited
the ladies'. Moreover, the rain has beaten upon it
and the wind blown upon it until between them
they have worked little holes in the putting
greens, which now look small-pocked. But the
spring growth is putting all this, which is a
winter vexation, to rights again ; and, winter
or summer, there is not a hole on the course
which is without its interest. The worst hole
is the last, as happens curiously often on golf
links, yet its faults are all negative—it is too
featureless. At present the links are too short.
They might be much bettered in the laying out.
It may be said that there is no good attempting
to lay out a first-class course when so few of
the golfers are even third-class ; but, on the
other hand, one cannot expect to attract a better
kind of golfer unless the course be laid out
for the best. In the long run it never pays to

cater for incapacity—it is no real kindness even to the incapable.

Nevertheless, taken as they are, the links are good—the best in France, so far as France as a land of golf is yet exploited. They have characteristics, too, which suggest the golf links of the North. Often there is a keenness in the air which may inspire the golfer by its likeness to that which has grown only too familiar to him on links of the British east coast; the sea of the Channel looks as if it belonged to the piece of water which beats on the shores by Bembridge and Hayling Island; all appearances conspire to remind him that he is drawing nearer home.

The links are divided into two parts by the rib of ground which shelters the club-house. It is not until the sixth hole that one comes in front of the club-house, and commences to play over the expanse stretching westward from it. Of this earlier part, the second hole and the fifth are so good that it is difficult to name better holes on any links. Indeed, it is easier and briefer to name the holes which are inferior: thus, the first is of little interest, beyond the chance of hitting a Frenchman or his wife, if the drive be far enough across the rib to reach the road. The third hole is rather flat and unprofit-

able, and we have already given scant praise to
the last. Of the rest, no one can be called anything but good, and some, notably the eleventh,
are excellent.   One selects the eleventh for
special praise by reason of its length, for it needs
a drive and a good long cleek-shot to reach it.
This is about the greatest length of any hole on
the course. Most of them, in all other respects
admirable, err on the side of being too short—err
in being of that worst of lengths, a drive and iron.
Both drive and iron shot, however, are full of
interest, the sand-bunkers lying in wait for topped
tee-shots, and the holes being well guarded by
hazards of bunker or whin. The twelfth, again,
is a very good hole. It is perched out on a corner
abutting the sea. A very long tee-shot will reach
it ; but he who would attempt it in one carries his
fate in his hands, for if he fail to hit a very good
ball, he will be lost among the rocks of the shore.
The safer way is to the left, inland. It is a path
of roses in the season, for the little white low-
growing blossoms cluster in the sandy soil; but
a bed of roses is too soft lying for the golfer's
comfort. Excellent, again, is the fourteenth hole,
and yet more so the sixteenth, both of which
require a very justly played second to find the
green. The seventeenth is one of the shortest
short holes, and one of the best on any green,

perched up at a quarter iron-shot distance, with a steep sandy face on the near side, so that you must be up; the putting-green itself at a gentle slope up away from you, and rather heavy with sand, so that if you play a well-lofted or well-cut stroke you can stop the ball close to the hole, though it be only two yards beyond the face of broken sand. It is a very cleverly planted little hole.

There are too many " blind " approaches. This, however, could perhaps not be avoided in view of the undulating nature of the whole ground—and, after all, it is only the stranger whose ignorance is thus handicapped. The course is rather too short, rather too sandy, and the putting-greens rather in need of more attention than the club is able to give them; but, taken for all in all, they are the best links in France, and from the whole number of links in Great Britain it is doubtful if one could name a dozen to be placed on a list of merit before them. Moreover, there are many links in Great Britain which are less accessible from its metropolis, for St Malo is within eleven hours of Southampton, and St Malo is divided from Dinard only by an estuary, across which the ferry-boats run half-hourly.

Should "staleness" overtake the golfer, he may spend an interesting day or two in a visit to Mont

St Michel, which is a place unlike almost any other. He will find the Breton caddie as quick and pleasant as the specimens which are grown in the country of the Bearnais or the Basques; and he may read, if he be a pious Englishman, sad omens of the times in the fact that Freemantle, the club professional, has abandoned his original calling as professor of cricket to turn professor of golf, which he practises, as well as professes, with a success that is altogether praiseworthy.

Without going into historical details, it may be sufficient to say that there are, in the neighbourhood of the French coast, certain islands named the "Channel Islands," belonging to England, and of which the most considerable is Jersey—Jersey, where the pears and the cabbage-stalk walking-sticks come from. Jersey is a very good halting-place on the way from Dinard to England. The crossing from Jersey to England is commonly very much dreaded; indeed, we have heard a sailor say that he had been all round the world and had never been sea-sick except when crossing from Southampton to Jersey. Nevertheless, it is quite possible to be sea-sick on this passage without having been all round the world, and again it is quite possible to make the passage on a sea as smooth as a pond. He that ventures abroad must

take his chance, and at all events one has a better
chance in breaking up the crossing into little bits
than in taking it all on one voyage. As the
golfer, having embarked at St Malo, gets clear out
into the open sea, it may happen that a stranger
will refer to his golf-clubs as an excuse for
addressing him with the information that if he
will cast his eye eastward along the coast, beyond
the cluster of houses which forms the watering-
place of Paramé, he will see a stretch of ground
which are the Paramé golf links. The stranger
will express surprise that a golfer should be
leaving Dinard without paying them a visit. The
golfer will reply that he had indeed heard of them
—had heard that in order to achieve such a visit
it would be necessary for him to take a train from
St Servan, and, after reaching Paramé, to drive
yet four miles farther, in any conveyance that he
might find, and that the conclusive piece of information given to him was to the effect that the
Paramé links were not a sufficient reward for so
much trouble. To this the stranger will reply,
that these observations are due to the jealousy
which the people of Dinard feel towards the
people and attractions of St Malo and St Servan;
that there is an excellent *auberge* at the edge of
the Paramé links, where one can get a very fair
déjeûner ; and that the links, though sandy, are by

no means such as Dinard detractors would describe them. The "though sandy" is a saving concession which dispels the gently rising regrets of the golfer who had left the links of Paramé unvisited, and he is able to devote himself with a free heart to the task of grappling with all the demons of sea-sickness. These are in their highest spirits and best energy in the ever-vexed neighbourhood of those rocks the "Minquiers"— "Minkies" in the mouth of the English tar— which, in days of less perfect chartography, were a harvest-field of death to the sailors of these coasts and islands. The French name of the western-most of these rocks, signifying "the reaper," is full of a very grim meaning. By this time the eye of the golfer, if he be able to lift it, may discern the whole extent of the southern coast-line of the little island, even to the neighbourhood of the golf links, which, it needs not to say, will be to him its chief attraction.

St Helier, where the golfer will probably stay, is a town which has no less than three daily papers, so there can be no question of its prosperity. It rejoices in the utmost freedom of trade, so that a man can smoke and drink at extraordinarily low prices; and no custom-house official invades the sanctity of his portmanteau in a search for dynamite or Tauchnitz editions. Nevertheless, he will find himself again in a land where they speak his native tongue, in a land of English newspapers and cookery and of penny stamps. In the town there is a good club ; but to reach the golf links it is best to make use of the railway which runs eastward along the coast to Grouville. There are trains about once an hour, and though they stop at intervals so frequent as to remind the golfer of the "Metropolitan and District," they achieve the journey in twenty minutes. The platform of the station is but the distance of a short putt from the golf club-house, which is as comfortable as could be wished. The newcomer is beset by the usual horde of small banditti, each impressing him with their individual merits as carriers of clubs. Some of them talk the two languages, but most seem to understand English better, and will stare with some amazement at the golfer demanding, as he infallibly will on coming from the Continent, his *petit fer*. It will take him some two or three rounds to realise, after his late experiences of caddies of the sabotted and berretted kind, that it is possible for these British urchins to understand the meaning of the "light iron." Recollection will be brought back to him by gentler means if he happen to fall upon one of the bilingual kind. Under either guise, however, and in whatever tongue they speak of it, these little boys of Jersey know something about the game. They understand its details and its spirit. In fact, the golfer will not long have been at Jersey before he will have discovered himself to be in a land where they have the traditions — the " doctrine," *golficè* speaking — as they have it not in any of the places, save Pau, of his earlier pilgrimage. Partly, no doubt, this impression is conveyed by the sound of the English tongue, which seems more suited than the gay accents of France to the stern purposes of Scotland's game ; but partly, too, it is due to the fact that golf has a more serious hold on the inhabitant of Jersey than on the sojourner of Cannes, Biarritz, or Dinard. At these latter places it is a new thing : it has not yet impressed the local devotees with a sense of its gravity. But in Jersey they have been playing golf for years and years, and not been playing it badly. Vardon, who has made a good show in the professional competitions of England and Scotland, lived and learned on the Jersey links ; and has a brother, less known to fame, who is his equal. The amateur talent is on a far higher level than on any Continental golf links. Pau may perhaps equal it—certainly will not surpass it—during its winter season ; but

in Jersey the golfer is resident and indigenous :
in Pau, he is only imported and migratory.

In point of fact, Jersey, as a land of golf, has
the respectability and conservatism which comes
of age alone. Golf was played at Jersey while
Westward Ho! Wimbledon, Blackheath and Pau
were the only golf clubs in existence south of
London; wherefore the golfer will not be surprised to find himself in a country where the
best traditions and manners of the game are
reverently cherished and observed. He will find
himself in a climate differing little from that of
Dinard, for though the Jersey winter is mild,
the spring east wind can nip shrewdly. In the
twenty minutes which the train takes to go the
very few miles to the course, he will have opportunity for observing pear trees in fine bloom,
cabbages with stalks like barge poles, and cows
of the true Jersey breed, on the landward side
of the track. Seaward, he may see a jagged
rock field, leading out towards those " Minquiers,"
in whose neighbourhood he may have confided
so many secret sorrows to the sea, and finally
the coast of France, dim and low-lying in the
distance. On close approach to the club-house,
the castle of Mont Orgueil will come in view,
like a Mont St Michel in miniature.

The links, less bold, and with less picturesque

views of bold seascape than those of Dinard,
are nevertheless of the right sandy soil and of
far better lies. This latter quality is, no doubt,
largely due to their greater age as golf links;
for of all known rollers, beaters and levellers of
the ground, none is so good as the human foot,
in sufficient frequency. The grass grows nice
and short, and the driver, where required, may
be taken for the second shot. The hazards, of
sand and whin, are of the real golfing kind.
You confess yourself at once, with gratitude, on
a golf links. At the first hole there is no sand;
you drive over patchy whins, and after a further
struggle with the mashie you are there. The
second hole is good golf; the first drive perfectly simple, the second endangered by a fort,
if the ball be pulled, by a bunker—one of the
best on the links—if it be short, and by a steep
bank beyond the hole if it be strong. The fort
again presents itself as a hazard for the tee-
shot to the fourth. A pull into it loses the
hole as fatally as a visit to the station-master's
garden at St Andrews. On the right lies the
sea-shore, and the stretch of good ground between is mighty narrow. Moreover, from the
corner of the fort to the beach runs a road, by
which men have hauled sand and seaweed, making big ruts, and it needs a stout shot to carry

it. The second shot is almost equally hazard-
ous, the hole lying near the sea beach, and
rifle-butts threatening a pulled ball with heavy
penalties. Then follow two holes which Rolland
would reach with comfort. Therefore they should
be threes. But those who are not Rollands are apt
to press to reach them, and with the aid of a
shallow bunker, just before the former hole, and a
keen plateau green, are likely enough to turn one
of the possible threes into a five. The seventh is
the longest hole. It cannot be reached in two,
and is a very sound hole in five. The eighth
and ninth are the normal drive and iron shot.
The tenth is aggravated by a railway on the
right hand to catch a heeled tee shot, or, again,
to catch the devious approach, for the hole is
very near the wire fence. One could play from
the railway with ease; but the wisdom of the
legislature has ordained that a ball wandering
thither should be treated as lost. Next is a
"blind" short hole. And here let it be said
at once that there are too many blind shots
on this excellent links of Jersey, and let it be
said without prejudice to any objector who says
that this is only when the tee is in a certain
place, and so forth. That may be true, but
one has to speak of courses as one finds them,
and not as they are arranged perhaps for cer-

tain weeks during the year, or at special
meeting times.   After this, one comes to a
long hole which sometimes is set upon a high
place, upon which it is almost impossible to
persuade the ball to remain—too high a test of
golf, in fact.   From this elevation, or a neighbouring one, you drive off, often into the
middle of a football match, and begin describing the letter Z as you zigzag backwards and
forwards, playing holes of a drive and cleek
shot, or drive and mashie shot, until the end.

If the spring is early, the golfer may find
the links covered with wild flowers and low-
growing thyme, among which the bees will be
buzzing and humming.   The numbers of bumble
bees so struck some golfer that he presented the
club with the "Bumble-bee" medal, which is
one of its permanent challenge prizes.   Amongst
the thyme the lies are very tolerable, but
scarcely first-rate, and the nature of the ground,
just a little too sandy, aggravates the difficulty.
A good shot sometimes misses its reward, and
finds its resting-place in a sandy pocket which
has no right to exist.   No doubt it is good
practice to have to play out of these sandy
drifts, but a better definition of hazard is to be
desired.   Over these links of Grouville broods,
as has been said, a portion of the spirit of the

classic saint of golf; nevertheless, in bigness and diversity of incident they do not compare with the links of Dinard, whose outlines you can almost make out, on a clear day, when rain is coming. Neither is their beauty on the same grand scale. It is all quieter, more peaceful, more homely.

After you have "done" the golf links, you have fairly well "done" the island. The other Channel Islands offer good sea fishing; but the coast off Jersey is shoal, and fish are as scarce at St Helier as at most seaside places. One cannot go on eating the big pears for ever, nor all the year round, and the joy of walking with a long cabbage stalk for a stick is one that palls. But you can go in a boat, or walk at low tide, to the fort named the Hermitage, opposite the Grand Hotel; you may have a look over the Gorey Castle; you may even take the Great Western Railway and run out to visit St Aubin and Corbière. And when you have done these things, you will be filled with a sense of satisfaction that they are accomplished and are not to do again. But if the golfer be a flower lover, his eyes and heart may have a feast of beauty and interest in the wild flowers which he may find in walks or drives over the island, or in masses in the shops of the market women.

Amongst those who live on an island you reasonably expect to find a certain insular prejudice, especially when the island of their habitation is so small an one as Jersey. Nevertheless, even among the conservative golfing men of Jersey you may have heard it said, in whispers, that the Guernsey links were better. It has happened to few, perhaps, to have even heard that golf was played in Guernsey; but such ignorance is merely due to the local prejudice of those who live in our greater island.

Apart from the golf, it is pleasant to make a half-way house of Guernsey on the way home. Your boat from Jersey starts at ten minutes to eight, if you choose the Southampton route; at twenty minutes past eight, if you elect to travel by Weymouth. Either hour is too early. You realise it more distinctly when you find yourself, after a hurried breakfast, on an unsympathetic sea, and by the time you have reached Guernsey —a run of an hour and a half—you are quite ready to be at the end of your journey. You cannot escape Guernsey. All the boats from Jersey to England call there, and take on board a few passengers, and an extraordinary number of baskets filled with fruit or flowers or vegetables for the home market. Will it be believed that thirty-two miles of glass houses for the growing of early tomatoes, potatoes, and other products were put up in the course of one year alone?

As an unsupported statement it will not be believed; the writer is not prepared to vouch for it, though it has been given him as a sober fact of statistics. But so soon as ever the visitor finds himself outside the houses of Peter's Port, and on his road to the golf links, he will be prepared to accept any statement whatsoever with regard to the extent of glass on the island. A waggonette conveys the golfer, at fixed and extraordinarily low charges, to the scene of his joys and sorrows, some three miles from the town; and after a mile or so has been traversed, he will find himself driving on a road which might easily be thought to have the sea close on either side of it, so continuous is the glint of the sun off the perpetual glass-houses. At the present rate of progress it may readily be computed how soon the island will be converted into one immense Crystal Palace, and shortly before that era there will be a very heavy premium on straight driving. On reaching the club-house, which supplies all that the simple soul of the golfer should require, you will be surrounded by a troop of caddies clamouring a chorus, in which shrill voices of little girls

will bear a part.   It is a discovery, on the part
of the Guernsey golfer, that the girl-caddie gives
more attention to your needs, more sympathy
to your misfortunes, than that most savage of
of all wild animals, as Plato calls him, the boy.
It is a significant fact, which should not be
overlooked by advocates of women's rights.   If
a small girl is competent to be a golf-caddie,
of what may not the grown woman be capable?

These caddies, the male and the female alike,
speak of preference a language of which you may
say with equal truth that it is French or English ;
for neither Frenchmen nor Englishmen can understand it.   They can understand your English,
however, and can answer you in a form of that
language which is within the comprehension of
the simple.   The first use which they will make
of this means of communication is to tell you
that you have to walk nearly half a mile to the
first tee.   This is the more annoying, because the
walk is over ground which is clad in whins, looking
as if they were providentially put there for the
trial of the golfer's soul.   But the commoner is of
a stiff-necked generation, whether he be called
potwalloper, or squatter, or "parishioner," which
is his title in Guernsey—a title which gives him
an interest in those whins, and the right of pastur-
ing his cattle.   With the true instinct of the

commoner, he puts as much value on the whin-
bushes as if they bore Jersey pears.   And the
second use which the caddie will make of his
power of communicating with his master, will be to
tell him that he is not allowed to play his ball out
of the whins into which he has topped it off the
first tee.   This is fiendishly exasperating, but the
rule has to be observed—lose one and drop behind.
Then you drive into the big high-perched bunker
before the hole, and have doubts of your enjoyment of the Guernsey links.   The doubts soon
vanish.   When you have given up the hole, and
are at peace again, you find yourself looking out
over a most glorious seascape, which extends to
three-quarters of your horizon.   The cliffs are bold
and rugged, and rocks in the sea relieve its blue,
and break it into foam.   The golf-course sweeps
down from you, and then away up on your right
hand, in a fine natural curve of beauty.   The
highest bends are crowned by great outcropping
boulders of grey rocks as big as a church; smaller
slabs jut from the tops of lower hills, here and
there forming a natural imitation of Stonehenge,
but they are so grouped together that straight
driving will avoid them.   Your hazards are varied
by whins, with the blighting rule attaching to
them; by sand-bunkers; by the sea and its
beach, on the north; by a huge walled enclosure

on the highest ground of all, an enclosure en-
closing emptiness.   It is said that it was the
encampment of the Russian troops, our allies who
came to govern Guernsey for us in 1815, when all
the British troops that we could spare—and a few
more perhaps — were busy trying to catch "the
little corporal."   Since then we have changed
friends, have stood shoulder to shoulder with
France, and our front towards Sebastopol.   From
that, again, it is something of a jump to the recent
demonstration at Toulon ; yet the wall still stands,
square and huge and grey, on the height of the
bare links, like a Russian column on the steppes.
All which historical facts and reflections are of less
importance to the golfer than that if his ball go
into the enclosure it has to be considered as lost.

This, again, is an exasperation ; but before the
wall is reached, and afterwards, the character of
the golf offers charming compensations.   The lies
are perfect : St Andrews cannot furnish anything
to compare with them.   The holes are full of
interest, and each has its individual interest.
There is no tautology, and there is but one cross.
The putting-greens are natural, and excellent.
There are many " blind " holes which will bother
the visitor, but they are of no account to the
habitué, who could find his way round in the dark.
For in Guernsey the *habitué* is a very ardent golfer,

though golf is a very late invention in the island. The ardour is not confined to a sex, for the ladies play at large over the long links. As in the neighbouring Jersey, there is no ladies' links ; but whereas at Jersey ladies only play golf under sufferance, and pain of being passed at every putting-green, at Guernsey they golf on terms of something like equality. They have tea in the drawing-room of the club. Instructed by their discovery of the capacity of the feminine intellect for golf-caddying, the Guernseymen have given the lady golfer a recognised position.

The visitor, if he admit the assumption that the male golfer is the nobler animal, will see reason in the difference of treatment of ladies in the two islands respectively. The Jersey links are often athrong with golfers, and the course crosses frequently. In Guernsey golfers are few, comparatively, and there is room and to spare for every one.

Of course, to a golfer who is playing badly the scene of his sorrow cannot be a pleasant one ; but it is inconceivable that to any other than him the links of Guernsey can give anything but the purest joy. They are so bold and breezy. The great rock-masses springing straight out of the green hill-crests are wonderfully charming in effect. They are just the sort of rocks which we see in the Biblical pictures illustrating the phrase "the shadow of a great rock in a weary land "; or again such as we see in illustrated books of African travel, so that our fancy involuntarily looks for a lion waiting on the top of them for his prey to pass below.   But there are no lions in Guernsey; were it not so, golfers would be even fewer.

If the golfing pilgrim be not delighted with the links of Guernsey, he must be very hard to please.   True, the drive out, whether all the way by waggonette, or by a complex connection of waggonette and electric tram, is troublesome; but what worthy golf links is not intolerably hard of access?   The electric car itself may be a novelty. There is but one other which we know in connection with a golf links—at Portrush, namely; and it only connects with the Giant's Causeway.   The wire of the Portrush cars runs close to the ground, and the incautious golfer may receive a shock. At Guernsey the wire is overhead; there are no such risks.

These Channel Islands extend to the migratory golfer the right hand of most liberal hospitality. There is a pleasant social club at Peter's Port, of which he may be made a temporary member. The sea-fishing is excellent; the views, the flowers, and the vegetables are lovely; alcohol and to-bacco are very cheap: what can the golfer lack to make him happy? If he need a change, he may even try golf in Alderney, where there is a soldiers' links, which abound in incident.

Beyond this, on the road to England, are no more links, for as yet they play no golf on the Casquettes. Four hours in the steamer will bring the golfer within the Needles, with a store of sunny golfing reminiscences which will fill with envy the souls of those who have golfed through the British winter. He will have served as one item the more to convince the foreigner of the inveterate lunacy of the Anglo-Saxon race; but he will have spent months of a perpetual spring at his favourite pastime, and learned how to ask for the "light iron" in French.

THE LIFE OF THE LINKS

THERE is a life on the links which has nothing in common with the golfer, nor he with it. He goes amongst it, and it passes him by on the other side. He exists, for it, only as an annoyance; and if it is regarded by him at all, it is in that light, mutually, that he views it. Perhaps it is right, for the golfer, that this should be as it is, that he should be all concentration upon the great game; and yet it seems that he misses much of beauty and interest and inspiration, much of which he might avail himself without interfering with the great purposes of his match. For those beautiful dumb things make no demand, they do not say "look at us!" They but go their own way, fulfilling their life, playing to no gallery—even as the golfer should—with an indifference that seems born of a conscious superiority. "We do not say 'look at us,' but if you do not look, with-

out our asking, what a fool you must be !"
That is what they seem to say. Are they not
right?   Is it not almost as interesting and
beautiful a thing as golf itself, this myriad-hued,
myriad-wise moving life which works out its
little day with such cheerful, such trustful, such
inspired industry—working to an end which
neither it nor the golfer knows? The golfer is
hostile to it all, no doubt, but it exists there,
in spite of him. It does not exist as richly as
it did before his coming, nevertheless there is
wealth enough of it, and to spare, to give him
joy. It is a place well famed in story—this
links—this Northam Burrows over which Mrs
Leigh looked from the windows in Burrough
House to watch for the homecoming of Amyas's
ship.   Across the estuary of the united Taw
and Torridge (up which his ship would sail,
past Appledore Pool and on to Bideford Bridge),
the yellow sand-hills, gleaming through the haze,
show the outline of the Braunton Burrows where
they buried the children's effigies ; and, beyond
the sand-hills, rises the slate grey roof beneath
which dwelt the maid of Sker.

I have chosen this links of Westward Ho!
to illustrate an incidental interest of the golfer's
pilgrimage, not out of arrogance, because it was
the course on which I learned my golf, nor

deeming it more richly endowed with life than other links, but simply because it is most familiar to me and because I believe that I can best sketch a picture there that may serve as a type of the life that exists on every golf links.

If the golfer be one of the earliest starters he may find a heron which has flapped its heavy way from beyond Fremington, still standing, as he has stood from daybreak, motionless in the shallow, muddy waters of Goosey Pool—motionless as a sentinel, save for occasional deadly lunges of the bayonet-bill, transfixing a small eel or stickleback or frog. Then there is a chuck into the air, a catch in the way most easy for the swallowing, and, with a gurgle or two in the throat of the heron, the eel's personality is lost for ever. In the old days, before the golfer came there, the wild duck used to resort in numbers to this pond; and the stream flowing from it, the stream so readily recipient of a "topped" first tee shot, was the favourite resort of a dab-chick. A grey phalarope, too, a rare bird, has been seen—alas, been killed—on it. The golfer will not see these to-day; only, if he heel his ball badly, he may scare from beneath the stone bridge a blue flash, which goes travelling down, very swift and straight over the surface of the stream—

a kingfisher. It is summer, and a wheatear
jerks himself out of the dry main ditch which
runs from the stream almost right across the
Burrows to the Pebble Ridge. He runs quickly
along, then flies low and swiftly; thinks he will
pass a certain molehill; changes his mind with
quick-turning motion; alights on it, jerking his
tail, jerking his head, jerking himself, finally,
altogether off the molehill again as you approach,
and so on, by similar methods of progression,
to the next hummock. On the left are wide
patches of low, greyish, sun-dried rushes. In
winter they stood rich-green and ankle-deep in
water, and snipe and jack-snipe sheltered in
them. Now they are crisp with the drought,
and no birds in them but skylarks and pipits,
which have nests at their roots. As you go
out to the Pebble Ridge the soil becomes more
and more sandy, the grass more yellow, everything drier. The wheatear has ceased to go before
you, for the ditch, with the necessity for it, has
ceased. In some hole in that ditch he has his
nest, with sky-blue eggs, or young ones probably, as the season is advanced, but it would
take too long in the middle of a golf match to
find it. The caddies will show you a pipit's
nest, horse-hair lined, under the cave of a
sand-bunker, later on. The third hole is at the

foot of the Pebble Ridge, where the old hut
was.   A pair of wagtails are leading about a
small following of greyer, more monotonous
images of themselves, chirping and peeping about
the stones of the ridge for the flies and hoppers
that have come out to bake themselves.   A
stone-chat is scudding about, perching on the
pinnacles of the ridge, flicking his tail, and
scolding uneasily in a way that tells one that
somewhere in the neighbourhood, under some
warm pebble, his mate, less dark as to back,
less ruddy as to front, is sitting on eggs or
fledglings.

After the third hole you turn westward, and
go parallel to the line of the great blue ridge
of pebbles.   The water has almost dried up
from the marshy pond on the left, and a few
small waders of the sandpiper or dotterel sort
are busy in search of sand worms.   After a hole
or two you get into more sandhills and more
serious country.   The sand burns hotly and
glares whitely.   The sheep are lying panting,
with tongues out, in the shadow of the bunkers,
their woolly sides heaving painfully.   They are
so loth to move that they lie still, regarding
you with anxious eyes, till you could almost
clutch them, then rush off in a distressful hurry
that makes you hot.   Great lambs, more than

big enough to crop for themselves, rush after the long-suffering mothers and aggressively pretend to be babies. In one of the bunkers the caddie shows you the pipit's nest, whence the little brown bird flies with quick, low, evasive flight. It is hung up, insecurely, beneath a wisp of dried grass roots, which hangs, like a bunch of woman's hair, over the bunker's edge. Farther on, amongst the sand-hills, the pipits are numerous, rising in broken imitation of the up-rising skylark who sings himself straight up out of the waving, yellow bent with which the sand-hills are clad, up, up, till he is lost in the radiance, has passed the portals of Heaven, still sending down his notes as he goes higher and higher into the Presence. But his mate is sitting in her close nest under the curl of the bent grass, and down he comes again, dropping out of the heavens, still singing his gratitude, finishing by a slantwise run down, as if along a slack wire, and so to the summit of a sand-hill, still singing, it may be, and running over the ground with crested head proudly erect. The air is full of the skylark choir. Overhead and seaward the gulls keep passing, deftly shearing their white way across the blue sky. Little flecky clouds are floating up over the far Exmoor hills; for the rest, the sky is an

untroubled blue. The foam of the breakers
gleams where they toss unceasingly on the bar,
and the white sails on the bay fleck the blue
of the sea, as the seagulls fleck the blue of
heaven. The ground is a carpet of wild thyme
and many low-growing flowers. The hive bees
are murmuring over it, visiting innumerable
honey cups; the humble bees, less frequent,
but more noisy, come buzzing about your head,
indignant at the intrusion. Occasionally a bee
passes, taking a straight, purposeful line, a "bee-
line," for its home. Little blue butterflies flicker
by and settle, living gems of brightest turquoise
blue. Folding their wings, the many mottled
hues of the under wings are almost more chastely
beautiful. Two meet, and a little dalliance begins of quick circling round each other. Sometimes they part quickly, sometimes the dalliance
goes on, leading them higher and higher into
the sky, until they are nearly lost to sight in
the blue air. Then one breaks away; drifting
aimlessly on a light current, a hundred feet off;
the other sinks to the flowers, as if wearied by
his ascent. Is it a game they play to see whose
turquoise-tinted wings are the more endurant of
the air climbing? Among the blue butterflies
two kinds of day-flying moths are moving, the
"gamma," with the alphabetical sign on its sober

wings, darting quickly, checking suddenly, and hovering, humming-bird-like, as he sips the nectar of a flower. With them some six-spot burnets, feebly flying, like rubies in the brightness of their splendid nether wing.

Swiftly scudding across the great belt of high rushes has come a peacock butterfly. Disdaining to settle on the lowly carpet, he hurries past. We may well know how he comes to be there, for on the way to the seventh hole it was not impossible to find one's ball in a thick clump of sting nettles. The leaves of the nettles were cut out in patterns even less regular than their own outline. Searching sting nettles is not pleasant, but had we undertaken it we might have found multitudes of black, spiny caterpillars, of whom one has found his apotheosis in the butterfly who is going scornfully over the lowly flowers of the links.

The eighth hole leads us, by way of a narrow passage, between the sandy desert and the sea. There, in the winter, we may have scared a little flock of light-brown birds, showing a bar of white on the wing as they made a hurried short flight. They were snow-buntings, not a common bird so far south. It is a bare, inhospitable shore, at that time, for the strangers. In the winter, too, there will be pools, often frozen over, in the great rush-bed landward of the seventh green. You may put up snipe and jack-snipe, possibly even a string of teal. The teal will string upward, straggling through the sky, and straight away from you. The snipe will rise with a scold, and begin zigzagging up—towards you, if you have flushed him down wind, up, and up, and up, in wider zigzags, eventually going into the rush-bed again, with a slanting dive, half a mile or more from you. The jack-snipe will imitate all these antics except the scold, in little. In winter, too, there are numbers of thrushes and blackbirds in the great rushes. You come on the thrushes' snail-breaking stones constantly. In the summer there are not many —only a few near the haunts of birds which have nested where a bramble has overgrown a rush-clump and made a thick tangle. A wren may be creeping about in these tangles, and the pipits will dart out away from you, and in, back again, on the "blind" side of the clump.

The rushes are terrible, with points like assegais, always hard and dry at the extreme tips, however juicy-full of sap below. Some patches grow taller than a man's head. It is easy picking one's way through, for there are continual open spaces, round and about the clumps, where a lucky golf ball may find a perfectly good lie;

but the rush-points have a nasty acrid juice in them, grey and dry though they look, which makes a wound smart painfully if they pierce you. All the heads have a constant stoop to the eastward, away from the prevalent west wind. One stem out of every ten bears a yellow-white cocoon of the burnet moth. Some cocoons are already empty, with the hole bored in them through which the perfect moth has escaped to flutter out helplessly over the flower-carpet. On the desert of sand beyond the seventh hole are frequent plants of the blue-leaved euphorbia, but no searching has found on them the caterpillars of the rare euphorbia-hawk - moth, though they are said to feed on the euphorbia of the Braunton Burrows opposite. Amidst the clumps of the rushes you may perhaps catch a fleeting glimpse of a vanishing brown form, and your caddie, with a glad shout, will declare it to be "the old hare"—the definite article sufficiently attesting that the species is not numerous.

After the ninth hole you bear away, past another big patch of the great rushes, to the more open common. The gleam of the high tidal water of Appledore Pool shines as if from a mirror, on which the coasting vessels pass, inward or outward bound. In the neighbourhood

of the outlying rush - patch one has seen the
weasels, a whole family, two parents and a half-
dozen of young, which evade, with marvellous
agility—lithe bodies darting this way and that
—the attempts of caddies to do them to death
with clubbed niblicks. Eventually all are likely
to make good their escape to the friendly covert
of the rushes. The greens and yellows of the
open common are dotted darkly with molehills.
No doubt there is a great deal of subterranean
life going on in the dark streets of the city
whose principal buildings are roofed by those
dark earth-lumps; but the golfer does not see
all that. Starlings rise from pecking busily
round and about the molehills. Some are
darker than the majority. These dark ones
are parent birds leading a troop of greyish
youngsters. Rooks are digging away in the
soft soil, for the surface of this dark earth is
always damp; we are leaving the most sandy
part of the links. There are rooks both old
and young. The youngsters may be known by
the all - black bill; they have not yet entered
upon the virile life - work of digging, whereby
the feathers have been worn from the base of
each adult beak, leaving a white scaly callosity.
They stand as helpless as children, occasionally
uttering a weak, pettish "caw," while the parents

dig busily. When father or mother brings back a beakful of wire-worm or fat grub, the babies open wide bills, "cawing" and fluttering high-shouldered wings in gratitude as the old one shovels the food down their gullets. The starlings grow uneasy as the golfers approach. One mounts a sheep's back, for a better survey of the situation, a proceeding which does not disturb the placid old ewe's cropping, but makes her big lamb gaze up at the bird wonderingly. A little further, the ground is alive with quickly-moving grey forms, sandpipers and ringed plover, all moving one way with quick little runs and sudden stops. One wonders what they can find to peck at as they stop. The sandier ground was covered with innumerable white snails, a favourite food of the mallard, but too well armoured in their shells for the soft bills of the small waders. Suddenly, as if at the bugle call, the grey forms begin running a little more quickly, rise in the air, sweep away with a flash of silvery breasts, wheel up into the sky with a plaintive cry, scud swiftly away down the wind to a more remote feeding ground. These birds seem always there, no matter the season. Frequently, too, you may see a small flock of golden plover, very tame, eyeing the golfer with the curiosity of their species, but, doubtless, per-

fectly discriminating between a golf club and a
gun. Early in the year, before the nesting time,
there is often a little troop of whimbrel (the
small curlew). Commonly they are as wild as
the curlews themselves, of whom they are most
perfect smaller editions, but in the season at
which their thoughts lightly turn to love they
are so intent on matrimonial arrangements that
the golfer may come, unregarded, within a putt
of them. In the cold weather, big flocks of
linnets fly up in a quick-rising cloud off the
ground, and jerk themselves along in the air
with a chirrup at each jerk. At all times and
seasons there is multitudinous life on the wide
stretch of common which is on the golfer's left
as he comes to the fourteenth hole. The fif-
teenth leads back over the big bunker, diving
again into the sandier section. On the left is
a rushy hollow, whence the wind, blowing pre-
valently from the west, will sometimes waft an
unsavoury odour from the carcase of an unfortunate sheep. A pair of crows rise, reluctant
and sluggish, from feasting on this rich banquet.
Likely enough they have hastened the fate of
the poor sheep, as it lay moribund and helpless, by digging into its dying eyes with iron
beak. There is no mercy in the ways of Nature.
And so the golfer turns back again, for the

concluding holes, homeward across the grey-green and yellow-green levels of the common, where a few starved horses and cows seek their famine rations. The little horned sheep fare better, since they are able to nibble up the close grass. Sometimes a cow, driven stark wild by flies and thirst, comes charging across the common from the sandy desert-land, where she has been lying in the shade of a bunker-cliff, galloping, with tail in air and tossing head, for the stream or pond.

Overhead, at the same phase of tide each day, will come three cormorants, leaving the tidal estuary for the rocks off the westward cliffs. They are as regular in their ways as the kestrel, who makes, twice daily, his round of the fields among which the golf-house stands. He repeats the same circuit constantly, hovering over the more likely spots, stooping down very close to the ground now and then, in the hope of spying a vole or beetle, occasionally swooping right down on an unfortunate insect or tiny furry thing. But he is soon on the wing again, wind hovering. For his resting-place he chooses the bare top of a tree. In the hedge and field around the golf-house one could see, at any time for a few weeks, some two years ago, a pathetic comedy — a wagtail, busy all the day in collecting food for a single big, unnatural nursling, who constantly pursued her, a young cuckoo, whose maw it seemed as if the active little foster-mother could never fill.

All this, and very much more, every golfer may see. It is doubtful if more than a very few see any of it.

THERE is no use telling who his master was,
for it might vex some poor sensitive soul
beyond the Styx, and to no purpose; but for
himself, he was a most familiar figure on the links
—tall, bent, somewhat one-sided — an infirmity
that increased with years and rheumatism—with
an angular face, clean-shaven (twice a week),
with a Scotch bonnet stuck awry above it, and a
short clay pipe insecurely held in the corner of his
mouth, for lack of teeth. Presumably he had not
been always thus. Doubtless there had been a
time when he was a barelegged gossoon scamper-
ing blithely with naked feet, and again a time
when he was a spruce young man, a favourite with
the lassies maybe; but if such times had ever
been, it was extremely hard to picture them
to one's mental vision, and "Slow-back" himself
never referred to them. It was impossible to
picture him other than he was when first we knew
him—shambling in gait, crooked of aspect, clad
in long trousers and inadequately short coat, with

132

a woollen scarf about his neck, and booted at such length that it seemed absurd to suppose his toes could reach the end of their coverings. He was a reserved man, and appeared to be without relatives. We did not trouble to inquire about his lodging, but every morning he was to be seen sitting on the bench that the older caddies occupied, smoking his pipe and waiting for his master to come, with the clubs, from the Club-house. Then he would "carry" the two statutory rounds of the links, and disappear again until the following morning. How he spent his Sundays we never thought of asking, but no one appeared ever to have seen him on the Day of Rest.

All this was in the years before the "boom" in golf which led to the game becoming the possession of all and sundry. Books had not been written about the game, and all the available maxims were carried in the heads of those who, like "Slow-back," made a profession either of playing or of carrying clubs. The maxims were, substantially, three: "Slow-back," "Keep your eye on the ball," and "Don't press." To these might have been added a fourth, "Be up"; but this applied more particularly to the short game, and it was the first of the maxims, concerned with the more glorious business of the drive, that was destined to exercise an important influence on

" Slow-back's " life.   There is no doubt, of course, that he had another name than this *sobriquet;* but it happened to none of us ever to learn it, and the manner in which he obtained his appellation was as follows : His master was never more than an indifferent player at the best.   He was conscious of his deficiencies, but rather than attribute them to what were, perhaps, their truer causes, of faulty eyesight or inadequate muscle, preferred to refer them to neglect of some of the important maxims of the golfing art, and especially to that first-quoted one of " Slow-back ! "   He conceived that he had contracted a fatal habit of hurrying the club away, in the back stroke, from the ball, and that this initial error was responsible for all the subsequent miss-hits and toppings with which the club visited the ball on its descent.   Maybe he was right; but in any case, the means by which he strove to clear himself of this fatal tendency was to make his caddie ejaculate the magic words of monition, " Slow-back ! " each time that he prepared to raise his club for the driving stroke.   The result, it has to be admitted, was not wholly satisfactory; one can say no more than that his execution might conceivably have been worse in the absence of the warning.

Thus it went on for several years.   At the end

of that time it happened that "Slow-back's" master—for already the caddie had earned the nickname by which alone we knew him — was called away for three weeks or so by the death of a near relative. Then "Slow-back" carried clubs for another master. But the habit that he had formed during these years of ejaculating his monitory "Slow-back!" as his master raised the club was not to be denied. Still, at the conclusion of each address to the ball, he uttered the solemn words, then found himself covered with most pitiful confusion at the rebuke which his uncalled-for interference had merited. For a stroke or two, putting great restraint upon himself, he succeeded in keeping his soul in silence ; but at the next the inevitable exclamation broke from him again, to the distraction and despair of the sufferer to whom it was addressed. During the three weeks of his master's absence several golfers made trial of "Slow-back's" services, for he was an excellent caddie, saving his single idiosyncrasy, and regarded with a certain affection as being somewhat of a "character" besides. But none could suffer him long. One after another had to give him up, after being reduced to impotence and despair by his raven-like croak. At length his legitimate master returned, and "Slow-back" was a man again.

A few more years dragged their length to a close, and then the hand of Death fell, this time on no near relative of his master, but on the master himself. "Slow-back," in a new suit of mourning, followed him to the grave, and came back, still wearing his apparel of grief, to sit during the afternoon on his accustomed bench, with the other caddies. In the morning he beset himself to find a new engagement. He was in receipt of a small pension from his late master, in recognition of so many years of faithful service, but the sum did not suffice to give him independence. He was soon engaged, for the links were thronged with players. This time his employer was a new-comer, who knew nothing of "Slow-back's" peculiarity. He was nearly stunned with surprise at what he deemed the caddie's insolence on his first utterance 'of the inevitable words. He said nothing, however, on the first offence; but when it was repeated, expostulated in un-measured terms. To his surprise his rebuke brought "Slow-back" to the verge of tears. Then, partly by his opponent, and partly by the opponent's caddie, the situation was ex-plained. He found himself able to mingle a measure of pity with his wrath, but throughout the round the ejaculation, many times repeated, in the speaker's own despite, spoiled his intended

stroke, and led to the immediate payment of the
caddie and rejection of his further services.
Several times during the ensuing weeks did now
one, and now another, in ignorance or in pity,
engage the unfortunate man to carry clubs, but
in no case could his idiosyncrasy be endured
beyond the limits of a single round. He made
efforts that were absolutely heroic to overcome
it, swathing the woollen comforter around his
mouth until asphyxiation threatened him; but
through all the folds of stuff came, with a
muffled lugubriousness, the hateful exclamation
which the man would have given worlds to have
withheld. Do what he would he could not rid
himself of this *damnosa hæreditas*, bequeathed to
him, along with his slender pension, by his departed master. Gradually he grew to recognise
the hopelessness of his condition, and ceased even
to seek employment. He spent his days sitting
dejectedly on the accustomed seat, growing thinner
and more gaunt as poverty set its grip more
firmly upon him, grateful if now and again one
of his friends on the bench would give him
a fill of tobacco for his seldom-replenished
pipe.

At length he ceased to frequent the links altogether. For some days no one seemed to notice
his absence. Then it was noted that "Slow-back"

had disappeared, and we began to ask questions about him. His cronies knew nothing, only that he had not been down to the links for a day or two. We inquired where he lodged, and with some difficulty found the locality. It was up a steep stair in a little house of a back street. His landlady told us that she feared he was not well. For some days he had not left the house, and had eaten next to nothing : said his stomach refused food, and that he had no appetite. We asked her whether she thought he lacked for money, but the woman said No, basing her information on the fact that he had kept his small rent paid up.

When we went in it appeared at once that he was very bad; he lay on the bed terribly wasted, scarcely more than the skeleton of a man. We asked whether he had seen a doctor, and being told No, sent off for one at once. He seemed to recognise us, and a strange smile of pleasure struggled across his thin features. He even tried to speak, but the only word that we could distinguish was his terrible ejaculation of " Slow-back," though whether he was trying to speak of himself thus by his familiar *sobriquet*, or whether he deemed himself still " carrying " for his old master on the links, we could not tell. Then he relapsed into silence, and seemed to sleep.

At length the doctor came. He took but one glance at the poor figure on the bed, passed his hand beneath the clothes, and laid it for a moment over the heart. Then he turned to us with a grave face. " Slow-back " was dead !

THERE is a certain practice of those nice barelegged little girl caddies of the Island of Guernsey on which I found it necessary to take the opinion of an eminent Scottish divine of St Andrews. He is a person celebrated for his breadth of view, and, indeed, his attitude towards the present question went far in itself to prove that breadth, for otherwise he must incontinently have dismissed the matter as pertaining to the Devil, or to the Pope, which, in the mouth of many of his brethren, would be only synonyms. But he did no such thing: he argued the matter out, dispassionately, on its merits.

The question arose in this way: We were all familiar with the methods of the ordinary Scottish caddie. We knew him, especially, that he was to be watched with peculiar care as we came to the last holes of the evening round, in the gloaming; for he had a habit, often detected, of inserting into the ground, between the opponent's ball and the hole, a green-painted pin, invisible among the grass, but which yet opposed the passage of the ball into the hole as effectually as a *chevaux-de-frise* resists the charge of a squadron. The ball broke itself on that salient pin; the player damned "that wiry blade of grass"; the caddie, as he picked his own master's ball from the hole, trod in the pin, and the episode was ended. That was a form of physical obstacle to the passage of the ball into the hole with which we were perfectly familiar—might even have been guilty of a personal familiarity with it, though we did not confess as much, in days long past; for it has happened, in some period in their lives, even to eminent Scottish divines, to have been boys, and boys are for ever mischievous.

This matter in question, however, was raised by the action of a girl—not by the action of one girl only, moreover, but by the action common to many girls—to so many girls, in fact, as carry clubs for the golfers of the Island of Guernsey. They make very charming little caddies, picturesque, with their bare legs and feet in the summer, talking a taking lingo, too, in which Gallicisms and golfing Scotticisms mingle pleasantly, with a piquant accent. And they are sympathetic — much more sympathetic than the boy-caddie of Great Britain. This may be partly a question of nationality, but partly also, no doubt, it is a question of sex. I consulted the eminent

Scottish divine on this side of the question also, but he put it hurriedly by him in a shamedfaced fashion. On the main question submitted to him, however, he deliberated seriously. The facts were these : As soon as the master of one of these girl caddies had holed his putt, and it became the turn of the opponent to play, the caddie would spit—prettily, in no offensive fashion—upon the ground, and describe a cross, with her forefinger, in the air, above the line of the proposed putt, to obstruct the passage of the ball into the hole.

Now, was this fair? It is evident that, on a question of this nature, one required the judgment of a theologian, no less than of one versed, merely as a layman, in the laws of Golf. For this suggested an interference not contemplated even in the most recently accepted rules of Golf, as revised by Lord Kingsburgh and his committee. Certainly it seemed like invoking the assistance of a person other than the player or his caddie, and this is expressly forbidden by the rules. But, on the other hand, where was this person, and who was to prove that he had interfered, or even that he was an agency included in the philosophy of Lord Kingsburgh and the other wise men? The pin, in the physical method of interfering with the run of the ball, remained as evidence, but there was no sign left of the crossing of the air, and if any unworthy agency had been invoked it vanished, leaving no trace, not even a smell of brimstone. And yet it seemed scarcely right to deny all power whatsoever to the invocation. The theologian whom I took into council scarcely thought it right to go as far as this: he admitted that "there might be something in it." Even on the merely rationalistic analysis, it is not without its force. We all know how it affects a man's stroke if he be led to imagine an inequality, which has absolutely no existence in fact, on the line of his putt: how much more fatally efficacious must be the suggestion that the devil bars his path! It is scarcely reasonable to doubt that the devil often does. There is no other rationally acceptable hypothesis on which some of the missed putts can be explained. On this point it might be well to consult "Old Tom."

But is his agency one that is tacitly, if not expressly, contemplated in the rules; and is it a breach of the rules to invoke his assistance, or to repel his services (in whichsoever significance we are to regard the invocation), in the manner practised by the little girl-caddies of Guernsey? It is a matter on which I have been able to receive no satisfactory assurance even from the eminent theological and golfing faculty which I have consulted ; but it is a matter that it concerns the golfer of Guernsey, for the sake no less of his soul than of his Golf, to look into very shrewdly.

All that the Scottish divine would say, by way of committal, was that, if it came to a close match, he would prefer to put his faith on the pin.

Despite all our boasted advance in science it is very difficult indeed not to believe, whatever the Divine may say, that the devil has something to do with the game, especially with the short game, which is just the insidious kind of business that he would meddle in.

A golfing maxim-maker has observed that "Driving is an art, iron play is a science, but putting is an inspiration." It is a very felicitous set of definitions. One has only heard it bettered once by the man who wrote, "Putting is the Devil." Of course, that is only another way of saying the same thing. Often one's putting suffers from "influenza"—a mysterious disease, which no one can diagnose—so that it is simplest to call it "influenza," in the tongue of mediæval Italy (where such manifestations were frequent), in English, "influence," the "influence," or "in-flowing" of diabolic currents. So that, practically speaking, influenza and inspiration are as alike as two golf balls, the only generally-accepted difference being that they come from different shops; and so, to say that "Putting is an inspiration," differs from saying that it is "the devil" only in that the latter seems to define the source of inspiration.

When you have studied carefully a putt of that troublesome yard-and-a-half distance, and succeeded at length in holing it, then you say to yourself, "Putting is an inspiration." But when your friend, who is watching golf for the first time, comes up, and says, "What nonsense taking all that bother about a thing like that! Here, give me the ball," and knocks it in from the same distance, or a little further, with his umbrella, then you observe at once, "Putting is the devil." There is no doubt of it. It cannot be an art or a science, for the more a man learns about golf the worse he putts, as a rule. Therefore it must be an inspiration; and no reasonable human golfer really doubts the source of the inspiration. When a man first begins golf he generally putts wonderfully; and ladies always putt remarkably well, which again supports the inspiration theory and the suggested source.

We may take instances. One would not like to adduce instances of special inspiration; but instances in which inspiration is noticeably lacking may be held up to the brightest light.

K

One knows the venerable story of the letter which the late Mr Wolfe-Murray addressed to "The Misser of Short Putts, Prestwick." It was taken, quite straight, to "Old Tom" Morris. Now no one could possibly conceive "Old Tom's" being inspired from the source suggested. No one more removed from possible influence from such a source can be imagined. His case lends a very decided support to the theory. Mr John Ball, jun., is another famous misser of short putts. (Of course it is always to be remembered that the missed short putt is observed and focussed in the "fierce light that beats upon a champion." The missed short putts of the average golfer escape the recording angel's book ; but, for all that, good golfers do putt badly.) Now, with the exception of "Old Tom," there probably is no golfer whom one would so little suspect of inspiration from Black Art sources as Mr John Ball. We may put him next to Tom Morris as an instance in support.

Another very fine golfer, who would be invincible altogether if he could get one of the inspired to putt for him, is Mr Leslie Balfour-Melville. He is even more remote from the inspiration (it is impossible to be more remote from its source) than either of the above named.

Tom Morris and Mr Ball, taking each at his best, used to lose strokes and holes on the putting green ; but usually because they could not hole the short ones, not because they could not lay the long ones dead. "Here the veteran laid a long putt stone dead, but subsequently missed it," wrote the shorthand recording angel, with humour that probably was unconscious. The veteran often used to do that. Now he is no longer at his best, alas! though, for his age, a wonder, so he does not miss the short ones as he used to. But Mr Ball is still at his best, virtually speaking—still good enough, at all events, to miss short putts, and to beat anyone he wants to. But these ex-champions could always hole the long putts. It was only at the short ones that they failed, even at their very best. Mr Balfour-Melville, perhaps, would have been better than either of them had he had but a share of the "influenza" or inspiration. But he lacked it even more than they, for at times he could neither lay the long ones dead nor hole the short ones. It only shows how complete is his mastery over the art of driving and science of iron play that he should have done such great things without a breath of the inspiration.

Mr Alfred Lyttelton has declared that the

man who wins a hole on the putting green "is guilty of a mean and ungentlemanly act." But it is obvious that he is something even worse —he is guilty of receiving aid from diabolical sources, and in the Middle Ages, in the green youth of the game, would have been most properly punished at the stake, had his methods been understood.

The inspiration is not a constant, but a capricious stream, so that those who have it in the fullest measure are sometimes left uninspired for a while. Then it manifests its returning presence, by new channels sometimes, such as putting over a daisy on the line, instead of straight at the hole; there is no end to its ways of entrance, and the spell that was effective yesterday may be valueless to-day. Some days no spell is of value—then it is best to go home to bed and consult a doctor about it, who will call it "microbes," for that is more modern than "influenza," and men of science are past the age of animism, though, of course, golfers are not.

They are perfectly capable however of conceiving in theory that dynamical laws control the flight of the golf ball, and are happy to read, if not to comprehend, all that Professor Tait has written on the subject, and to imitate, if not to equal, Mr F. G. Tait's practical application of the paternal theories. They are apt to speculate, perhaps none too acutely, on the operation of the law of motion, and amongst its details none seemed fashioned to perplex them more than the function of the "undercut."

"Why is it," I asked the other day, "that it is so much easier to pitch a full iron shot dead than a half-iron shot? Why are the half-shots so much more apt to run, after pitching, than the full, though they be cut never so shrewdly?" I had often asked this question before, and the answer had always been, "Yes; funny thing, by Jove! It is so, certainly; but can't quite make out why."

So one had begun to put this problem down in the number of those "things that no fellow can understand." And then, on the occasion of which I write, a pilgrim in our company answered, quite casually, "Oh! of course it is quite simple why it is so. You hit the full shots a quicker, sharper blow, that makes the club go through after the ball better, and so puts more under-spin on, presuming that the ball be hit below the centre."

There seems to be nothing amiss with this as an account of the matter, though the answer did not seem to cause the answerer a moment's thought or pain; and though, in all the weighty treatises that we read and write—or, does anybody read them? —about the great and good game, the point does not seem to have been attacked at all. Probably there is no general doubt about the fact—that it is easier to pitch a full iron shot, or full mashie shot, comparatively dead than a half-iron shot or half-mashie shot. Certainly, to most people it is easier; but that is not to say that there may not be singular exceptions who can pitch the ball deader off the half than off the full shot. There are paradoxical exceptions to every rule that is worth stating, and for every one real exception there are a score of persons who believe themselves to be exceptions. The reason of the deader fall of the full shot, however, has always hitherto seemed obscure to the present writer; therefore, it is possible that it may also have been obscure to others, who will be grateful perhaps for a little light thrown upon it. The writer does not answer for the quality of the light; it may be only a Will-o'-the-wisp, and no true light or account at all; but, at all events, it seems to fulfil certainly one condition of a workable hypothesis, namely, that it explains the effects. If any other hypothesis will explain them equally well, I am sure we shall all greet it with gratitude. There is, I think a

certain interest in understanding the "why" of
a ball's behaviour, though whether the understanding of the theory will result in our being
able to better our practice is quite another
matter. Often in these matters ignorance is
bliss, and a little knowledge a dangerous thing,
to the golfer; but the reasonable human being
(quite another person) likes to know reasons,
and, after all, it is not impossible that he,
understanding that it is helpful to dead pitching to hit the ball sharply under the centre,
may help us to achieve the dead pitching in
practice.

Observation, I fancy, confirms the deduction.
Taylor, for instance, who pitches his ball very
dead off his mashie, seems to strike the ball
more sharply than most strike it. Sayers, on
the other hand, seems to get the same result
of a dead pitch by other methods, namely, by
clubs so lofted that the ball goes very high and
has very little way on when it pitches. Of
course, other things being equal, the ball which
has least way on—which describes the steepest
parabola—will fall the deadest. But then, other
things are not always equal; for instance, the
amount of cut on a ball sent up to the hole by
Taylor, and one scuffled along with a sort of
putt with the iron by the ordinary duffer. The

queer thing about Taylor's approaches is that they fall so dead, although they fly comparatively so low; and if anyone can suggest a better theory to account for it than that of my friend which I have quoted above, I think many of us will be obliged to him. I wonder if, after reading this, we shall all go out and approach like Taylor? At all events it seems to me that my friend's answer started a good hare, if anyone will catch him.

And besides these questions of science which the pursuit of Golf is apt to raise in the mind of the philosophic pilgrim, he will not fail to recognise the value of the game, or, at all events, its force, as an ethical factor.

At one time St Anthony kept a pig. This he did because he found that the trials of ordinary life were insufficient for him. He tried his virtue yet more highly by living in the uncongenial companionship of this rude animal—for it was not a learned pig. It is a significant fact that this happened a very long while ago, when St Andrew was the patron saint of Golf.

On coming down to days which, in view of the antiquity of the Royal and Ancient game, are but as yesterday — the date of "*Les Contes du Roi Cambrinus*"—we there find the Golf of the period (under the name of "*Chole*," as played in French

Flanders) flourishing beneath the protection no longer of St Andrew, but of St Anthony. And the great point is this—that had the change taken place earlier St Anthony could have had no possible use for his pig. The pig, as we all know, is a difficult animal to drive—"especially when there's many of him — very." This is a dictum which has become historical. But the difficulty is as nothing compared to the difficulty of driving, in the way it should go, a golf ball. If St Anthony had taken to Golf a little earlier he would not have wanted his pig. He would have found Golf a sufficient substitute for all other ways and means of exasperation, of mortification, and of crosses. If there be a use in adversity there must be a use in Golf, and a moment's consideration will compel us to elevate the so-called game to the horrid position of a "moral factor."

But there is no doubt that we may overestimate the value of adversity, though this is more often done in precept than in practice; and on the principle of one man's meat being poison to another, the effects of adversity are different on different temperaments. And it is so in Golf. The "moral factor" is liable to abuse, and its results differ. There are persons who even go so far as to argue that its general effect is not moral — that the temper is injured, rather than

improved, by the practice of Golf.   They illustrate
their pernicious theory by pointing to kindred
games, such as billiards, and they assert that
players are far more tetchy, more particular about
"silence on the stroke," more furious if people in
the gallery move or light a pipe, than they used
to be before Golf, which so imperatively demands
perfect concentration, became an element of daily
life.   They point, too, to the fact that the bats-
man pauses when anyone in the pavilion at
Lord's moves within a radius of thirty feet behind
the bowler's arm ; and this they say was never
done in the good old days before men caught the
hyperæsthesia of Golf.   Also, they say that the
golfer carries this hyperæsthesia into all the
details of his daily life, and that his wife,
his cook, and his dog all suffer from his missed
putts.

Now, there is nothing in a philosophical disser-
tation such as this which is more to be deprecated
than dogmatism.   All this may be true, but there
is another view which it is possible to hold and
to support by cogent argument, namely, that as
the game of Golf is indisputably the most vexatious of all the ills that flesh is heir to, it makes
such smaller annoyances as the talking, moving,
match-striking spectator of a billiard match, the
disturbance behind the bowler's arm, the exasper-

ating wife, the unpunctual cook, or the dog who makes night hideous by baying the moon, sink into utter insignificance. The extraordinary thing about this argument is that there really is some truth in it. It is not altogether whimsical. Every golfer probably admits that Golf is not the most important avocation in life; yet when he is engaged on it it at once assumes that position, and there is no pursuit which has such capabilities of raising the temper. This is a postulate; but it is one which is not likely to be denied. The very unimportance of the issues enhances the aggravation. You know that it is so very foolish to get angry over such a matter as putting a little lump of guttapercha, approximately globular, into a small hole in the ground. Surely this is a thing that cannot greatly affect the progress of humanity? And that you—a person of fair, average intelligence—can be incensed over such a matter is the most incensing thing of all. It is impossible that one should bother about it.

Yet it is impossible not to. At all games men get angry. There once was a man who grew so evil-tempered over games that he gave them all up and played nothing but patience, and even that enraged him so, when it did not come right, that often, when he left off, he was not on speaking terms with himself. And if this is possible at

patience, how much more possible — how much
more inevitable even—is it to grow angry at Golf?
There are so many causes of vexation, so many
things to be angry with; there is the way the ball
falls, the kick it gets, the lie it gets.   Then there
is your caddie and your opponent, and his caddie,
and, if it be a foursome, your partner, and twice as
many possibilities of vexation from your opponent.
Also there are the parties in front and the parties
behind, and casual — very casual — spectators.
Finally, there is the worst offender of all—yourself.   After all, the only righteous wrath is wrath
with self, and the patience player may have been
justified.

So the chances of vexation are infinite, and one
or other is always to the fore.   Also, in this game
of Golf, there is plenty of time for them to take
full effect, and sink deep and rankling into your
soul.   It is not the sudden death of cricket or
tennis—a stroke, a profane cry of pain, and there
is the end of it.   It is a slow, lingering, torture-
some death, in which the sad wounds are continu-
ally made to smart afresh by the crocodilian salt
tears of your opponent, the insidious venom of
your partner's sympathy, the incisive surgery of
your caddie's comment.   So when all this has
been endured, can it be but that the golfer must
go to his home purged of all his evil tempers, as

if he had passed through a very fiery furnace?
What is left that can anger him after such an
ordeal as this? But here it is that the difference
is seen in the effects of adversity. The noblest
nature of all, which can despise and throw off
from it even such poisoned arrows of offence as
these, must necessarily endure all minor scourges
with lofty scorn. But these are heroes—perhaps
mythical. Of mortal golfers there are two classes,
whereof the one fails to keep its woes pent in its
bosom, and must needs give them voice, which
is a frequent subject of subsequent regret. This
class exclaims, "Tut, tut, tut!" or words to that
effect, after the bad stroke, however occasioned.
But there is another class which does not vent
itself in these dreadful exclamations. It keeps
the escape valve of its wrath closely shut down,
but it is simmering away with a fearful pressure
underneath. On this latter class—the simmerers
—the effect of the adversity is dubious. They
may come back with nerves on the twitch, hyper-
sensitive of the minor annoyances of life, and for
them Golf may be indeed no "moral factor."
But of the others—those who open the valve to
steam forth in fiery "Tut, tut, tuts"—the effect
is beyond all doubt. Their wrath flies freely to
dissipate itself in the pure air of the links, and
their heart is left light to meet their lesser trials.

And this latter class is in a great majority, so that adversity and Golf may triumphantly vindicate their uses.

After all — and this is a point which is very likely to escape the golfer — adversity and Golf are not absolutely synonymous. There is, when all is said, a small margin even of pleasure in the game — it is in this that it differs from other "moral factors"—for occasionally it happens to almost everybody to win a match, or at least a hole. So that by none need it be altogether neglected, and it is abundantly evident that to the many it must be invaluable as a means of teaching them to keep their temper.

Whether this is worth the learning is quite a subsidiary question. "You, Sammy, as a bachelor," said Mr Weller, senior (or words to the same effect), "cannot be expected to know anything of the ways of women. When you have been married as long as I have, you may perhaps know more about them ; but whether it is worth while to go through so much to learn so little, as the charity schoolboy said when he had finished the alphabet, is a werry open question."

And that is the dubious position in which the science of Golf stands towards the art of keeping the temper.

There are certain matters of etiquette, rather

than of rule, that are governed, slightly differently, by the custom of different greens. To learn the whole of these is beyond the power even of the most scrupulous of pilgrims; and chief of these points of etiquette, in its variation and its importance, is perhaps the term of mercy that is extended, at each locality, to the "Sitting Hen."

When Dr Johnson was not abusing something nearer home, he solaced himself by abuse of Scotland. The poor Bozzy was once moved to remonstrate, "After all, sir," he dared to say, "after all, we must remember, must we not, that God made Scotland."

It was a brave stroke, and at first sight the answer is not obvious to the ordinary man. But it did not trouble Dr Johnson.

"Yes, sir," he replied, instantly; "but we must also remember that He made it for Scotsmen."

The next move is yet to seek. The published gambit ends here.

Much of Dr Johnson's dissatisfaction with Scotland is explained when we consider that he never seriously adopted Golf. As a professional lexicographer, he was no doubt the man to have edited the rules, and to have supported his emendations against the attacks of Englishmen. For, of the

rules, as at present constructed, if one (the gentleman of Auchinleck, or another) had dared to point
out to him that their origin was—not, indeed,
divine—but the tradition of those who had
played the game for centuries—that is to say,
of Scotsmen—he would, doubtless, have retorted
in his old manner, "Yes, sir; but we must also
remember that it is for Scotsmen that they were
handed down."

For this makes a deal of difference. If there
is a quality of the Scot which even Dr Johnson
might have excepted from the universal ban, it
is his patient long-sufferance and forbearance
under hardship and wrong. This is doubtless
why the game of Golf is so well suited to the
Scottish genius, and why one is sceptical if they
will ever play Golf equally well in Ireland—
except in Ulster.

But now the English pilgrim, less long-suffering,
is sitting in the shadow of a great cloud. He has
studied—at least a few of him have—the rules
published by the Royal and Ancient Club, and
finds a clause therein which conjures horrid
visions. Under the old dispensation greens were
blocked. We sat, and we watched, and we
waited, and we swore, while M'Foozle and all
his tribe crawled, snail-like, over the links.
But we knew there was a bright time coming.

So soon as ever M'Foozle and his companion had played their second strokes we could take a great, glad shot at them, emphasised by a blood-curdling, premonitory "Fore!" For that was the beneficent rule—you were not to drive into parties in front unless first (*nisi prius*) they had played their seconds. But now, within the last half dozen years—by all that's scarce sufferable by the Scot, intolerable to the Sassenach, and infuriating to the Celt—the rule has been made absolute, we are not allowed to drive into them at all! Imagination darkened with the fearful prospect of waiting, helpless and hopeless, upon the tee, while the golfer who had taken to himself the methods of the sitting hen brooded in halcyon security over his ball until the abortive, addled result had at length been hatched; then he pursued it, as a hen chases an unmanageable duckling, and we took in fresh microbes of influenza and pneumonia while he once more gathered it deliberately beneath his wing.

When a hen wants to sit, the remedy is to make her sit longer than she wishes—to shut her up—just as they give the confectioners' boys sugar-plums until they hate them, or as you tie up a sheep-worrying dog to an aggressive old ram. But a golfer, even one who has adopted the methods of the sitting hen, does not thereby forfeit his rights as a British subject (though he ought to have), and if we treated him on the lines of the sheep-worrier or fowl he would have us up for false imprisonment. Moreover, it is doubtful if it would be any real discipline for him to be shut up — even indefinitely — so long as a golf ball was his companion.

Yet we are not delivered over absolutely to his mercy; for—mark this—the clause which bids us spare him is not a rule, though in the old days of chaos it was confounded with rules. It is but a maxim of courtesy, and as such, under the new dispensation, it finds its place. We are at least thus far advanced since the chaotic age: it is not open to the opponent, as heretofore, to claim the hole from us because we have driven into the sitter. But is there any degree of offending—any length of sitting —which can justify us in the breach of such a maxim? We think there is. Even here, in a warm comfortable room, we can record this as our honest opinion; and when we have waited a quarter of an hour, in a bitter wind and rain, upon the lethargic sitter, there can be no doubt that we shall be absolutely convinced of it; which point of casuistry is to be approached with the following test—if we see the sitter brooding over his ball with a clear field a hole or two before him, and behind him a telescoped muddle of exasperated golfers, then cry "Fore!" and spare not. For this is indeed no breach of courtesy. In such extreme cases the obligation becomes reversed. It is in no rules or code of courtesy, but in a far older book, that no man may annoy his fellow-man too unconscionably; that we are but poor worms, but that it is a long worm that has no turning. And if the sitting hen continue to brood over the nest egg regardless of the sufferings of fellow-creatures, he must expect that the sufferer will turn and rend him — speedily if the sufferer be a Celt, after a certain sober interval if he be a Sassenach, and eventually even if he be a Scot.

Wherefore let the sitting hen take warning, nor arrogate to himself, with much cackling, an indefeasible position, in virtue of the clause in his favour in the new rules; but let him be assured that after a time human nature will assert itself and proclaim its prior existence to maxims of golfing courtesy, even though it be a Scottish nature, and it is for Scotsmen that the rules were made. Either the halcyon period of brooding must not be indefinitely prolonged, or the brooder must let others go past him. Otherwise of a surety the sitter will be slain as he sits, and a jury of good golfers will hold the homicide justifiable.

How long and how often a man should be allowed to sit before he is shot is a question which perhaps does not admit of a general answer. Each case must probably be judged on its individual merits and by the degree of tolerance that it is customary to give the sitter on the green whereon for the moment it so happens that he sits.

Golfing trials of patience, however, are like the making of books—of them there is no end. The Golfing Pilgrim, in the course of his pilgrimage, is sure to be accused some time or other, though he be a Cæsar's wife for guilt-lessness, of the heinous vanity of the hunting of the pot, and this, be it observed, is an offence with which the Scotsman is especially fond of charging the Sassenach golfer.

An English young lady, once returned from a visit to Scotland. She remarked to her friends at home on the wonderful extension of the game of golf. "It is played every-where now," she said; "it has even spread to Scotland."

In the winter of our discontent, when the ground was frozen so hard that club-shafts snapped, a compassionate friend told us this tale to cheer our *ennui*. Poor Scotland! She had been badly treated, that year. An Englishman—one and the same Sassenach—had won both amateur and open championships; but there was hope for her even then, for, as the young lady assured us, she was learning to play golf, and since she has had many a signal vengeance, wresting from England the championships of her own game. Yet she has criticised, very hardly, young England's methods of playing golf. No doubt she has been right. She says hard things and witty things about "the cult of the biscuit box," and the English golfer selling his soul somewhat even below its value —Sassenach thing, though it be—for a few points more in the handicap. There is some truth in Scotland's criticism, no doubt, but it is not all truth. She has rather gone ahead of the truth. The Englishman does hunt the pot a little more than is good for him, it may be. He would be more ideal, as a golfer, if he were content to play the game for its honour and its glory and its half-crown. Sir Walter Simpson has suggested the formation of a club—an esoteric society—whose formula of initiation should contain, amongst many others, the following strange oaths and self-denying ordinances:

That its members should play for no pot, and should play at least three matches a year for not less than five pounds each. It is this last proviso that fills us with surprise. This, surely, is not Scotch. "English, quite English, you know," this reckless plunging appears.

But, after all, what is it that Scotland has to criticise? The English golfer is a pot hunter, Caledonia says. Let us discuss the manners, if he has any, of the English golfer. He sits in a club in the West End, or his office, in which there is sometimes leisure, in the city, and in foggy weather or holiday time it strikes him that God made the country—including golf links —and that man made the town. So he looks in his *Golf* for the notices of meetings of the different clubs of which he is a member, and then, having focussed one which fits in with the fog or holiday, he makes his arrangements forthwith for pouncing down upon the most suitable carcase. Then he goes down, in a flock with other eagles, and fights with them horribly over the carrion. This is the conception that the Scotsman has of the manners and mannerlessness of the Sassenach golfer. But, really, it is not all quite true. It is true that golfers collect in flocks over the carcase, but, indeed, it is not merely, or even mainly, the carrion that attracts them. They go, not nearly so much to rend the carcase, as to enter into a friendly rivalry with the other eagles who are gathered together—not a rivalry in which the carcase is the ultimate prize, but a rivalry to which their incentive is the valueless (to gross hearts) bay leaf of glory. For consider the nature of the unholy grail whose pursuit is so condemned by Scotland. The ordinary golfing prize is no precious article of *vertu* or *objet de luxe*. Its worth is, generally, about a fiver. How many fivers does the golfer not expend in the pursuit? What a shockingly bad investment of capital it is, if he really does all this travelling and staying at hotels and purchase of golf clubs and golf balls—to say nothing of the minor matter of compounding with what he is pleased to call his conscience—if the object of it all is a very problematical five pound pot. It really is a little in the nature of an insult to the finance of the Sassenach to attribute to him such methods as these. They are far enough removed from those of Caledonia, and compare indifferently even with the precipitous ways of Argentina and her friends.

There was once a golfer who won a second prize in a half-crown sweepstake. He realised a sum of seven and sixpence. He asked the committee of the club for permission to "add to it, and buy something that he could keep." (He did not often win second prizes in sweepstakes.) The committee accorded their gracious permission, and the golfer added to the original seven and sixpence fifty-nine pounds twelve and sixpence. For sixty pounds he then bought a golden eagle, of solid silver, as large as life, and shows it with remarkable condescension as "my golf prize."

Surely there is nothing of the taint of filthy lucre love in such a proceeding as this. It is a vanity so innocent as to be clearly amiable.

So that it seems that we have a case for submitting to Caledonia, and justification in asking her to reconsider her verdict about the Sassenach and his pot-hunting—more especially as, with her native canniness, she has left herself that back door out of her dilemmas—the attitude of "not proven," in which, nevertheless, as Charles Lamb tells us, her sons are so unwilling to abide. For when we come to make any valuation and careful scrutiny, we find that the golfing "pot," as a thing of value, will "slowly and silently vanish away." In fact, Caledonia, the pot "was a Boojum, you see."

Any golfer will tell you so. Any who has

been engaged in this fascinating and, as we maintain, almost perfectly innocent chase, will join us in giving evidence that the "pot," even when we have got him for our very own, will always slowly and silently melt and vanish away, engulphed in expenses, so as to leave, proportionately, a profit account of 7s. 6d. against a loss of some £59, 12s. 6d.; and if this is so of the pots which we win, how much more of those even more numerous ones which we pursue and miss. These, yet more undeniably, are "Boojums" unredeemed.

There are many valuable challenge prizes, it is true, but these are the most veritable "Boojums" of all. They live in the strong room of a bank or in the house of the man who has been unfortunate enough to win them, and who trembles every night lest the fire is coming down to burn them, or the burglar to enterprise them away.

Occasionally, a really valuable prize is given to keep. It were much better that there should be none of these. But most of them are not under handicap conditions, so they demoralise, comparatively speaking, a few—not that great English golfing army against whose rank and file Scotland has levelled her scathing criticism that they have been sworn into the service of the "pot."

In the course of our pilgrimage we have enjoyed some rather interesting, if idle, discussion as to which, in the world of golf, is the most trying hole. It is to be premised that the world of Golf is limited to the world of reasonably good Golf, for if the world of unreasonable Golf be included there is a certain hole, on a course that shall be nameless, for which the record minimum is 15. And yet this would scarcely, after all, come under the description of a severe hole, for the purposes of the discussion raised. This is evident, for among those holes that are mentioned as the most severe is the Himalayas hole at Prestwick— by no means a long one. Therefore it appears that what is meant is a hole that presents great opportunities for disaster; not a hole that takes many strokes to reach. Now there are no opportunities of disaster in this hole we know of for which the minimum is 15, for there is no hazard throughout the entire six hundred yards or more of its length—or, it is only another way of looking at the same fact, its whole length is continuous hazard. At all events, after the tee shot you only want one other club all the way through—the niblick—not excepting the putting green.

So much depends on the way of looking at things—the point of view! And this is why we

hear men make such startlingly divergent state-
ments about this or that hole or links. It all
depends on the point of view from which they
consider it: from one point of view a hole that
we ought to do in 3 may be a peculiarly dangerous one, by reason of the dire penalties that may
be entailed by any inaccuracy, while a hole for
which 6 is an extremely good figure may be
simplicity itself from the point of view of the
man who is considering perils by bunker. As
an instance ˉof the former class take a certain
cleek-shot hole at Archerfield, or, since Archerfield is a private green, and not familiar to the
general, take any one of several of the holes
on the old North Berwick green, before its extension. For an instance of the other kind of
hole, the hole that is not bad in 7, and yet is
a simple hole, it only needs to mention the long
hole at Blackheath.

And what is true of holes is necessarily true
of links—which are, after all, but the hole multi-
plied by eighteen. There is a character of links
as of holes, and one hears disputes arise, as to
the relative difficulty of links, between two players
equally qualified, as it would seem, to judge, just
because they do not recognise fully enough that
their difference of opinion comes from the difference in the character of the greens discussed.

The discussion of the relative difficulty of links is perhaps interesting and idle too, but there is a measure of purpose in it, for if any man, about to visit a new course, shall learn a fact or two about its character from the discussion, he may learn, at the same time, what kind of strokes he ought to practise in order to negotiate the characteristic features of the strange green. Thus it will boot a man but little to waste his energies on bringing to a high pitch of perfection his running-up strokes with the putter when he is on the point of visiting a green where no approaching can be brought to any perfection without high pitching.

Men argue till they are purple in the face and sultry in the temper about the relative difficulties of Sandwich and St Andrews,—the Sassenach, as a rule, declaring that you can play all round the St Andrews course (granted that you ever cross the Burn) with a putter, while the Scot is equally fervent in asseveration that Sandwich (once you have driven a decent tee shot and carried its bunkers) presents no further difficulty, whereas, says he, see how each hole at St Andrews is guarded. Those discussions are always the most heated and longest lived, in which each side is right. Therefore, this mode of quarrelling will endure for ever, for, obviously if a man cannot drive the Sandwich bunkers, the course must be very much more difficult for him than the St Andrews course. At St Andrews there is a complete absence of bunkers to be carried from the tee ; the accurate approach stroke is the important feature. Thus it often happens that a man makes a good score at St Andrews, though he be badly off his driving — instances are not far to seek in recent medal competitions of the Royal and Ancient—but it is scarcely conceivable that the same anomaly could occur at Sandwich. At Sandwich he might do better to be a little "off" his approaching, by which deficiency he would, at St Andrews, suffer a deal more than from weakness of the drive. The old North Berwick course was an extreme instance of premium attaching to the approach play. It may almost be said that the Golf consisted of nothing else. You approached, or failed to approach, most of the holes from the tee.

The severest course of all will of necessity be that which taxes very highly both the approaching and the driving — and in the approaching must be understood as included such approaching as is done with clubs as long as a driver, not merely the short approaches. Of all the courses within the writer's knowledge, he is inclined to think Brancaster the most severe in both these characters, needing good driving, to be followed by strong and accurate second strokes. The lengths of the holes are good—it beats Sandwich in this particular. It requires a good carrying ball from the tee in most instances; and in almost every case the approach to the hole is guarded not merely by a bunker, but by a precious bad and deep one. The greens are not quite as good, perhaps, as the Sandwich greens (let us be just, since odious comparisons have been provoked), certainly not so good as the very excellent greens of St Andrews.

Another characteristic difference, seldom recognised, depends on the gradients. Some courses are a deal flatter than others, and on the flatter greens a low ball will take you over the ground as well as a higher one. This is a truth and a truism in a calm; but, supposing a high wind, a low ball will take you over the ground, not only as well, but a deal better. But it will not serve you where you have to drive over great sand-hills, as at Sandwich, at Prestwick, and, often, at Brancaster. Westward Ho!, Muirfield, and St Andrews seldom need the driving of a high ball. Carnoustie more often requires it; Luffness and Gullane seldom, despite the "Gullane hill"; and the flattest of all, perhaps—where "wind-cheaters" may be driven with best effect — is Hoylake. Along its flat surfaces it seldom boots to drive the ball more than a few feet above the ground; and at the autumn meeting, in 1896, when Mr John Ball returned the wonderful score, which surprised even himself, of 76 in half a gale of wind, he explained it to the writer by saying that he "happened to be driving the right sort of ball for the day—never above six feet from the ground." At Hoylake you can do this; but at Sandwich, Prestwick, Newcastle (County Down), and so on, these very low raking shots will not carry the sandhills. You are bound to put the ball into the air. Therefore, these latter greens are far harder, relatively, to play in a high wind than the flatter greens; and this, too, is a feature of comparison that commonly escapes notice. Unfortunately for most of us, Mr John Ball very often, both on the flat greens and the mountainous, "happens to be driving the right sort of ball for the day."

Thackeray is credited with the generous observation that "no dinner is bad, though some dinners are better than others"; but we claim a mental reservation that he must have abused his dinner now and then. However that may be, it is certain that, though no links are easy, yet some are easier than others; and it may be a help to those who cannot agree about the comparative hardships to analyse links into their component features, and so find out the simple factors that make up their difficulty.

IN the following chapters I have endeavoured to give a picture of the spirit in which Golf was accepted in England, after being introduced on the glorious links of Westward Ho! I say this without any detraction from the honour due to Blackheath as the oldest club, not only in England, but the world. The game, however, remained stationary there, and did not win proselytes as it did when Englishmen first began to play it on a seaside links. I need scarcely say that the personages and details of the picture are purely fanciful. Nothing, for instance, could bear less resemblance to the winning personality of the late young John Allan than the grotesque imaginary figure of "Old Blobb," yet I believe that I have drawn a fairly faithful sketch of the veneration with which we at Westward Ho! regarded the traditions of St Andrews, incarnated for us in poor John Allan, as, for the persons of my fiction in "Old Blobb."

There is no doubt that, under Providence, England is indebted for her Golf to Colonel

Burscough. Pebblecombe was the first links on which Golf was played in England, for Blackheath is not a links. Soon after we started the Pebble-combe Golf Club, Colonel Burscough, who had seen something of the game in Scotland, had a professional down from St Andrews. He lodged the man in a very nasty little cottage on his property. There was a pond of greenish stagnant water near the door, and some of us even ventured to suggest to the Colonel that it was scarcely a fit habitation for so good a golfer. The Colonel, however, declared that it was quite good enough for a "jammed scoundrel like Old Blobb," and that we did not know what we were talking about.

Curiously enough, "Old Blobb," as the Colonel alway called him (he was years younger than the Colonel, and Blobb was not his name), seemed quite pleased with his new home, and he and his wife and two small boys lived there with great satisfaction, and they all loved the Colonel very dearly.

The Colonel, I ought to say, was a widower, retired from the Indian Service. He had lost an eye in his country's cause, but it was replaced by an excellent imitation in glass. His face was extremely red ; his hair and moustache strikingly white. His whole appearance was all that could be imagined that is most military—stout and upright. He had a volcanic temper, and a heart of gold. His habitual costume was a tweed suit of many colours, knickerbockers very loose and long over the knee, stockings of a fine bold pattern, and white spats. His cap was usually cocked at an angle over the glass eye, giving an appearance of remarkable ferocity.

The Colonel lived with Robert, his orphan nephew, at the manor house of Little Pipkin, some three miles out of Pebblecombe. It might therefore be thought that "Old Blobb" was rather far from the scene of his labours, but the Colonel's zeal left nothing to be desired; for every morning, without fail — rain or shine — he would be seen driving into Pebblecombe in a dogcart, with "Old Blobb" on the seat beside him and the groom behind. Then, during most of the morning, the Colonel and "Old Blobb" would walk the links together, condemning mole-hills and levelling sheep-tracks, with the view of making of these links a perfect work of art.

"It's been jammedly neglected, this links, Blobb," he used to say, impressively, about once every half-hour — "jammedly neglected; but I mean to make it the finest links in the world." To which "Old Blobb" invariably answered gravely, taking his pipe from his mouth for the occasion, "Ou aye."

We had no regular club-house in Pebblecombe then—early Victorian Golf was very primitive in England—only just a room in a farmhouse bordering the links. I remember that it had a stone floor sprinkled with sand ; but we could keep our clubs and coats there, and drink whisky, and tell each other what bad luck we had had—so what did we want more ? But in those early days we did not drink so much whisky. We had just the same bad luck, however. It was largely " Old Blobb" that taught us to drink whisky. To do him justice, he was a very sober little man himself ; but he told us that all good golfers drank whisky, so we began to drink whisky too.

We were wonderfully unsophisticated. We had a walk of about a mile over a rough common, from the farmhouse with the sanded floor, to the first tee. We used to trudge out there, bending our backs to meet the wind, often with a storm of hail pelting us. Then, when we arrived, we would throw down our overcoats beside the last hole and off we would go. We had to leave our coats there, lying on the ground, all the while we played the eighteen holes ; but they were always safe.

Of course there were no flags in the holes, but we knew about where the holes should be. When we came within fair range, one or other would run on (it was seldom that we were able to get caddies) and stick in one of his Golf clubs as a signal post, then run back again and play at it. The first couple to play over the course for the day were expected to put in crows' feathers, or any like marks for the benefit of their followers.

Nobody used to play with an iron putter, nor did people approach much with the iron; but we had a nice gradation of spoons. We began with a driver, which we also called a play club. Next to the driver was a grassed club—very like the driver, but with its face very slightly laid back—then came a long spoon, then a mid spoon, then a short spoon, and then a baffing spoon, or baffy. "Old Blobb" used to encourage us to play with all these clubs, though he did not use nearly so many himself. But we felt that we should be guilty if we failed to possess ourselves of one of this finely graduated series, and that Blobb would speak with less respect of what we used most respectfully to call our "game." It would have needed a very delicate eye to distinguish between some of the varieties—the driver, the grassed club, and the long spoon—but we were extremely dogmatic in those days of extreme ignorance.

"Sir, I maintain that you ought to have taken

the grassed club," we would say to a partner who had failed us.

"Not at all, sir. I insist that that was a lie for a long spoon."

When we came in we used to lay the case before Blobb, with a considerable difference in our several descriptions of the lie. Blobb was a very diplomatic man. He used to listen to the one party with a bland smile, wagging his head with immense intelligence. When the speaker had finished, Blobb would take his pipe from his mouth and say, with a chuckle, "Ou aye." Then it was the turn of the other party. Blobb listened with the same bland smile and the same wise wagging of the intelligent head, and at the end he again took his pipe from his mouth and said "Ou aye," with identical intonation.

Then the parties left him, perfectly satisfied, but with an added element of discord between them, for each was utterly convinced that "Old Blobb" had agreed with him only to the confusion of the absurd contentions of the other. It was Blobb's great merit, as an oracle, that he so seldom expressed an opinion. Nobody could point to an occasion on which he could say that Blobb had been wrong. It did not occur to us that it was equally difficult to find an occasion on which Blobb had been right.

His attitude through life was one of inspired neutrality and non-committal.

Personally, Blobb was not an attractive man. He was extraordinarily like a gnome. Indeed, he had spent much of his life underground, mining in the neighbourhood of Musselburgh, and very probably he had brought up with him some queer power of terrestrial magnetism. His head was very large and square, his body also square, and about the same size as his head. His legs were thin and bowed. His hair was remarkably black and straight, but rather scanty, and this applied equally to his beard and moustache. His face had rather the appearance of having a large claret mark all over it, but his features were not ill-formed, and his large eyes were open, honest and kindly. Mrs Blobb and the little Blobbs loved him affectionately.

Such was Blobb, and we took him as our conscience. Misshapen as the little creature was, he was a remarkably fine golfer. We all thought him the very finest golfer in the world, and nothing that Blobb told us tended to disabuse us of this opinion. Moreover, he had been to St Andrews, and we had a veneration that was almost superstitious for a man who had been there. Not only had Blobb been there, but he had scarcely been anywhere else.

"Have you ever been to London, Blobb?"
Colonel Burscough told us that he had asked
him, before he brought the little man to Pebblecombe.

"Na'," Blobb had answered, simply (they were
at St Andrews then),—"Na', but I've been to
Musselbrae, an' I've been to Pairth."

Blobb could talk familiarly, as of personal acquaintance, of "Old Tom" and "Young Tommy,"
and Admiral this and Sir Robert that—names
which inspired us with reverence for Blobb—that
he should ever have even spoken to the great
originals.   As it seemed, however, he had done
far, far more than this—he had played Golf with
them—it had even happened to him, occasionally,
to have beaten them.   But chiefly he regaled us
with stories of their wonderful feats of driving or
steadiness, adding a little postscript of his victories over them, upon which victories his previous
generosity in praise shed a glorious lustre.

We modelled ourselves upon "Old Blobb" in
all possible particulars.   We imitated, very in-
effectually, his swing.   When a golfing problem
presented itself, we said to ourselves, "Now, how
would 'Old Blobb' play this?   What club would
he take to it?"

Even when we did not put the question to ourselves thus directly there was always an uncon-

scious reference in our minds to "Old Blobb's"
opinion. Sometimes we startled ourselves in dis-
covering this result of our introspection; and we
confessed as much, *sotto voce*, to one another. We
even carried into other departments of life this
sincerest flattery of "Old Blobb." In church (he
always attended church) on Sunday morning, with
his wife and the two little Blobbs, all singing
lustily, I found myself copying "Old Blobb's"
manner of holding his hymn-book, and his general
attitude. We consulted "Old Blobb" on the
correct cut of golfing garments, the number of
nails which it was advisable to have in one's
boots, and the way in which it was best to have
those boots made. I really think we often, in
secret, grieved that we were not made in the
extraordinary proportions which distinguished
"Old Blobb."

Before "Old Blobb" came among us we had
always looked to Colonel Burscough as our great
oracle. For the Colonel had been to St Andrews
too—as he took very good care to let us know—
but of course he had not had the remarkable advantage possessed by Blobb of having been born and
bred there. But in everything the Colonel was
careful to speak of St Andrews as the standard,
with an implied superiority which we fully admitted, to us who had not been there.

"They say at St Andrews," the Colonel would observe impressively, when his partner in a foursome was short in his putt, "that the hole will not come to you."

"'Never up, never in,' as they say at St Andrews," was another ever-ready axiom which he often applied on the same very familiar occasion.

But, of course, as oracle, he, immediately on the appearance of "Old Blobb," took second place. We all felt it to be very generous and large-minded of the Colonel to have been at the trouble of bringing "Old Blobb" all the way from Scotland for the general behoof, when he must have known how much he was doing to eclipse his own glory. Of course, we never uttered any such sentiments, but unconsciously they were at the heart of each of us, and tended to raise, if that were possible, our opinion of the Colonel.

You must not suppose that we played with feather balls. That age was past before Golf got any hold on England, save for Blackheath. We began in the early gutta-percha age. The "mashie," of course, had not yet been heard of, and we even looked upon a man with some suspicion—as a Radical—who used a niblick. It was then comparatively lately that the niblick had been evolved out of the sand iron.

"Old Blobb" supplied us with clubs. He had brought a great many down with him, and we bought them all up directly, and showed them to each other with grave pride, quoting the rare eulogiums, which nothing but his own play, or something for which he wanted a purchaser, could win from his lips.

"'Old Blobb' told me that he thought this was the finest shaft of all those he brought with him from St Andrews," you would hear a member say as he exhibited a new driver.

On comparison, we found that "Old Blobb" had said this of a good many of the clubs he had sold us; but this did not diminish his credit as an oracle, for each one of us believed that to him "Old Blobb" had spoken the truth, and each was secretly a little flattered to have been taken, as it were, into the oracle's confidence for the delusion of the less favoured.

Professor Fleg mentioned to "Old Blobb" that the same form of praise which he had bestowed on a recent purchase of the Professor's had also been bestowed on a weapon in the hands of Captain Saxby.

"A weel, Professor," "Old Blobb" replied, "he's just a puir sailor buddy, ye ken; het's no just fair to launch him oot wi'oot confidence i' his timbers."

Colonel Burscough actually had a shaft which

had been made by Hugh Philp, the prince of all
club-makers. We all considered it a great favour
when the Colonel handed us this club and allowed
us to "waggle" it for our edification and instruction. No one among us dared to criticise the
club. We should have thought great scorn of
the man whose sense of criticism was not utterly
overpowered by his joy in the creation. The
awe-struck ejaculation of a single adjective, such
as "Marvellous!" or "Miraculous!" was the
utmost to which we could trust ourselves, as we
handed the club back, with reverent care, to the
Colonel. As St Andrews was the standard to
which the Colonel referred everything in Golf, so
did this club of the Colonel's become our standard
of excellence by which we measured less ideal
efforts.

If "Old Blobb," as occasionally happened when
he was playing very well, so far favoured us as to
take from our hand a club recently bought from
his stock, and after a knowing waggle, to remark,
"Eh, het's a braw club, yon," then we would
sometimes presume to answer, "Yes, Blobb, there
is a spring in it near the whipping, something like
the Colonel's club, don't you think?" (there was
no need to specify the club further). And Blobb
would always reply, "Ou, aye, het's that," and
then relapse into his taciturnity.

I have since grown to know that the clubs which "Old Blobb" sold us were most parlous bad ones. They were not particularly badly made, though even in this they were not ideal, but the material was abominable, the wood was green, the horn was always cracking, the lead was always coming out, the glue was always giving way. But we never knew that they were bad clubs — it is one of those lost illusions which I regret, that "Old Blobb" supplied us with the very best clubs, next to the masterpieces of Hugh Philp, that a golfer ever handled. Now we know better, and we do not play with "Old Blobb's" clubs, — but neither, alas! do we play with so much pleasure.

At first "Old Blobb" had not very much to do in the way of making clubs, for it took us some little time, though the clubs were such as they were, to use up the stock he had brought with him; but he used to perform wonderful surgical operations on the broken limbs and heads in a little shed adjoining the cottage at Little Pipkin. He used to trudge away home in the evening, laden with a bundle of cripples, which used to come up fairly active in the morning. He rather encouraged a disposition which was very strong in all of us to keep an old club going so long as it could look a ball fairly in the face at all. It involved less cost of raw material, so that all the pay went to the workman. He was almost a genius at this kind of club cobbling. He would fix in a loose lead with a screw. If the horn was coming off, pushed out by the wet getting in between horn and wood, he would rivet it again by driving tin tacks into the pegs by way of wedges. In all such things as leather faces and long splices he was unequalled.

Now and again, on great occasions and under strenuous persuasion, he would make a club for one of us. Then (it was not part of the bargain, but it was tacitly understood on both sides that it was the graceful and proper thing to do), we used to go over to Little Pipkin for the special purpose of seeing "Old Blobb" at work on our club. The room used to smell very strongly of pitch, used for the twine which whipped head and staff together, and of melted gutta percha. These were the salient smells—the associations which endeared it to us as golfers. But there were also the ordinary smells arising from "Old Blobb's" tobacco and from the green oozy pond just outside. In this room we used to stand and watch "Old Blobb" fashion the club, from the earliest processes of planing down the shaft and shaping the head, down to the running in of the lead, the joining of head and shaft to-

gether, and the fixing of the horn. The vigil
was a solemn thing—a kind of silent prayer,
such as a savage might breathe while the arrow-
maker was chipping the flints for his arrow-
heads. Sometimes "Old Blobb" would let us
take the half-finished club in our hands to see
how it felt. It was a pure formality. We never
dared, or indeed cared, to make any adverse
criticism, for we knew that "Old Blobb" would
have disregarded it.

When the club was finished we used to walk
back very proudly to Pebblecombe with it, taking
tremendous care not to touch the still liquid
varnish on the pitched twine. But sometimes
"Old Blobb" did not so far favour us as to
work on our club, even when we had taken the
trouble to come out from Pebblecombe. He
would say, perhaps: "Eh, but I've an awfu'
sicht o' ba's to mak' the noo," and he would
sit on his bench turning with finger and thumb
the ball, which was held in a semi-circular
wooden concavity, while he plied with the other
hand a hammer, of which one side of the head
was worked out into a broad chisel-like tail.
With this he could nick a ball all over most
symmetrically in two-and-a-half minutes. All
balls were hand-hammered in those days, one
at a time.

And the gutta-percha was as bad as the clubs. The ball used to flatten visibly after each drive. "Old Blobb" would not allow us to say this. He insinuated that it was all our fancy. With the balls that he played with he was remarkably cunning, for he always examined them carefully before teeing them, so as to place them with their most salient bump facing [the club-head. In this way he would beat a ball quite round again after it had looked like a potato. It was but another of the great gifts which we revered in "Old Blobb."

We used to have superstitions about golf balls. Occasionally we got hold of one which seemed to know by instinct its way into the hole. Then we would pocket it affectionately and carry it about with us for weeks, and put it down just for a hole or two at the very crisis of the match until it got black with age and careworn, and had long ceased to be fit to play with. But this, too, we had learned from "Old Blobb," so that our conscience was at peace about it.

Certainly Colonel Burscough had gone down in our estimation, as an oracle, since the appearance of "Old Blobb." In another way, however, he commanded from us even an added respect—he knew Blobb so intimately well!

About five days a week, upon an average, they used to play in singles, "Old Blobb" giving the Colonel a stroke a hole. On these occasions all was not always peace between them, though it is true that the war was all on one side. But often the Colonel, in his volcanic wrath, would seize "Old Blobb" by the coat collar and throw him upon the ground and stamp upon him. "Old Blobb" never made the slightest remonstrance. He lay quite still till the Colonel had done with him, then he rose up and shook himself like a little dog, whom a big dog has charged and rolled over, and the match continued as if nothing had happened. Of course it was no action on Blobb's part which called down this condign punishment—it was merely his own bad play that roused the Colonel's wrath. He admitted it himself. He never pretended that he blamed Blobb at all; only he punished him for playing so much better than he could play. It never seemed to occur to either of them that "Old Blobb" could have any cause for complaint about it. Indeed we used to think that he took it rather as a compliment.

One day when the Colonel was playing very badly, and "Old Blobb" was a good many holes up, the former said he believed that the clothes Blobb wore had something to do with it: "It's that jammed coat of yours, I believe, Blobb; take it off, and let me see if I can play in it."

Of course Blobb said, "Ou aye." So they exchanged coats and played out the round so. The Colonel was very much taller than Blobb, but the little man was so fearfully and wonderfully made that his coat was not much too narrow for the Colonel's swelling chest. But then it was indescribably too short. It was so short that it did not look like a coat at all. It was shorter for the Colonel than the shortest of Eton jackets looks on the biggest and fattest prefect.

On the other hand, the Colonel's coat, while it lay fairly well on "Old Blobb's" square shoulders, hung straight down, like a monk's gown without the cincture, to his heels. His foot just came out from under it when he stepped forward, then disappeared again beneath it. He looked marvellously like Noah in some of those wooden figures of the inmates of the ark. But the Colonel did not win the match.

Of course the Colonel was our best player, after "Old Blobb." No one ever dreamed of questioning that. When we started for any match the "honour" was always accorded to

the Colonel "as an old St Andrews player."
In point of fact he had not played much at
St Andrews, but it was just so much more than
any of the others.

The Pebblecombe course in those days was
rather a sociable one. It turned this way and
that, so that you were constantly seeing something of the other players. It was not like some
of those all-round-in-a-circle links, where you have
no company but your own match from start to
finish. We had nice opportunities of seeing each
other's play—and we were very critical. "Poor
old Saxby," we would say, "he will never play so
long as he goes on in that cramped style of his.
I asked 'Old Blobb' yesterday if it were not so
and he said 'Ou aye.'"

Or perhaps it would be Professor Fleg whose
performance we were watching—then "Too much
science," we would say, "too much science. I
really think our learned friend a little overdoes
it. I spoke about him only this morning to 'Old
Blobb,' and he said, 'Ou, aye.'"

For Professor Fleg had taken the game up in a
very remarkable way. He was a very learned
man, but anatomy was his special branch of
knowledge. All his life had been devoted to
science, and he proposed to approach the game
of Golf from a scientific standpoint, deducing its

practice from first principles. We were not altogether sure about Professor Fleg in this matter;
it all seemed a little unorthodox. Our first principle, a fully sufficing one, was incarnated in "Old
Blobb," and we could not understand the necessity
of looking further; indeed, we thought it distinctly
wrong. We had to make allowances for Mr Fleg,
however, in this as in other things. He did not go
to church, and this we could only overlook in consideration of the long study he had given to bodies,
and its probable materialising influence on the soul.
But though we were thus far tolerant, we let him
fully understand how truly thankful each and all
of us were that we were not learned men. With
this implied rebuke we satisfied our consciences.

And now we had to adopt a similar attitude
towards Professor Fleg's method of learning Golf.
He had in his room a very fine human skeleton,
nicely hinged and jointed. He would inveigle
"Old Blobb" up to this study of his, and there
get the little man to attitudinise, golf club in
hand, while the Professor bent into a more or
less similar position the creaking limbs of the
skeleton.

"I propose, my dear sir," the Professor had said
to "Old Blobb," in his manner of the grand old
school of courtesy, "I propose to take up each
club in turn, and so become master of the game

in detail. I shall commence, my dear sir, with
the putter."

So "Old Blobb" said "Ou, aye," and got himself into position for putting; and the skeleton
creaked piteously while the Professor tortured it
into an attitude somewhat resembling Blobb's, and
finally the Professor wedged himself down, too,
into a like attitude, and there were the three—the
gnome, the skeleton, and the sage—as if they had
all begun to "putt" at the word of command.
"Will you be kind enough to inform me, my
dear sir," the Professor would then say to Blobb,
"whether the figure is now in the correct
attitude."

And Blobb would say, "Ou, aye," and the Professor would let him go. But after he was gone
the Professor would prolong the *séance, tête-à-tête*
with the skeleton, often for an hour or more. By
the morning he had tortured the figure into an
entirely new attitude, and had evolved an equally
new theory about putting, deduced from first principles, which he communicated with very great
courtesy and at vast length to "Old Blobb."
"Old Blobb" said "Ou, aye," and the Professor
came among us and told us that he had *discovered
the secret of putting*, which Blobb, "a man of more
than average intelligence, my dear sir," had fully
comprehended (when explained), and with which

he had cordially agreed. Was it to be wondered at that we congratulated ourselves on our tolerance that we accepted these radical tendencies as the forgiveable and inevitable accompaniment of vast learning ?

But there was one among those whose swings we watched as they approached us on the round who rather baffled our criticism. This was young Robert Burscough. We used to see his ball go skimming away, as if it had wings, over bunkers which we could never hope to carry. We used to watch this wonderingly. The wretch was such a stripling—his little wrist looked as if it must break if it tried to waggle a full-sized club ; yet the ball flew like a swallow from his driver. We none of us quite knew how well the boy did play. We did not take him into any of our matches. "It is not a boy's game," Colonel Burscough said when we proposed taking Bob into a match. "You never see a boy playing in a match at St Andrews."

So Bob Burscough was ostracised as a golfer, though he was a nice boy. But he used to play with "Old Blobb" in the evenings. Then we used to ask "Old Blobb" how he played, and "Old Blobb" used to reply, "Eh, he's the makin's o' a gran' player, yon "—but as there were few of us on whom Blobb had not passed a like eulogium this did not indicate very exactly his place in our golfing hierarchy.

Still, that he could drive farther than most of us was undeniable. If one of us wished to make an opponent press a little we used to say, "I saw young Bob Burscough drive a tremendous ball here yesterday ; he carried that further bed of rushes." But, as a rule, we made it our study to ignore his driving. We left off looking at him, finding, instead, some great preoccupation close at hand. When we spoke of him at all we said, " A boy is always so uncertain in the short game." Afterwards I found out that this was diametrically opposed to facts ; but I don't think we were to be blamed for knowing no better, because none of us had ever seen a boy play.

One night there was a dinner party at Mrs Eccleston's. Our dinner parties were quite small, homely gatherings. We all knew each other. The carving was done on the dinner-table.

Mrs Eccleston was a widow, but her husband had been dead so long that she had ceased to mourn very fiercely for him. Indeed, he must have found many compensations in going to any other world than that in which Mrs Eccleston existed. Miss Mary Eccleston, however, her daughter, was charming.

Of course our talk was principally of Golf.

"Who do you think is the best player here —I mean, of course, after Mr Blobb?" Miss Eccleston asked, with the charming insolence of youth.

"My dear, my dear," said Mrs Eccleston, bowing and mincing with innumerable affectations from the head of the table, "what can you be thinking of? Surely you do not forget that the Colonel" —with a bow to Colonel Burscough, who sat on her right hand—"has been to St Andrews!" Her emphasis upon the saint's name was most impressive."

"'Old Blobb' told me that Bob could beat him any day," said Miss Mary sturdily, rather forgetting, in the spirit of combativeness, her best company way of talking.

"'Old Blobb,' my dear Mary!" said Mrs Eccleston, with a shudder of horror, "That horrid man! I am sure *nothing* that that man said could possibly be true."

"Oh, jam it all, my dear Madam," the Colonel exclaimed, generously bursting out when he heard his old friend thus attacked, "Jam it all, you must not say that. He's a most excellent fellow, I assure you, my dear Madam, though—hum—heh —ha, what in the world he meant by saying that, I cannot conceive. Are you sure, my dear Miss Mary," he continued, turning to Miss Eccleston,

"are you sure that that is what our old friend
said? Did you not misunderstand the words,
eh?"

"Oh, no, Colonel Burscough; really I am sure
I didn't. You see it is so very seldom that Old
—I mean that Mr Blobb—says anything, that it
is quite easy to remember all he says."

"I should think it is—yes. Hum, yes, jammed
old scoundrel!" the Colonel muttered under his
breath.

There was a very painful little pause when this
interchange of remarks was over. We all felt
considerably shocked—first that anybody should
have dared even to report such words as coming
from Blobb's mouth, and, secondly, we were much
shocked to find that it was possible for anyone to
speak of "Old Blobb" as Mrs Eccleston had
spoken of him. Of course we knew that she
was an affected, foolish woman, but still, to dare
to speak so of "Old Blobb"——! It was beyond
words. Perhaps it was most painful of all to poor
Bob Burscough, who was dining, and who sat
through the discussion silent and ashamed, and
with burning cheeks. We wondered what he
would say about it to Miss Eccleston afterwards,
for they were great friends; and we wondered,
too, what the Colonel would say to "Old Blobb"
about it.

At first we all told each other that Miss Mary must have been mistaken about the words. Then a horrid doubting spirit crept in to take the heart out of this wholesome conviction, and we began to wonder whether "Old Blobb," by some accident, in a rare moment of thoughtlessness, really might have said so. Finally the most horrid doubt of all suggested itself —could "Old Blobb" not only have said it, but could it, even by the barest possibility, be true?

This was indeed the ultimate phase of scepticism. After this, what belief could we possess unmarred?

The day of this dinner party at Mrs Eccleston's marked an epoch. From that day we began to watch Bob Burscough's play more openly. If "Old Blobb" could have suggested such a comparison as Miss Eccleston had indicated, what shame need we feel in seeing the boy perform feats which we could not rival? The more we observed of his game, the more horridly reasonable did that, our last phase of scepticism, appear. It was not difficult to believe that "Old Blobb" might really have said of him that his uncle "would not be in it."

Then we began to palliate this horrid view by

telling each other that Bob's talent must be inherited. "Wonderful!" we would exclaim, as we saw his ball soar over the bunkers, "wonderful; he must get it from his uncle."

Then we used to compliment the Colonel vicariously on his nephew's skill. "It is easy to see whose pupil he has been," we used to say, until the Colonel began to take a pride in Bob's prowess which he had never shown before. He used to take him into matches sometimes, generally as his partner, always, however, striking off at the holes which gave the longest carries and giving Bob the short ones. It never suggested itself to us that any other arrangement would be proper. The only chance that any of us had against such a combination, however, lay in taking "Old Blobb" into partnership. Then we generally managed to win. Indeed, we had a belief that it was, humanly speaking, almost impossible for Blobb to be beaten, even in a foursome, and he did much to justify it. He would say, "Eh, I'm thinkin', Mr So-and-So, thet you and me'd mak' just a gran' match wi' the Cornel and Maister Robert."

It was not always the same Mr So-and-So to whom Blobb made this suggestion. At the time we did not realise the principles on which he made his selection; but I have since suspected that it was on the principle of selection of the fittest. I am pretty sure that he carefully watched to see which of us were playing fairly steadily, and would choose as a partner the man who was playing most nearly what he considered his "game."

Miss Mary Eccleston took a remarkable interest in the games in which Bob was concerned. This gave no particular occasion for comment, because they had been like brother and sister since they were quite little things. But Miss Eccleston had been told that at St Andrews there were ladies' links. She asked Colonel Burscough if this were not the case, and when he had answered in the affirmative she told him that he could never rightly call Pebblecombe the " St Andrews of the South "—a name which in moments of somewhat irreverent levity he had been heard to give it— until he had provided it with a ladies' links. Miss Eccleston was a great favourite with the Colonel, and she did not allow him peace till he had promised that a links should be laid out under the Argus eye of Blobb. Blobb was something of a ladies' man, and his heart had been captured by Miss Eccleston through the medium of certain baskets of fruit and tins of beef tea, which the young lady had been in the habit of personally conducting to the cottage in Little Pipkin, when the little Blobbs were convalescent from the scarlet fever.

Now, hitherto, amongst us there had reigned comparative peace. We had been of the number of those happy people whose annals are dull. But with the establishment of the ladies' links there came a great spirit of discord; Miss Eccleston laid siege to old Blobb, and soon induced him to give a great deal of time to the laying-out of the ladies' links. Hence there arose rows and rumours of rows amongst those of the men who said that Blobb was not working as he ought to work upon the long links. The ladies' links, in fact, became a great *casus belli*, and in some unfortunate instances the arena of the contest; but the bitterest feud of all, which was there fought out, had its origin, singularly, in a monkey.

The monkey was the property of Professor Fleg. Professor Fleg was an anatomist—a comparative anatomist, it should be observed. It was with the view of studying the comparative structure of man and his forefather that Mr Fleg first became the proud owner of Mr Johnson. Mr Johnson was the monkey's name, and Mr Johnson was a married man—there was also a Mrs Johnson. Mr Johnson was not beautiful, but he was better—he was good. He was an affectionate husband, in the absence of any rival to Mrs Johnson in his affection, and in fact he had so many merits that it appeared to Mr Fleg not impossible that, with patience—which is always needed for that great study—he might learn to play Golf. Professor Fleg went further, he not only said that Mr Johnson might learn to play Golf, but he maintained that the style, the purely natural style, which Mr Johnson would evolve, would necessarily be the ideal (because the natural primitive and unspoiled) style in which man, his degenerate descendant, ought to golf.

"You will observe, my dear sir," said Mr Fleg, "that my friend, Mr Johnson, is what I may term the natural man. He is physically unspoiled by our nineteenth century civilisation." (He had not even had a chance of reading the Badminton book on Golf.) "Doubtless we shall see in him the perfect, because the perfectly natural, golfer. It remains only in doubt whether I shall be able to impart to him a knowledge of the intricacies and the beauties of the Royal and Ancient Game."

We all had so profound a confidence in the Professor's knowledge and skill, that we doubted not of his ability to impart these great truths to Mr Johnson. We even envied the latter the advantages he enjoyed from his close and constant

companionship with Mr Fleg. But at first the
pupil made but ungrateful progress. Mr Johnson
was immensely pleased with the little club which
Old Blobb, by the Professor's direction, had made
for him, but he used it for every possible purpose
except the right one. He used it as a walking-
stick, as a toothpick, as an assegai. Once it
inspired him with such sudden rage (which seems
very human when we consider that the instrument
was a golf club) as to make him forget his usual
virtue and courtesy, and give his wife a very severe
beating with it—apparently for no sufficient cause.
Professor Fleg undertook the responsibility of
interfering between man and wife, and for a
while Mr Johnson was not permitted the use or
the abuse of his golf club.

The truth is that domestic matters in the
Johnson family were nearing a crisis, and about
a fortnight after the beating, Mrs Johnson had
a baby. This innocent baby was the first occasion
of one of the bitterest feuds which has ever
vexed the tranquillity of Pebblecombe.

Mrs Eccleston, a woman of kind heart but
infinite affectations, had taken into that which
did duty with her for a brain the idea that it
would be an artistic success if she were to be
seen lavishing all sorts of *petits soins* upon that
curious imitation of humanity, the baby Johnson.

For she belonged to that large class of women who are always thinking of the stage-effect of their actions, playing more or less consciously to a gallery—the class of women who want to write a book or keep a bonnet shop or a livery stable. She was always trying to appear literary or cultured or philanthropic—anything, in fact, which she was not; and into each of these motives there really did mingle a slight taste for the pursuits which she affected, imparting a measure of security which made the affectation so much the more specious. It was in the spirit of mingled self-consciousness and philanthropy that she "took up" little Master Johnson. She assured Mr Fleg that it was impossible, nay, even almost indelicate, to suppose that a bachelor, even though he were a professor of anatomy, could know how to deal with the peculiar domestic circumstances beneath his roof. She spent much of her time—more perhaps than Mr Fleg fully appreciated—in running in and out of his house, to see to the wants of little Master Johnson. It was in vain that Mr Fleg suggested the impolicy of such interference with the maternal methods of Mrs Johnson. "Are the many thousand years of evolution to go for nothing," Mrs Eccleston plaintively asked, "that Mrs Johnson should be considered equally capable, as a mother, with a woman of the nineteenth century?"

This was an appeal to Mr Fleg's love of science to which he could oppose nothing but the most courteous hints, to all of which Mrs Eccleston, who was fond of the society of "a man of intellectual attainments," as she rightly described Mr Fleg, presented a sweet, wilful blindness which nothing could perturb. Therefore Mr Fleg, sorely tried by the perpetual sweetness of Mrs Eccleston's presence in his house, could bethink him of no better plan than to make a present to the kind lady of the cause of all her kind assiduity. So, little Master Johnson, having arrived, most precociously, at such an age as to be able to feed himself, Mr Fleg determined to give him away to the lady who took so great an interest in him. This he was the more ready to do, because Mr Johnson began to show a jealous disposition, and to resent the natural affection which, as he seemed to think, Mrs Johnson had sufficiently lavished upon their child. The offer was made to Mrs Eccleston in such a way that she could not fail to express her appreciative acceptance of it, and Mr Fleg at length thought that he saw his way towards regaining peace both for his own domestic circle and for that of his Johnson dependents, when circumstances, most unkindly, suggested to him a joke.

It so happened that neither Mr nor Mrs Johnson was the possessor of a tail. Some bare six inches—scarcely enough to measure a stimie—was the utmost extent of caudal appendage which they could boast of between them. It therefore appeared somewhat in the nature of a reflection upon the parents that young Master Johnson should have been ushered into this vale of tears and bunkers with a fine prehensile tail some eighteen inches long. Mr Fleg had often spoken gravely of this curious fact, and had reflected upon it with particular severity on the eve of the day upon which Master Johnson was to be given over to his self-appointed stepmother, Mrs Eccleston. It so chanced that Master Johnson was in the room while these severe observations were incautiously passed by Mr Fleg, and whether he had overheard, with pain, the tenour of the strictures, and of his own will determined to rid himself of the compromising appendage, or whether it were the result of some unexplained operation of nature, it is certain that on the following morning he presented himself to Mr Fleg's astonished vision absolutely tailless. Mr

Fleg scarcely knew whether to be pleased or distressed, but he rang the bell for the housemaid, and observed in his usual courteous way : " Master Johnson has been so unfortunate as to lose his tail. Would you, please, be so very kind as to see if you can find it ? "

The girl went off on her Bo-peep mission, and presently returned with the missing appendage, in a perfect state of preservation, in her hand. Whereupon Mr Fleg sat down and wrote a note to Mrs Eccleston, in which he said, " I send you a small instalment of the monkey. The rest shall follow in the course of the day."

This note he enclosed in a small packet containing Master Johnson's tail, and sent it off to Mrs Eccleston's villa.

Now this joke, which, if humble, was, at all events, most innocent, made Mrs Eccleston very angry. She was a lady who seldom saw a joke, except of her own making, and this fact it was Mr Fleg's duty to have considered. But he incautiously overlooked it, with that neglect of detail which is characteristic of some great minds, and the monkey's tail was sent. Mrs Eccleston's refined mind was filled with horror. When her daughter endeavoured to soothe her, telling her that it was all meant as a joke, she did but respond, severely, that "it was a joke in the worst possible taste." She affected to deem herself personally insulted by Mr Fleg, and not even the due arrival of the rest of Master Johnson went any appreciable length towards pacifying her delicate wrath. Never, thereafter, did she treat Mr Fleg with anything but the most distant politeness, and the seed of discord thus sown by the tail of the monkey was destined to bear fruit upon the ladies' links.

As soon as the ladies' links were opened they became a very popular resort—more especially for the young people of both sexes. Of the most assiduous in their study of the game of Golf among the beautiful sandhills were Miss Eccleston and young Burscough. Unhappily for the young man, he chanced to be a great friend of Mr Fleg. It was but natural, therefore, that Mr Fleg should often join in their matches, and should also, sometimes, play single matches, in which he got greatly worsted, with Miss Eccleston herself. This, in the condition of Mrs Eccleston's feelings, induced by the receipt of Master Johnson's tail, was sufficient to make the whole game of Golf, as played by Miss Eccleston, to be viewed with abhorrence by the young lady's mother. That good lady, therefore, from the depths of her delicate sofa

cushions, issued her absolute veto against any
more of these matches with young Mr Burscough; and when the daughter suggested that
as a rule they were played under the surely
sufficient chaperonage of Professor Fleg, the
mention of this learned name did but serve to
add fuel to the maternal wrath. Mrs Eccleston
even went so far as to hint at the impropriety
of Mr Fleg's playing in single matches with
her daughter, and signified her intention of
personally speaking to that famous man upon
the subject.

So Mr Fleg, greatly to his surprise, for the
lady had of late been treating him with excessive
coolness, received a summons from Mrs Eccleston,
which informed him that she would be glad to see
him on a certain named afternoon. It happened
to be a day and an hour on which Mr Fleg was
engaged to play at Golf with Miss Eccleston, but
it appeared to him, in his exceeding courtesy,
scarcely right to allow a previous engagement
with the daughter to stand in the way of the
summons from the mother.

Mr Fleg opened the interview, rather infelicit-
ously, by an inquiry after the health of Master
Johnson. Mrs Eccleston answered him in a tone
which suggested that the welfare of Master Johnson was a matter to be arranged between herself

and Providence, and that even verbal interference on the part of Mr Fleg was nothing less than an impertinence. The professor then proceeded to refer, in touching terms, to the grief of Mrs Johnson at the loss of her son, and this occasion was skilfully seized by Mrs Eccleston as a masked advance towards her point of attack.

"Ah, Mr Fleg," she said, with a deep sigh, from the depths of the sea-green cushions on which she was reclining, "you can know little, indeed, of the anxieties and sorrows which beset a mother's heart."

"Naturally, my dear madam," Mr Fleg rejoined, "my experience of such emotions is not personal. I trust, however—— "

"Ah, there you are wrong, Mr Fleg—so wrong," the lady interrupted him, with an approach to vivacity. "Had you but an inkling, but the faintest notion of the anxiety which wrings a mother's heart, you could never be so cruel as to subject it to the pain you do."

"I, my dear madam, I!" said Mr Fleg, in sore distress and perplexity.

"Ah, Mr Fleg, you men but little know the hopes, the sentiments, which you lightly arouse in a young girl's heart."

"Young girl, my dear madam?"

"Ah, Mr Fleg, must I be explicit? Is it

necessary that I put the dots on all the i's? Do
you not, Mr Fleg, frequently play Golf—in single
matches sometimes — with my daughter on the
ladies' links?"

"Certainly, my dear madam ; but—— "

"But, Mr Fleg—but do you think nothing of
the hopes—the emotions so easily aroused in a
trusting young heart?"

"Emotions! I! My dear madam! Arouse
emotions?"

"Alas, Mr Fleg, can you doubt it?"

"But, my dear madam, my years, my grey
hairs, my exceeding shortness of sight—surely all
these put a gulf which the most far-reaching sus-
picions could never cross between myself and
your daughter. As for emotions—— "

"Ah, Mr Fleg, you forget your intellectual
attainments," said Mrs Eccleston, with a very deep
sigh, as though these were the devil's engines for
the snaring of maidens' affections.

"Really, my dear madam," replied Mr Fleg,
with somewhat less than his usual courtesy,
"really I had failed to realise that a knowledge
of anatomy was likely to exercise a fatal fascina-
tion upon a young lady's heart. For the future I
will be more careful. I wish you good-day, Mrs
Eccleston."

Thus, with the invention of the ladies' links

there was introduced into our golfing midst a spirit of discord which had before been alien to it.

Almost concurrently with the appearance of Master Johnson there came among us another new thing—a St Andrews man. We had known little heretofore of St Andrews men. Colonel Burscough, it is true, had played golf at St Andrews, and for this we regarded him with all proper veneration; but he was not, in the full sense of the word, a St Andrews man. He had not been born and bred on those classic links, as had our new guide, philosopher, and friend, Mr Fraserburgh. I think I am disclosing no confidences in saying that our common feeling, as we watched his play, was surprise that one who had enjoyed so great advantages could play so badly. He partially accounted for this, how-ever, by explaining that the nature of his pro-fessional work was such as to keep him much in Edinburgh, away from the city of the great links. His profession was that of Writer to the Signet, an honourable title which we but dimly understood, supposing it to have reference to some form of literary work in the service of the Crown—a subordinate post, perhaps, to that of Poet Laureate. In appearance he was a small, ferrety-eyed man, with sandy hair and whiskers;

but the prominent feature of his face was a peculiarly bulbous nose, which looked as if it had been coloured with much artistic care and Scottish whisky.

But while we observed his golfing execution with a criticism of whose audacity we were painfully conscious, we regarded his methods with unmixed reverence. For of these methods many were quite new to us. Especially were we impressed by his treatment of his caddie, which struck us as a remarkable combination of deference and ferocity. Hitherto we had been accustomed to play the game in our own way, taking the club which seemed best in our own eyes, and altogether conducting the game on our own responsibility, or with an occasional reference to the methods of Old Blobb or Colonel Burscough. But now, greatly to our astonishment, we saw this golfer, whom we all regarded with the awe due to a St Andrews man, gravely consulting upon his stroke with his small, ten-year-old caddie. He would solemnly ask, and defer to, the opinion of this little rascal, released for the time being from the Voluntary school, with regard to the club he ought to use for an approach stroke, or even such a delicate matter as the line of a curving putt. At first the caddie was no less surprised than ourselves, and being more or less dumb

with awe of the great man, and speaking in a
broad South-Country dialect which had no affinity
to Mr Fraserburgh's trans-Tweedish speech, it
was with difficulty that they arrived at anything
definite, even in the way of a misunderstanding.
Therefore, when Mr Fraserburgh would ask :
"What club am I to take, boy ?" the caddie
would first look at him in mute amazement.
Then, when by dint of loud and frequent repetition the question had found a home in his small
intellect, he would say, " I don't know."

"Don't know," Mr Fraserburgh would repeat,
with fiery Gaelic wrath, "is it a cleek or an iron
shot ? "

Then the boy, comprehending the alternatives,
would search for both the weapons mentioned
and timidly offer to Mr Fraserburgh that which
came to his small hand first. After which Mr
Fraserburgh, having made an indifferent stroke
would say to his opponent, "I knew it was a
cleek shot, but my confounded caddie *made me
take the iron.*"

"Made me take the iron !" It was a new and
a blessed idea to us—this of making the caddie
responsible for our misdeeds. We were quick to
recognise the virtue of the new phrase, and to
make it our own. Henceforward this form of
explanation was a frequent one at Pebblecombe.

We seldom of our own unskilfulness now made a bad stroke. We learned, with gratitude, to say that "the caddie had given us a wrong club."

But there were other things in the same regard that were taught us by Mr Fraserburgh. Hitherto we thought that we had done well if we contrived to make our caddies keep comparative silence and very comparative immobility upon the stroke. For Mr Fraserburgh it was not sufficient that the caddie should be immobile. He must be immobile on a certain spot, like a piece at chess. If the caddie stood behind his arm it was cause for his righteous indignation and for the caddie's summary removal. Not only so, but he told us that it was no less baulking to have to speak to the boy and request his removal than it was to have him standing upon the offending spot. All these minutiæ were a subject of our zealous study. Hereafter the caddie's life was no longer the peaceful thing that it had been before. For we grew to be mighty particular about the exact position, relatively to ourselves as we played a stroke, in which the caddie should stand. Nor was this all, but each developed some special and individual taste, one being unable to play if the boy stood to his front at all; another finding the striking of the golf ball an impossible thing if the caddie stood anywhere behind him. So that these little boys had not only to learn the whole duty of the caddie, but, in addition, the special duties required by the exigencies of each individual's temperament; and our nervous apprehensions of the misconduct of the caddies increasing and becoming more sensitive through indulgence, as ever happens, we soon grew to expect of these small boys more than boy-nature is capable of satisfying, to the end that the carrying of golf clubs became little less trying to the youthful brain than the ordinary curriculum of the Voluntary school. Hence arose murmurings and a newly-found love of learning in the boys, together with a difficulty in obtaining caddies, so that some of us were occasionally driven to the humiliating straits of carrying our own clubs.

But the strain thus put upon their intellects developed a wonderful cuteness and aptitude for the game in these small rascals, so that Mr Fraserburgh's treatment had its compensations for them. "Ice-cream," a boy who had thoroughly merited this *nom de guerre* by undauntedly devouring thirty-six penny ices and a whole week's pay at a sitting, was especially attached to Colonel Burscough's service, and soon became quite an indispensable adjunct to the gallant gentleman's golf. He would even rate his master severely when he was off his game, and an exhortation of "Come, come, old man, this won't do," on the occasion of the Colonel's missing a nine-inch putt, became historical. "Ice-cream," partly because of his distinguished position as Colonel Burscough's henchman, grew to hold some sort of monitorial authority over the other caddies. He it was who, when "The Bengal Tiger" (a very small and puny boy, so called from the felinely striped neck-comforter which he was in the habit of wearing) threw down Capt. Lazenby's clubs, saying, "I be going home; there's goose for dinner"—"Ice-cream" it was who took upon himself to chastise the offender for this gross crime. "Ice-cream" undoubtedly was a born leader of men.

Thus, painfully, under Mr Fraserburgh's influence, our caddies grew in golfing intelligence, and in a very just contempt for the frequent imbecilities of our play. Ourselves, too, gained much from the inestimable boon of listening to the many comparisons which Mr Fraserburgh drew — naturally to our disadvantage — between Golf and its surroundings at Pebblecombe and at St Andrews.

"It is maist deleterious," he would say, "to an auld St Andrews player like myself to see nane aboot him with the true St Andrews swing. You will obsairve that I have the true St Andrews swing. I'm no' saying," he would modestly add, "that there's nane at St Andrews that could na' beat me, even at my best; but play he well or ill, ye'll always know a St Andrews man, supposing that ye have any golf experience, the first moment that ye see him swing."

The weighty words, and a sense of our own in-adequacy, sank heavily into our hearts. If there were any to whom it occurred to think that, St Andrews swing or no, young Burscough could give Mr Fraserburgh close upon a stroke a hole, at all events the reflection was allowed to die in silence.

"An' is it no' true, Mr Fraserburgh," Old Blobb responded, "het the caddies at St Aundries are fine, clever buddies, an'll no', by the veriest oustest of a chaunce, pit t' wrang club intil yer haun'?"

"Oh, aye, Blobb, it's verra true."

"An' is it no' true, Mr Fraserburgh, het t' whusky at St Aundries is o' t' finest an' maist pooerfu' quarlity?"

"Oh, aye, Blobb"—with rising enthusiasm—"it's verra, verra true."

"An' is it no' true, Mr Fraserburgh," Blobb pursued, after one solemn, capacious wink at the rest of the company, "het the rats an' mice at St Aundries are t' maist ferocerous arnimals i' t' warld?"

"Oh, aye, Blobb, it's true, it's true," Mr Fraserburgh said, with ecstatic excitement. " It's true—though I did na' know ye knew it. The rats and mice at St Andrews, sir "—and Mr Fraserburgh turned his nose to us defiantly, as though he challenged contradiction — " the rats and mice at St Andrews are the largest and most voracious of their kind in the known world."

But no one contradicted him. Colonel Burscough only inquired whether these were *real* or only *alcoholic* vermin, and then we all sighed heavily, for we knew that he was embarking for a long, long voyage upon his favourite old story about the imaginary mongoose.

At the very outset, however, he was mercifully interrupted. Mr Fraserburgh, with his nose a few tinges warmer, inquired volcanically whether the Colonel presumed to doubt his word.

" Begad, no, sir," the Colonel returned. " I would have believed you if you had said the same of the lions and tigers of St Andrews. No gentleman ever doubts another's word, no matter how many lies he tells."

" Lies ! sir, lies !" Mr Fraserburgh exclaimed, with terrible excitement. " Do you mean to tell me I tell lies, sir ? "

" Certainly not, sir," returned Colonel Burscough.

"All I said was that I would not doubt your word if you did."

"I don't understand you, sir. You have cast reflections on the honour of a Scotsman and of a St Andrews man."

"To you as the representative of Scotland and of St Andrews," said the Colonel, drawing himself up very stiffly, "I beg to tender my apologies for anything that I have said derogatory to the dignity of either; and "—with sudden collapse of his majestic style of address—"and you may go to h—— for a little red-headed lawyer."

The Scotsman's fury was propitiated by the deference paid to his home and country; his keen Gaelic sense of humour was touched by the Colonel's breakdown from the heights of grandiosity. His small eye twinkled appreciative of his repartee, as he said, turning to the consolation of his whisky and water: "Na, na, Cornel, I'll no' go there. I'll go somewhere where there's less chance of meeting yourself." The Colonel joined in the laugh, and all was peace where a moment before we had been threatened with bloody war.

By the time that Mr Fraserburgh came among us we had advanced far beyond the primitive simplicity of a room in the farmhouse beside the common, and the crows' feathers dimly marking the holes. We no longer threw down our unnecessary coats, exposed to all the winds of heaven, at the first tee. We had subscribed for the purchase of a gold medal, which we played for once a year, in the autumn; and on these occasions of annual enterprise it was not enough that we should cast superfluous coats unguarded on the ground. So at first we hired a bathing-machine to give shelter on such occasional meetings. Later we went to the extravagance of purchasing a tent, and soon after the arrival on our South-Country scene of Mr Fraserburgh, we blossomed into the full magnificence of a corrugated iron hut. Here, with a man in charge dispensing whisky, we took our royal leisure when Golf was over, explaining to each other the hardness of our luck — how but for some accident which could be ascribed to nothing short of diabolical intervention, we should have made the finest round which ever had been chronicled. Here we joined with Mr Fraserburgh in a new chorus, of which he was instructor and precentor, about the "disgraceful state of the putting - greens." But before we made use of our new house of refuge for these homely purposes, it had seemed right that we should inaugurate our corrugated iron magnificence by a ceremonial dinner in the edifice

P

which we now proudly spoke of as "the club-house."

The materials for this function were carried out from Pebblecombe in many donkey carts to the spot where our club-house stood pictur-esquely situated among the sand - hills. We dined well, as befitted the greatness of the occasion, and drank many loyal, patriotic and golfing toasts. The name of Mr Fraserburgh was coupled with that of St Andrews, "the golfing metropolis," and his health drunk with prodigious enthusiasm. Mr Fraserburgh re-sponded with much feeling, and so overcome was he by his emotion, that at the close of his speech he failed to seat himself securely on his chair, and rolled off, with much detriment to his best dress coat, upon the floor. On this, Colonel Burscough, who, of course, was in the chair, shouted loudly to those on either side of Mr Fraserburgh to "tee him up again." This, however, was found to be impossible, as the gentleman persisted in his preference for the floor, so there he was permitted to remain until the close of the proceedings, which ter-minated soon afterwards.

In the course of the dinner it had been deter-mined that the new era of our club—its corru-gated iron age, as one may call it—should be inaugurated, on the morrow, by a very great match—the Burscoughs *versus* United Scotland as represented by Mr Fraserburgh and Old Blobb. The match was first mooted during the fish course. By the time the cheese was on the table it had been arranged as a definite fixture, and with the dessert many bets were recorded on the result. On the first blush it had appeared that the redoubtable Scotsmen must inevitably have the best of it.

Who could withstand the indomitable prowess of Old Blobb, the imperturbable cunning of Mr Fraserburgh? Mr Fraserburgh, himself, indeed, gave a grudging acknowledgment of their probable superiority, for when the Colonel in his hearty way called out, "Why, jam it all, Fraserburgh, it's a certainty for you; you'll have to lay us two to one," Mr Fraserburgh had answered, in words which have since become historic: "Na, na, Cornel; Gowf is not a game to be degraded to the vice of gambling, like your horse-racing, your pigeon-shooting and the rest. It is a game to be played amongst gentlemen for the pure love of the sport. Besides," he added, and therein showed his belief in the prowess of himself and his partner — "besides, there is no two to one in it, *but I'll lay ye sax to fower.*"

Later in the evening, however, and especially when notice was taken of Mr Fraserburgh's recumbent position, the betting, which was on the mildest scale, somewhat fluctuated, until slight odds were actually laid against "the gentleman on the floor." And when this great night was over, and we were all bethinking ourselves of the walk home over the Common, it appeared quite impossible to make Mr Fraserburgh realise the necessity of returning for the present to the shelter of any other roof than the corrugated iron one. He explained to us that the effort of speaking had been rather much for him, and that he would be greatly obliged if we would leave him to walk home by himself in the moonlight an hour or so later. We did not venture to disregard his express wishes, and there Mr Fraserburgh remained, the lonely guardian of that lonely corrugated iron building, while the rest of us, with some trouble, stumbled, in twos and threes, homeward to our beds.

"Mind you're in time for the match to-morrow," Colonel Burscough had shouted, as we left him ; and the fearless answer had come back from the darkness, with tolerable distinctness, "I shall be there."

But when the morrow came and we called,

about ten o'clock, for Mr Fraserburgh at his lodging, the appalling news was told that no sign of him had been seen that night. Nevertheless, we all went forth with confidence, relying on that undaunted answer, "I shall be there," out over the Common towards the clubhouse and the first tee, to witness the great match. And, "there," sure enough, Mr Fraserburgh was—but in what figure for his game of Golf? In the snowy shirt front, somewhat crumpled, and the dress clothes, slightly soiled, of the previous night! Seldom had a more singular spectacle been seen than Mr Fraserburgh, with admirable *sang froid*, practising a few preliminary putts in this costume, which, in the broad light of day, strongly suggested the Christy Minstrel. No, he had not been home, he said, had spent an excellent night beneath the corrugated iron roof, had breakfasted well, but plainly, off dry biscuits and whisky, was in every way prepared and eager to do himself justice in the great match. His valiant nose showed no pallor from the discomfort of his night, his ferrety eyes were as keen as ever. Old Blobb looked at his partner with taciturn disfavour. He was perhaps less unused than most of us to see his yoke-fellow in a golf match present himself in these conditions.

It needs not to be said that the honour of driving off the first ball was, by unanimous consent, accorded to our president, Colonel Burscough; neither need it be told that a goodly crowd of onlookers was collected together, attracted by the greatness of the occasion. Until the putting-green of the first hole was reached, no remarkable feature presented itself. Either side had played faultless Golf. It was young Burscough's turn to play the approach putt, and here the first symptom of the young fellow's not unnatural nervousness was apparent. He went forward doubtfully to examine the nature of the ground.

" It's roughish, isn't it ? " he asked of the Colonel, timorously.

"Yes, it's roughish a bit, and then again its keen," the Colonel replied, " whatever you do be up, and, for Heaven's sake," he added impressively, " don't be more than a foot past the hole."

Now, whether the heroic nature of this counsel cast despair of its achievement into the young man's soul, instead of the confidence which it was intended to inspire, or whether it was, as he explained, "that confounded blade of grass," which, none but himself could plainly see—at all events, the result was that the ball did but go some two-thirds of the way towards the hole.

The Colonel was filled with gloomy indignation. As a just retribution upon a partner who had treated him in such a manner, it was his habit to make but the merest semblance of an effort to hole out with the next stroke. He went wide of the mark, and Old Blobb having laid Mr Fraserburgh stone dead, the first hole went to the Scotsmen.

"Confounded young fool," the Colonel ejaculated. "I told you, whatever you did, to be up."

For several holes following young Burscough played, for him, exceedingly badly, in spite of the solicitous and sagacious counsel which the Colonel repeatedly pressed upon him. They were now two down, and, approaching the fifth hole, young Burscough took in hand his iron.

"Iron!" his partner exclaimed, in high scorn, "what are you doing with your iron? You'll never reach that with your iron."

"What club would you advise?" young Burscough asked, with a beautiful submission which might have suggested suspicion.

"Take your long spoon, and I doubt if you'll get up with that the way you're playing."

So, with that, young Burscough took his spoon. He set his teeth, and swung with the first really free, fearless swing he had given that day. The ball flew away like a rocket. Straight it went

over the flag, which, in these days of our glory
had superseded the old crows' feathers, and on and
on it went as if it never were going to stop, ending
some hundred or so yards beyond the hole.   Then
Colonel Burscough never said a word.   He gave
a look at his young partner—a look of terrific
ferocity, which was answered by a bland smile,
and, " I always take the club you tell me."   Then
he smothered his wrath and walked after the ball
to drive it back again.

This little episode marked the turning of the
match.   That hole was lost, and the Burscoughs
were three down, but, after that, young Burscough
got his nerve, and all his strokes were pictures.
The Colonel said not another word to him of
advice.   Gradually they regained their lost
ground, though the Scotsmen struggled dourly.
At the eleventh hole the match was all even.
Then, as Mr Haggard says, a strange thing
happened.   As the Colonel was studying, with
his usual stern deliberation, the line of a two-
foot putt, some one in the crowd of spectators,
a stranger to most of us but a friend of one of
the party, exclaimed in a shrill voice, which had
an unmistakable American accent : " She has the
mange in her hind leg, which detracts considerably from her appearance."

The Colonel withdrew hurriedly, and in visible

wrath, from the post of observation of his putt. Several shocked " hushes " from the onlookers in the offender's immediate neighbourhood did not appear to the Colonel to be a sufficient rebuke of the crime. He sternly addressed the offender : " I do not know to whom you may be referring, sir, but I would tell you that even that unfortunate malady is no excuse for your mentioning it upon the stroke."

" Very sorry, I'm sure," the American answered, " I was only speaking of a dog."

" Then let me tell you, sir, that no dogs, not even mangy ones, are permitted upon a golf course," the Colonel excitedly replied.

" But, gracious me ! " said the stranger, " I have brought no dog. I did only mention one."

" Then let me tell you again, sir, that the moment you selected for its mention was an exceedingly ill-chosen one. Probably, as a foreigner, you know nothing whatever of the game of Golf."

" No, sir," returned the American, unabashed. " It is a form of lunacy from which I have not yet suffered. I have had chicken-pox, I have had measles, I have even had philanthropy ; but, thank goodness, I have never yet had Golf."

Then let me tell you, sir, yet again, that the time will come when every man of an English-speaking nation (and I include the American nation)," said the Colonel, with majestic irony, "will suffer from what you are pleased to call this form of lunacy." And, having satisfied his soul with this tremendous prophecy, since amply fulfilled, the Colonel returned, amid an awful silence, to his putt, which, after some further study, he failed to hole.

This disaster, which put the Scotsmen again one ahead, was soon atoned for by the transcendent play of young Burscough, and all went smoothly until the sixteenth hole, at which point the Burscoughs were one to the good. Here, however, another unpleasant little incident occurred. Colonel Burscough's study of his putt was, at this crisis, prolonged even beyond its wont—so much so as to be unendurable to the nerves, now greatly excited, of Mr Fraserburgh.

"Come, come, Cornel," the Scotsman exclaimed, as the Colonel, for the third time, went to the back of the hole to make sure of his line. "Come, come, Cornel, putt it out."

Colonel Burscough withdrew himself from the hole with majestic dignity. "Confound it, sir!" he said, "I shall putt it out when I like, and how I like, and with what club I like. You hold your tongue, sir."

After which he addressed himself, yet again,

to the stroke, and holed the ball with the courage of a lion.

One up and two to play! And the last two holes being halved, the Burscoughs won this never-to-be-forgotten match by one.

This match had revealed, amongst other revelations, the astounding fact that young Burscough was a better player than Old Blobb. Mr Fraserburgh said so himself, pointing his assertion by many an illustration of Old Blobb's deficiencies in the great match. Hereafter, it began to be a recognised fact that young Burscough was the best player in Pebblecombe, and we had a notion that he was the best in the world. Therefore they turned the match about, Colonel Burscough playing with Old Blobb and Mr Fraserburgh with young Burscough. It was all the same, however—young Burscough's side won the great majority of the matches.

For a while the Colonel ascribed this result to supernatural agency. "It was all luck," he said, with an emphasis on "luck" which made it seem much as though he had said "the devil."

Later, this theory became exhausted. He could not believe in such persistent working, in one line, of luck or the devil. He then began to ascribe it to bribery. "Old Blobb sells you," he said, "that's the worst of these professional fellows—they're always ready to sell their matches."

The puzzle was to find the buyer. If Old Blobb was venal, who was it that bribed him? To whom was it worth while? For there was seldom more than a half-crown on the match. But, of course, we never presumed to put these questions to the Colonel. We listened with respectful silence.

After a while, however, these matches fell through—not so much by reason of Old Blobb's scandalous venality as because of a tremendous row between the Colonel and Mr Fraserburgh, which began, so to speak, in a sardine tin. It probably was the only sardine tin on the whole of the Pebblecombe links, so there is every reason to suppose that it was especially put there by the evil one in order to engender strife. For it lay in a little ragged patch of rushes, and close behind it lay the Colonel's ball. There were no sardines in the tin, but that is a detail.

The Colonel was stooping down to remove it when Mr Fraserburgh called out, "What are ye going to do, Cornel?"

"I am going to remove this biscuit tin, sir."

"And I maintain, Cornel, that ye are lying in a hazard an' have na right to move yon tin—and it's no' a biscuit tin, but a sardine tin, at ony rate."

A few minutes were spent in pursuing the side issue of the original purpose of the tin. This was determined by Old Blobb's going down upon his knees, sniffing sagaciously at the tin, and pronouncing with confidence "Fush!"

"There now, Cornel," said Mr Fraserburgh, triumphantly, having scored this first point in his favour. "May I ask, if ye please, on what grounds ye propose to remove this *sardine* tin?"

"On the ground, sir, that it is in the way."

The very simplicity of the answer made Mr Fraserburgh very angry indeed. With question and answer they went on from hot to hotter words. Old Blobb paced apprehensively around them, doubtful how to act, and wondering whether it would be safer to run home. Young Burscough lay on the ground and rolled about in the ecstasies of his laughter. Eventually Colonel Burscough seized the stumbling block, the sardine tin, and threw it furiously and crookedly at Mr Fraserburgh's head. Then he played his ball, in triumph, while Mr Fraserburgh, calling to his caddie, marched home with his nose very high in the air and warm in colour. After this, for a long while, they were not on speaking terms, and we all regretted the breach of harmony and the cessation of these interesting matches.

About the same time came the first institution among us of handicap prizes. They owed their origin entirely to the ingenuity of Colonel Burscough, who knew that their invention would grievously vex the Gaelic soul of Mr Fraserburgh. The Colonel himself disapproved of handicap prizes, but this disapproval was not nearly so strong as his approval of any measure that could annoy Mr Fraserburgh. So we began to have biscuit boxes and butter dishes and monthly medals, and selling lotteries, and many, many things which were an abomination to Mr Fraserburgh. Personally he never competed for these honours.

"Na, sir," he would sternly say, "Gowf is not charity." Another reason for his non-competing, which he did not mention, was the enormous handicap he would have required to make him win.

There came among us, too, men who bet large sums upon a match—and paid them. Distinguished city men came for an occasional holiday to golf at Pebblecombe. Once we even had a member of Parliament. The city men introduced ingenious ways of betting. They would lay ten shares in the Great Desert of

Sahara and Central African Railway Company, Limited, against fifteen shares, not fully paid up, in the East Lincolnshire and Fen Countries Irrigation Company, Limited. They spoke of these great investments with a strange familiarity, under the terms of "Sarahs" and "Lincolns." Then they invented the plan of purchasing back from an adversary who might be a hole or two ahead his holes of vantage. For instance, if the layer of "Sarahs" were three up and nine to play, the layer of "Lincolns" might, with proportional justice, say, "I'll give you four 'Lincolns' and we'll call it all even."

Such were the *fin de siècle* modes of betting which were introduced among us about the time of the invention of the Eclipse golf ball.

Young Burscough was the first to play with one of these balls. It will be remembered that one of their peculiarities is to fly silently off the club, like a thief in the night. He happened to be playing with the Colonel when he made the first experiment with the new ball. He had said nothing of it to the Colonel, who, as the first flew off, looked suspiciously at the flying sphere but made no remark. At the second tee shot, however, he could no longer keep silence. "What is the matter with that ball, sir?" he sternly inquired.

"Nothing particular," the young man replied; "it is just a new sort of ball they have sent me to try."

"New sort of ball, sir! why, jam it all, it's rank cheating. You didn't hit that ball at all —you know you didn't—it made no noise, and yet it flew off the club as if you had hit it perfectly. It's not a fair ball to play with."

When the hole was finished the Colonel looked at the novelty with curious disgust. He was very silent during the round, but when they had returned to the Iron Hut, and young Burscough was discussing the merits of the ball with some friends, the Colonel observed again, "I tell you, sir, it's not fair playing Golf with a ball like that. No gentleman, sir, plays Golf with a lump of putty."

For the ball was rather soft, and gave some grounds for this description, and the appropriateness of the epithet was so fully recognised that from this remark of the Colonel's the term "putty ball" came into general use as a designation of the Eclipse patent.

So, now that we have brought the history of our club so late down as to the days of putty balls and great handicap prizes, we are treading closely on the threshold of contemporary golfing history as written in the chronicles of the

Badminton Library and other great books. It remains only to relate how that great sundering of hearts which took place over the disunited caudal appendage of Master Johnson was mended, and the heartstrings rejoined, by the medium of a piece of rope's end.

Amongst the golfers who came into our circle was one by name Mr Lazenby. This gentleman was a brother of Mrs Eccleston. Further, he was of a round full figure, a puffy face, and a melancholy disposition—a little troubled with some fatty sort of degeneration of the heart— just such a man, in fact, as one imagines Hamlet to have been. In the case of Mr Lazenby, however, there was no Ophelia—at Pebblecombe, at least. Golf was his Ophelia, his only love, the subject of all his thoughts by day and of all his dreams at night. His soliloquies, his ecstasies, and his melancholia, all had regard to the great and ancient game. He was fully conscious of this himself, and sometimes spoke of his absorption with a touching mixture of self-pity and of pride. A short putt missed at a crucial point in a match would be with him, in mental vision, during whole days of torture. But he never broke his clubs or indulged in the violent manifestations of grief which were the safety valves of Colonel

Burscough's volcanic wrath. Mr Lazenby's
sorrow was too deep and too subtle for these
gross remedies—it was beyond medicament, it
preyed upon him and ate into his inmost soul,
to the detriment both of bodily and mental
health. Mrs Eccleston was seriously concerned
for her brother's welfare.

And now there came on a very great match,
long arranged, between Mr Lazenby and Old
Blobb, on the one side, against the two Burscoughs on the other. Mr Lazenby was not
a player of very high class, inferior, probably,
to Colonel Burscough. It was thought, amongst
those who knew, that there was but slight
chance for Mr Lazenby. Nevertheless, he had,
at the first, expressed himself with confidence
as to the result. As the day drew near, however, he began to grow less satisfied. He was
in a vein of unsteady play. His nights were
made miserable by his anxiety, his face grew
more pallid and flabby, his step more vacillating.
The day before the great match Mrs Eccleston,
going into his bedroom, after he had gone
forth to Golf (for he was staying in her house)
was horrified to perceive, lying upon the floor,
a long coil of stout rope. Not for one single
instant did Mrs Eccleston deceive herself as to
the purpose for which this deadly coil was in-

tended. She knew well the melancholy bent of her brother's mind, and the terrible strain which the only too probable loss of the morrow's golf match would put upon it. Already he had taken his fatal measures. Even now Mrs Eccleston saw him pendent, over her mental horizon, his neck encircled by the fatal noose. In her anguish of spirit the poor lady could think of no adviser better than her old friend (now, since the Johnson episode, somewhat estranged) Professor Fleg. Again, therefore, the Professor received the lady's gracious summons, and again, with his usual courtesy, he punctually obeyed it.

"Mr Fleg," she said, very sadly, from the depths of her sofa cushions, "you see a woman in very great trouble."

"Indeed, my dear madam," the Professor answered, with some trepidation, owing to a vivid recollection of a former interview, "I sincerely regret to hear it. May I be permitted to inquire its nature?"

"Ah, my dear Mr Fleg, you know my affection, my anxiety for my dear brother. Can nothing, do you think, be done to save him?"

"Save him, my dear madam—from what, may I ask?"

"Ah, Mr Fleg, from this fatal golf match." And

then Mrs Eccleston proceeded, at great length, to lay before Mr Fleg her fears, grounded upon the unassailable evidence of that terrible piece of rope.

" But, my dear madam," Mr Fleg asked, when the lady's moving narrative was finished, " have you any reason to suppose that the rope of which you speak is destined for any such deadly purpose?"

" Ah, Mr Fleg, I know my dear brother so well —know so well the effect of this dreadful game upon his curious disposition."

" But could you not conceal or destroy the rope, my dear madam ? " Mr Fleg naturally inquired.

" Again, Mr Fleg, I must repeat to you, I know my poor brother's disposition far, far too well. Once he has determined on a course of action he is like—like—what shall we say, Mr Fleg ? "

" ' A mule,' my dear madam ? " Mr Fleg courteously suggested.

" Let us rather say ' adamant,' Mr Fleg," the lady corrected him. " At all events, I perceive that you understand my meaning. How, I ask you—you, a man of commanding intellect—how are we to save him ? "

Mr Fleg took his leave, promising to call again later in the day, by which time he hoped to have thought out a means for Mr Lazenby's preservation. He was doubtful whether the rope might not, after all, have denoted some less deadly purpose than that which Mrs Eccleston had surmised. Nevertheless, he was not without his apprehensions. He had suggested that Mr Lazenby might have some boxes to cord, but had been checkmated by the answer that the gentleman always travelled with portmanteaux. On his way home he met the Pebblecombe doctor.

"Have you happened to have seen Mr Lazenby lately, my dear sir?" he asked the medicine man.

"Lazenby; yes, by Jove," said the doctor, who was a jovial little man, "saw him day before yesterday. Getting jolly fat, ain't he? Eats too much, drinks too much, sleeps too much—told him so myself. That old Golf of yours" (the doctor was not a golfer), "not enough exercise for a man of his habit. Advised him to get a skipping rope and skip for a quarter of an hour every morning when he gets out of his bath. Jolly pretty sight he must be—ha!—ha!—fine study in comparative anatomy. Good morning, Professor."

The Professor made no answer, but stood thoughtfully, with an expression which was as nearly a wink as a very learned man can be expected to get it. Then he walked away delicately, like Agag, revolving subtle schemes in his head.

He had been very sincerely vexed by the gulf

which had been set by Mrs Eccleston between those two young people, who had bid fair to make so fine a pair of lovers, young Burscough and Miss Eccleston. Then he wended his delicate way back in the direction of Mrs Eccleston's villa.

"There is but one way that I can see, my dear madam," he said, "for the preservation of your brother's most valuable life—that is that he should win this great golf match."

"Ah yes, Mr Fleg," the lady responded very sadly. "Alas! how is that to be done? Young Mr Burscough is so magnificent a player."

"But, my dear madam," Mr Fleg resumed, with *finesse* — "but young Mr Burscough might perhaps be persuaded to play, for the nonce, less magnificently."

"But how, Mr Fleg—I do not understand you —you would not have the young man poisoned? Bad as he is——"

"Good gracious, no, madam!" said Mr Fleg, much horrified. "Poisoned, good gracious no—unless it were," he continued, regaining his courtierly tones, "that he should be poisoned by the exceeding sweetness of the manner of your request."

"My request, Mr Fleg?"

"My meaning is, my dear madam, that you should lay the case—the sad case—before young Mr Burscough, and request him, in the interests of humanity and of your favour, to permit your brother to win this match in which he takes so keen an interest."

"But to ask a favour of that—of that young man, Mr Fleg!"

"Of my friend, my dear madam," Mr Fleg answered, venturing to correct the tone of the lady's speech.

"Quite so, Mr Fleg—of your friend."

"Consider, my dear madam, the horror of the circumstances. Supposing that on entering your brother's bedroom your were to find him ——"

"Oh! spare me, Mr Fleg," the lady interrupted, with some vivacity. "Yes, yes; indeed I will. I will ask young Mr Burscough myself."

"And consider, also, if you please, my dear madam, that this is a great favour which you will be asking. It is no little matter. Think of the light in which your brother would view it were one to ask him to give up, of set purpose, his chance in so great a match."

"It is true—indeed, it is true, Mr Fleg. Surely, though, the young man will not be so iron-hearted as to refuse."

"That, my dear madam, must entirely depend upon your powers of persuasion," said Mr Fleg, in a gallant way, which left no doubt about his opinion of those powers. Then he took his leave, and proceeded to give his instructions to young Burscough.

Young Burscough was at first very averse to the part which Mr Fleg proposed to him. "What good am I to get out of kidding and losing this match to please the old lady? I don't care whether old Lazenby skips, or hangs himself, or what he does."

Mr Fleg expressed his horror at such inhuman sentiments, and further said : "It will be for you, my dear sir, to make your bargain with the lady. If I might be permitted to suggest, I might perhaps hint that permission to play Golf, on all convenient occasions, with Miss Eccleston upon the ladies' links, might be not an unfair remuneration for a few topped tee shots."

Young Burscough started, and turned red with joy as the whole meaning of the Professor's stratagem came to his stupid young brain.

"By Jove! Mr Fleg, you're a regular Mac— Mac what's his name? some Scotch name — Machiavelli. You're a regular brick — by Jove, you are!"

"I thank you, my dear sir. I should doubt, however, whether Machiavelli had ever before been, even indirectly, dubbed with that soubriquet."

In the afternoon young Burscough had an interview with Mrs Eccleston. Later in the evening the young man walked out over the sands with Miss Eccleston, and it was said in Pebblecombe that they had been unrebuked.

The following day was the date fixed for the great match. Colonel Burscough played exceedingly well, which made the young man's task all the harder; but the Colonel's wrath against his young partner was excessive, for Mr Lazenby and Old Blobb won the match on the last hole by 1.

Never saw such a thing in my life as that boy, sir," the Colonel said, describing the match. " Why, jam it all, he topped two tee shots running; and at the last hole, when he had the match for the taking, he foozled his iron shot right into the bunker. It's the way with all boys, sir; you can't trust 'em. They ought to be destroyed."

So Blobb and Mr Lazenby won the match, and Lazenby did not hang himself. He skips about every morning after his bath so noisily that Mrs Eccleston has had to inquire the meaning of it all. But still she believes that the original purpose for which he had destined that rope was the fatal one of her first surmise; and now she speaks of its use as a peaceful skipping-rope with a pious reference to the turning of swords into reaping-hooks, as foretold in Scripture.

And young Burscough and Miss Eccleston play Golf, almost daily, upon the ladies' links.

THE GOLFER IN ART

NATURALLY the pious pilgrim will desire
to see the object of his piety enshrined in
the most worthy manner possible through the
medium of those arts of representation whose
province is as wide as the scope of human interest.
And yet we are not quite certain whether, even
yet, we have seen it so handled to the full extent
of its possibilities. We have seen it treated dra-
matically—*pour rire*, as by Mr Arthur Roberts
or incidentally, as by Mr Barrie, if we mistake
not. Elsewhere the golfer may have appeared
on the stage and escaped our notice : it is only a
wonder that we have not had more of him. He has
not left music quite alone ; golfing songs have been
many in number. Mercifully, perhaps, he has not
yet invaded the sphere of operatic music, though
the notion suggests possibilities—of tender treatment, as he addresses himself to the short putt
with a *smorzando* movement, followed by the
finale furioso when the putt is missed. And
throughout the action the dreadful stimy motive,
suggested or realised, might recur hauntingly—

the idea is not copyright! It would be a hard
thing to say, after so much has been written about
him, that he plays no part at all in literary art;
yet the hard saying is very nearly the true one.
We know of no golfer, as such, artistically portrayed, unless it be perhaps in that old story from
the *Contes du Roi Cambrinus*, named *Le Grand
Choleur*, of which we have spoken before. And,
after all, *chole* is not Golf, though possibly a lineal
ancestor. The great Golf novel, like the great
American novel, has yet to be written, and we
may confess to a secret doubt whether, even then,
it will be read.

But there is one art—an older and more primitive art than any of these, probably—in which the
golfer has figured often, and figures more and
more frequently as he becomes more popular—
the limner's art. We find him in many of the
pictures of the old Dutch artists, a familiar figure
to Van der Veyde and to Van de Neer. (We
know that Holland was an old home of Golf—
possibly even its nursery—for does not a protec-
tionist Act of the Scottish Parliament forbid the
importation of Dutch-made golf balls?) In most
of the Dutch pictures the golfer is portrayed playing on the ice. But this is not always the case,
and in a small drawing of an interior, by Rem-
brandt we believe, a glimpse through the open

door shows us the figure of a golfer playing on the lawn before the house. Earlier than the time of these Dutchmen, however, we find the golfer depicted occasionally in old missals. That which is prefixed to Mr Andrew Lang's historical intro- duction to the game in the Badminton Library book is an instance; though in the case of this particular illustration it is not impossible for the sceptical critic to suggest that the game might equally well be hockey. It may be that the designer suffered under a similar confusion of ideas about the two games to that which pos- sessed many Englishmen until about a decade or so ago. But there exists another missal, which the indefatigable Mr Lang routed out of the British Museum comparatively lately, in which Golf, almost exactly as we know it, is, beyond all question, the game portrayed. Curiously enough one of the performers seems to be kneeling down to putt, and it looks as if one of his opponents, moved to just indignation, were expostulating with him on such a gross breach of golfing etiquette, though on what rule of present-day Golf he could convict him we are rather at a loss to know. For the most part, these old Dutchmen, and the rest of them, are not playing with any very dashing driving· Of course, they suffered under the inestimable dis- advantage of living before the days of the Badmin-

ton book.   All allowance is to be made for them.
Still, it is singular that few of the rather grotesque figures portrayed on the Dutch tiles and
elsewhere seem to have got much beyond the
half-swing.   Certainly, this seems to show want
of enterprise on their part, which may be taken
as a significant coincidence with the decadence
of their naval strength.   Of the pictures that
survive to us of Golf since it made its home
in Scotland, it is very noticeable that few of
them depict the golfer in the act of making
the stroke.   Most of the artists seem confined
by the classic tradition, and portray rest in preference to movement.   Charles I. is receiving
the news of the Irish rebellion on the Leith
links, but he is breaking off his game to read
the letter.   Modern golfing manners would dis-
approve of such disturbing intelligence being
imparted in the course of the game.   The
messenger should have waited till it was over.
Many other pictures are familiar to us — the
gentleman with his club over his shoulder, with
the three - corner - hatted caddie behind, and no
lack of a subtle humour in the lines of either
face.   Then there is he with the epaulettes and
golf clubs, and many others; but in none of
them do we see the swing depicted.   The man
was the picture, not the style.   Mr Clark has

indeed reproduced for us the quaint figure of
the "Cock o' the Green," so early out on the
links that he has had but time to tuck in his
nightgown and clap on his hat over his night-
cap; and he is addressing himself to the ball.
But this is evidently something in the nature of
caricature, rather than of sober portraiture. In
none of the graver pictures do we see the game
in progress. There is indeed one most animated
picture, in which action is everywhere — that
picture of putting out at the old Ginger - beer
Hole at St Andrews, wherein players and spectators are crowding forward, more irrepressibly
than even a St Andrews gallery of to-day, and
endeavouring by all manner of excited gesture
to affect the laws of dynamics by which the ball
is taken towards the hole. But even there the
stroke has been already played, the ball has
left the club, and the volition of the player
has no more influence over it; even this short
putt we are not allowed to see in course of
execution. It detracts considerably from the
interest of this picture, in which many of the
figures are portraits, that we cannot readily believe that the crowding and animated gestures
are a true representation of a scene in a game
which we have always learned to associate—
especially in the days of the older school—with

all that is courteous and dignified in demeanour;
and the bench and the ginger beer are so singularly close to the hole!—but perhaps the artist
had to compress his space for the purposes of
his picture.

Thus, in all the older pictures it will be seen
that the swing was not regarded as a suitable
subject for representation, except in the missals
and in those paintings of the Dutchmen in
which the golfer only appears as an auxiliary
incident.

Exception might have been taken in the instance of the drawing by Raphael, shown in the
gallery at Venice, depicting a nude figure swinging
a rude club at *something*. The something might
well have been a ball, and in that sense the action
was taken by those who were good enough to
make the tracing of the figure in question, and
in that sense it was published and discussed by
the present writer. Later, it happened to him to
see a photograph of this drawing, taken previously
to the tracing, and showing the faint but indubitable outlines—which, perhaps, photography alone
could reveal—of a bullock's head. The beast's
head, beyond question, is the object of the club-
man's aim. To lay a bullock, not a golf ball,
dead, was the purpose of the mighty swing,
which imitated so perfectly the swing of a golf

club.   As a study, even for golfing purposes,
the recognition of this very different aim makes
the figure scarcely less interesting, though de-
priving it of any place in the history of Golf, or
of any allied game.

It is singular that a pose lending itself passably
well to the purposes of the painter or the sculptor
should have escaped the attention of artists so
long.   It is not necessary to go back to the
Discobolos of Myron or to the "Gladiator" of
Agasias, to find imitations of athletic poses
plastically reproduced.   Mr Hamo Thornycroft
has a fine figure of a youth, bent back, with
the gathered-up knitting of the muscles prepara-
tory to "putting the stone."   The pose may
lack grace, but certainly is vigorously suggestive
of the power about to be exerted.   Similarly in
the golfing drive, there is a moment, at the top
of the swing, when the attitude of a fine driver,
if not disclosing lines of perfect grace, suggests
vividly enough the force with which the club is
about to be brought back towards the ball.   It
is a moment well worth a sculptor's catching,
yet no sculptor fully qualified to do it justice
has, so far as we know, given it attention.
Figures we have indeed seen plastically representing this moment, but none of them inspired
with the vivid movement of which this moment

of rest is so suggestive. Some we have seen
modelled with sufficient knowledge of the sculptor's art, but inadequate appreciation of the art
of the golfer. Others we have observed deficient
in the converse sense, and some inadequate in
both. Though the writer has endeavoured to
model figures in this movement himself — he
cannot find, even in them, reason to restrict the
general nature of this criticism.

But the golfing swing has another moment
than that which we call the "top of the swing,"
that lends itself even more kindly to the sculptor's
purposes, namely, the end of the swing. Here we
do not see, indeed, the suggestion of power about
to be applied, as in the former instance; but we
do see the suggestion of power just recently
exerted, and, moreover, with certain players, the
pose is remarkably a graceful one. This pose has
lately attracted the attention of the modeller, and
a very charming figure has been the result. It has
a drawback, however, and that is, that the attitude
is not immediately convincing. For a moment we
are disposed to imagine ourselves regarding a representation of a left-handed golfer about to make
his swing down upon the ball. The next instant,
when that false impression has been corrected, we
see the figure for what it is, composing itself gracefully, with pleasantly flowing lines of limb, and, in

R

the case of female figures, drapery, and the face turned forward expectantly, to view the flight of the ball.

This, if we mistake not, is the most artistically pleasing moment of the golfing swing. It is unfortunate that we are not able to regard it as the most characteristic. It is a moment to which, as we watch the course of a game, we pay little attention; we are commonly absorbed in anxiously following the ball's flight. Instantaneous photography, however, has often fixed it for us, sometimes with the most fortunate, as sometimes with the least flattering, results.

Other attitudes, more than equally representative, do not so readily suggest themselves for artistic treatment. To the initiated there is a grace in the manner in which a finished player addresses himself to the approach stroke, but this is a grace that is suggested by association only. The golfer who understands the game perceives, by the player's way of standing to the ball and wielding the club, a guarantee that the stroke in prospect will be executed gracefully. To one who has not this special knowledge the lines of the figure in this attitude do not commend themselves as revealing peculiar grace—we have even heard the attitude most irreverently spoken of. Neither is there a large share of classic beauty in the commended pose of putting : all these useful details of the short game demand a certain crouching attitude which seldom sits so gracefully on a man as on the *felidæ*. The full driving stroke is the athletic glory of the game, and the supreme incident which the artist, in whatever medium, will be most concerned to portray.

If in these remarks I have dwelt at length on the point of view of the artist whose medium is the plastic clay, I hope this length of discussion will be forgiven me in virtue of the consideration that the whole is greater than its part—the round greater than the flat. No factor that will determine the painter in his choice of subject is alien to the sculptor so long as the former is confining his consideration to form alone ; but the sculptor in the round has to consider his composition from every possible point of view, while the painter is concerned only with that outline which he represents on the flat.

As a subject of pictorial art the golfer has chiefly, of course, occupied the attention of the caricaturists. Mr Harry Furniss has considered him. Major "Shortspoon" has depicted him —sometimes by way of portraiture, singly or in groups, sometimes as a merely incidental feature of a landscape, and sometimes again in a lighter vein whose spirit matches that of Mr

Furniss. Finally, Mr T. Hodge, the chief illustrator of the Badminton Book, has treated the golfer with a peculiarly subtle and appreciative humour. Others, too, have found the golfer a fitting subject for their humorous fancy, as Mr Ralston, Mr Hillingworth, and several of the artists of *Punch*. *Punch's* appreciations, however, have scarcely been worthy of the greatest and oldest of comic illustrated papers dealing with the greatest and oldest of games.

Perhaps it can seldom be said that portraiture is a true example of the golfer in art. Such a portrait as that of Mr Whyte-Melville, in the club-house at St Andrews, has a golfing interest of association merely. No golfing action is depicted. It is merely the portrait of a gentleman, who happened to be very well known as a golfer, who wears a red coat, and has the Swilcan Burn and St Andrews Club House for the accessories of his portrait. There is art, indeed, of a higher order, in such a picture as this, but the golfer, as such, is scarcely its subject-matter. Nor can we say even so much as this of those strange groups of golfers compounded by the separate photographing of each unit and the pasting together and subsequent photographing off, on one large plate, of the aggregation. In this there is certainly a grotesque

likeness of each individual, grotesque by virtue
of the utter absence of all art, all composition,
all proportion, all perspective. It is a reversion
to the infantile days of Persian group painting.
Something more we may indeed say, though
perhaps no great deal, for the generality of
those groups which have been taken, at first
hand, by the camera. But we must make a
great distinction between the generality of all
such ₁groupings and a certain picture executed
by Messrs Dickenson & Foster of Bond Street.
This is a golfing group representing most of
the best known players of the Royal and
Ancient Club gathered around the house on
the occasion of Mr A. J. Balfour's driving off
the first ball, as captain. Though the artist's
hand has no doubt been held by the primary
necessity of producing good portraiture, the
total effect is artistic in every sense, and ex-
hibits, moreover, if not the game in progress,
at all events an interesting moment of expectation before the actual firing of the gun and
striking of the ball. Photography has been
used as an aid to the artist in his attitudes and
portraits, but it has not been allowed to have
the master hand. The same firm has produced
an excellent portrait in oils of "Old Tom"
Morris.

Instantaneous photography and the ubiquity of the camera have been in many ways of great assistance to the artist, enabling him to take notes with wonderful quickness and, with a certain reservation, exactness. So long as the artist recognises the necessary reservation the camera is invaluable to him. As soon as ever he allows himself to forget, or lose sight of it, it becomes an evil influence that cannot be over-estimated. It distorts, with an insidious subtlety that is all its own. As Mr Bagehot divided modes of falsehood into "lies, d——d lies, and statistics," so false drawing might be put into categories of "bad drawing, d——d bad drawing, and photography." No artist, probably, that has ventured to attempt any except miniature work from a photograph will dispute the justice of this—though it may seem a paradox to the irreflective—or have failed to realise the inimitably convincing falsity with which the camera exaggerates that which is near, and diminishes that which is afar. Photography is to the artist an excellent servant, but the worst possible of masters—invaluable for note taking, but its notes to be constantly subjected to the most watchful supervision and correction.

Some very pleasing pictures have been pro-

duced by Mr Douglas Adams, named "The
Tee Shot" and "The Putting Green." Possibly
these are not the precise titles; but they indicate the character of each representation.
These are correctly described, too, as having
Golf for their primary subject, though the landscape—the ground driven over—is perhaps a
more important and striking part of the picture
than the little group of golfers. With the treatment, in the case of the short game picture, we
have no fault to find; but, where the drive is
the principal object, we may confess ourselves
aggrieved that the painter did not take a few
liberties with the style of his model, if the
picture truly represents it; for, though he has
shown us the drive as it is often done, he
might equally easily have shown it to us rather
better done. No doubt the model was at fault;
but then, whose fault was the selection of the
model? Major Shortspoon, among his larger
efforts, has one or two of similar style to Mr
Adams' pictures, though in almost every case
they have the added interest that their figures
are portraits. A year or two ago a girl caddie,
in red Tam o' Shanter, if we mistake not, was
shown in the Academy; but even in this, the
golfing interest was rather incidental than
primary.

Messrs Dickenson & Foster's portrait group is so well composed and executed, and the colours of various golfing dress are made to harmonise so successfully, that the result is a very artistic whole.   But the picture in which the golfer in art receives his most adequate treatment, so far as we have yet met him, is one which Mr Dollman painted, and which was exhibited at the Fine Art Gallery in Bond Street.   It is a figure picture emphatically, though St Andrews is seen in the distance. It deals with a golfing question that has greatly troubled the minds of many, especially in Edinburgh, within the last months, yet for all that, the date of the subject treated is some three hundred years back.   Herein the player is depicted in the very act of Golf, heart and soul absorbed in his putt.   The old costumes, which have been a matter of careful study, lend a charm to the picture, which has at once much topical interest and a very high degree of artistic merit.   But the aspects of Golf are very many, and so are the methods of art. The painter and the sculptor may work at the golfer till they are tired, they need have not the least fear of exhausting the opportunities that, properly considered, he may be induced to afford them.   There is work for them yet to do.

PROFESSOR FLEG'S methods with the
golf club were remarkable. He was in
every way a remarkable man, and in every de-
partment of his life a methodical man. If he
ever erred, it was, as in the present instance,
by regarding all things as capable of being
brought into the domain of exact science; for
it was in this attitude that he approached the
game of Golf, which is scarcely susceptible of
such treatment.

The occasion has now become historical on
which he sought the counsel of the wizard—the
great medicine man—of Golf, in the following
terms:—" I like, my dear sir, to do everything
methodically. All through my life I have
approached things in that way, and I have
not yet been completely beaten, if I may say
so, by anything. Now I am taking up the
game of Golf club by club—each club in turn.
Hitherto I have devoted my attention solely
to the driver. I now propose to make myself thorough master of the iron. Would you

therefore have the kindness to show me, my dear sir, exactly in what manner you hold your hands while playing an iron stroke?"

Such are the methods of a conquering intellect; but the club-by-club system did not exhaust the peculiarities of Professor Fleg's fashion of mastering the game of Golf. For he put himself into what he conceived to be the position indicated by the best authorities and illustrated by diagrams in many highly scientific treatises on the game, and had in attendance the Pebblecombe carpenter, who then and there constructed around the Professor's feet a wooden framework. This framework the Professor's caddie (a long-suffering and much-to-be pitied person) carried round with the Professor whenever that great man engaged in the game of Golf, and planted it upon the *teeing* ground, so that, if, as sometimes occurred, the Professor *topped* the ball or otherwise misconducted himself with regard to it, he could at least be sure of erring on the most approved methods.

Now Colonel Burscough was not a man of science, and greatly preferred hitting the ball in a style which the most charitable critic could not call orthodox to missing it in the correct fashion affected by Mr Fleg. "Brute force, my dear sir,— no science," was Mr Fleg's whispered soliloquy

(for even in soliloquy his speech was studiously
courteous) whenever the Colonel in his attitude of
Philistine drove beyond the limits of the Professor's
highly-cultured power.   And this frequently happened, for the Colonel's physique was better
adapted than that of Mr Fleg to the complex
purposes of the noble game.   Nevertheless Mr
Fleg's scientific perseverance was rewarded by a
steady though gradual improvement such as did
not attend Colonel Burscough's more rough and
ready methods.   Therefore in the many matches
that they played together, though Colonel Burscough had always up to a certain point had the
upper hand, yet his advantage grew less with
every match, until there were critics to prophesy
(under their breath, be it said, and far, very far,
behind the Colonel's back) that the day would
eventually come when science would make its
power felt and the Man of Learning come in a
hole ahead of the Man of War.

In prospect of that day all Pebblecombe held
its breath in an awful silence, for it was shrewdly
thought that on such a day as that it would be
evil for any who came within reach of the warrior's
wrath.   For though the Colonel's methods with
the golf club differed absolutely from those of Mr
Fleg, they were not one whit less remarkable.
The game of Golf is one which demands peculiar

equanimity of temper and the long-suffering patience which is so eminently characteristic of the Scot. Now, excellent man as Colonel Burscough was, equanimity of temper was not one of his natural gifts. A game of Golf with the Colonel was therefore a mixed form of pleasure—a fearful joy. A measure of amusement was assured, but it had need to be amusement carefully disguised, for golf clubs are formidable weapons in the hands of an angry man. When things were going well all was sweetness and light; but golf links are treacherous places with dire pitfalls, named bunkers, into which the ball sidles like an ant into the lair of the ant-lion. In the first bunker Colonel Burscough was as good as gold; in the second he began to talk in Hindostani; and in the third he sometimes grew a little angry. Then his caddie, who knew him well, would hand the Colonel his niblick, and place in a convenient corner of the bunker an old umbrella, which he always carried with him to perform the office of a scapegoat. For if the Colonel failed to extricate his ball from the bunker on the first attempt his mood grew dangerous. The niblick strokes fell faster until the ball flew from the bunker, and the Colonel, being now very angry indeed, would look around him for some object upon which his wrath could spend itself. Whereon he would see the umbrella, to which, as having "caught his eye," he would at once attribute his calamities, and summarily execute it at the edge of the niblick. The caddie, having kept himself in the background until the extreme fury of the Colonel's wrath had spent itself, would come up with discreet humility to receive the tail end only of the storm, and to retrieve the umbrella which had been the vicarious sufferer in his stead.

The occasions on which the Colonel had sworn once and for ever to abandon the game of golf are almost beyond counting. He would wave his hand with tragic pathos towards the links of Pebblecombe and declare with sad solemnity —"This place has seen me for the last time"; and in this black mood he would remain till dinner. With the soup, however, life began to wear a brighter aspect, with the joint he began to repent him of his determination, and with the dessert he was ready to play any man in the world, on any terms that were at all reasonable, on the very next day.

But besides these numerous occasions on which he had set no outward and visible seal to his immutable resolve, there were other greater ones on which he had confirmed himself therein by a solemn burning of his ships—his entire set

of golf clubs. Twice he had built a small bonfire on the edge of the links and then and there
made a solemn holocaust of his clubs, his balls,
his red coat and all his golfing paraphernalia.
Many times also he had broken all his clubs
over his knee, that he might never be tempted
again to play the game which cost him so much
mental anguish: but always on the morrow
morning he had appeared at the club-maker's
with an order for a new set.

So that now these two methods of treatment
were familiar to Pebblecombe—the Ordeal by
Dichotomy (or division in two), as Mr Fleg
humorously named the club-breaking plan, and
the Ordeal by Fire, which was the Professorial
name for the holocaust—for it was the Colonel's
constant contention that his clubs were possessed
by some malign witchcraft so that they would
not hit the ball. There remained yet another
in the Colonel's repertory—namely, the Ordeal
by Water,—and this was put into execution on
the day on which the Colonel was first beaten
in a match with Mr Fleg. For the day which
all Pebblecombe expected in fear and trembling
came at last. The methods of science proved
triumphant, and Mr Fleg, with a proud flush
on his brow, and not without a tremor at his
heart, walked into the Golf Club *one up* against

the Colonel at the eighteenth hole, having added
insult to injury by laying an iniquitous *stymie*
at the very end when the Colonel was lying
dead at the hole and certain of a half.

There is no measure in the good gifts of Providence. To many it would have seemed that
the blessedness of having at length attained the
mastery over one who had so often beaten him
would be enough to fill the cup of happiness for
any ordinary professor of anatomy to the brim.
But Mr Fleg was no ordinary professor, and fate
dealt with him in no ordinary way. About a
twelvemonth after this first and epoch-making
victory, he began to make some very singular
and interesting discoveries.

There is on the beach at Pebblecombe a stretch
of bluish grey mud, of no very great extent. It
is far out upon the sand—so far that only at the
lowest tides is it uncovered. It happened that
on a Sunday Mr Fleg was once walking in a
pensive, Sabbatical mood along the sands by the
sea. The tide was unusually far out, and this
mud was uncovered. Mr Fleg prodded the mud
thoughtfully with his stick, and suddenly began
to consider it with greater interest. It contained
woody fibres in a fair state of preservation —
the fibre in many instances of quite large tree
trunks.

Now there are people to whom this fibre would have said nothing, unless possibly *decayed cabbage*, or something unpleasantly suggestive of that kind. But it was crammed full of meaning to such a mind as Mr Fleg's. It said *a submerged forest*—and a submerged forest included remains of the denizens of that forest, of who could say what interest and antiquity! For a moment Mr Fleg's imagination peopled its once mighty shade with quite impossible denizens — pterodactyls, icthyosauri, megatheriums. Then his archæological sense smiled at the anachronisms into which his scientific fervour had launched him, and he corrected himself with softly-spoken soliloquy—"Cave-bear, my dear sir, cave-man, at the earliest; more probably old British ox and Irish elk; almost certainly modern fauna."

Then his anatomical imagination saw himself constructing out of a *humerus* or *tibia* mighty ruminants of primeval days. Mr Fleg went home that Sabbath evening in a state which in any other man the vulgar might have ascribed to the effects of alcohol. To say he was in a fever of wild excitement is to give not the faintest suggestion of his mental condition. To say that he was covered from head to foot in blue mud is to express but feebly his outward aspect; for never had Mr Fleg so bitter reason

to bewail his shortsightedness, which, fortified
with double spectacles as he was, compelled
him to go upon his hands and knees, grovelling
almost like a serpent, in order to make a close
enough examination to reveal the treasures of
which he was in search.

Suffice it to say that he returned in a state
of general disorder, which was a pain to the
faithful whom he met on their way to evening
church, but with a scientific joy without bounds
in his heart, and a small piece of the decayed
horn of a deer in his pocket. Nor would he
ever have ceased from his search until the shades
of night had come upon him, had not the jealous
sea come lapping up to him and driven him
back step by step over the mud until its nearest
limit was swallowed by the envious waves. Then
Mr Fleg went slowly home with the one treasure-
trove in his pocket, and elsewhere, impartially
upon him, the blue mud.

After this auspicious beginning Mr Fleg bought
a nautical calendar which gave information of
the behaviour of the tides; and whenever the
sea was sufficiently far out to discover even a
portion,—and for a few minutes only,—of the
precious blue mud, he would neglect the royal
and ancient game of Golf itself to go down with
a coadjutor, in whom he had inspired a small

share of his own enthusiasm, and dig and delve in this dirty clay.

And to tell truth, he made several interesting discoveries in the shape of bits of bone and horn and flint arrow-heads and a portion of a human skull. Then he would sit hours into the night poring over his bits of bone, examining them through a microscope, comparing them with the descriptions and pictures in certain very large and heavy books, containing fearful representations of huge skeletons of animals such as no living man has been so unfortunate as to meet. Then on a vast sheet of paper he would begin, with pencil and scale and compasses, to map out a huge skeleton of his own devising—leaving only a little gap, generally somewhere down upon the shin-bone, into which, when all the rest was finished, he would fit the little bit of brown bone which was the basis of the whole mighty superstructure, and would say proudly. "Such, my dear sir, was the creature who roamed in the primeval forest of which we see here to-day the few submerged and wonderfully preserved remains."

Sometimes it would be only a tooth that would supply him with the data for the construction of a whole mighty skeleton—so great,

so inconceivable to lesser minds are the achievements of science and the knowledge of men so
richly endowed as Professor Fleg.

But even as it was in the days of old, when
that hero of *Henry's First Latin Book*, Balbus,
feasted the town at twenty sesterces a head and
there were still found some, as historians tell
us, who laughed—so too now, in Pebblecombe,
there were found persons so unappreciative of
the great discoveries of science as to scoff while
Mr Fleg drew his majestic skeletons.

Chief, perchance, among the scoffers was
Colonel Burscough, as kind-hearted a volcanic-
tempered man as ever lived, yet a British
Philistine to the very backbone of him.

The Colonel would stand before the fire with
his hands behind his back in Professor Fleg's
study, examining, with head thrown back, the
Professor's latest masterpiece in constructive
anatomy. So he would stand for a while in
silence—then take the cheroot from his lips to
say with all the air of eulogy—"Jammed extraordinary imagination you must have, Fleg—eh ? "

"Imagination ! my dear sir," Mr Fleg would
reply, permitting the slighest note expressive of
the shock which the word bore with it to modify
the habitual courtesy of his address. "Imagination ! Pardon me, my dear sir, if I venture, with

all deference, to take exception to the term you are good enough to employ with reference to that drawing. I assure you there is no imagination used or needed in the construction of such a skeleton on such convincing evidence as the splendid molar which you see restored to its appropriate jaw. It is, my dear sir, as capable of scientific demonstration as any one of Euclid's theorems. Let me refer you——" Here the Professor began turning over the leaves of one of his ponderous volumes, with a running fire of extracts and commentary, while Colonel Burscough took a seat in the armchair and began wondering how he had lost his last match.

When Professor Fleg had triumphantly vindicated himself, the Colonel would rise from the chair, examine the molar as if he were comparing it with the essence of all the scientific reading to which he had not listened, and say, " Yes, Fleg—you are right, of course. Jammed like an old sheep's tooth though, after all — eh ? "

Mr Fleg courteously admitted that there was some superficial resemblance, and began to talk to the Colonel — as to one professionally interested in small artillery—about the flint arrowheads.

The more important of his discoveries—if one

may speak so of a matter in which every discovery was of great import—Mr Fleg communicated from time to time to a certain learned
journal which no one in Pebblecombe, except
himself, was able to read with intelligent appreciation. Hitherto, however, Mr Fleg had been
fortunate enough to make no discovery which
ran counter to the deductions of other scientists.
With the flint arrow-heads he found the skull
of the cave-man, the bones of the cave-bear, the
horns of the great Irish elk, and the remains of
other creatures, all of whom, as is well known,
lived together in love and unity.

Then, unheralded by any miraculous premoni-
tion or unusual circumstance, the sun dawned—
quite in its ordinary manner—upon a day which
was to be credited with a discovery at once
epoch-making and epoch-breaking—a discovery
perhaps the most portentous of any that had
been known since men began to read the world's
history that is written in its stones and clay.
Among the mass of decaying vegetable fibre and
blue mud — of a consistency somewhat thicker
than chewed tobacco — among the relics of the
cave-man, the cave-bear and the elk, Mr Fleg
came upon something that beyond question was
a lump of iron!

Possibly every reader may not at once appreciate the tremendous, the appalling significance of this discovery. But remember the circumstances. Remember that this lump of metal, more than a pound in weight, was found among the flint arrow-heads, among the remains of creatures the history of whose life was part of the story of the world when it was very young — when, in fact, it was in its stone age. So at least it had ever been supposed. Science had given its united voice in favour of the opinion that the cave-man, and these animals who were found to be of his time, had existed in the very infancy of the age of stone—that his weapons were at best of flint, and those not of a high finish. Science had asked sympathy for the cave-man in his apparently unequal fight with the great denizens of the forest in which he lived. But now—what did this discovery say? No less a thing than this—that Science had been mistaken in the matter from first to last—that all previous theories must be cast to the wind (for one negative condemns an hypothesis, no matter by how many affirmatives it be supported) — that the comparatively sophisticated age of iron must be put back perhaps thousands of years in the world's story— must be put away back into the fancied simplicity of the age of stone. With this iron weapon (for doubtless it was in the manu-

facture of weapons of offence that Tubal Cain,
in the early struggle for existence, first exercised
his art)—with this fairly adequate iron weapon
the cave-man, who had so long and so nefari-
ously usurped our sympathy, might have felled
to the earth perhaps no less mighty a quarry
than the Great Irish Elk itself!

In such manner did Mr Fleg expound his theme
to his admiring listeners while he held, in a hand
that trembled with infinitely more sense of the
preciousness of its burden than if it had borne a
nugget of like size, the miraculous iron weapon
that he had delved from the blue mud.   True, the
exact nature and outline of the weapon were as
yet somewhat shrouded in mystery, and in what
Mr Fleg referred to as " ferric oxide, my dear sir,
or rust," but it was abundantly evident, from its
mass and rough shape, that it had been intended
for a hitting weapon of some kind.

Next day, by special messenger, Mr Fleg sent
this wonderful relic to a shop in London, with
which he had had frequent dealings, and where he
could trust the care and knowledge of the work-
men, with orders that the ferric oxide should be
removed with such skill and science as these
specialists had at their command.   Meanwhile
he wrote off to all the scientific and leading
papers in the country, giving an account of the

discovery, with photographs of the weapon in its rough state (encrusted with mud), and minute descriptions of the nature of the clay and other relics in whose company it had been found.

A perfect storm of correspondence followed, both in the public prints and in the shape of private communications, to the Professor — so that he found himself obliged temporarily to engage a special clerk, to answer at his dictation the mass of his correspondents.

Meanwhile all Pebblecombe, and Mr Fleg particularly, held his breath in expectation of the return, cleansed of its swathing of "ferric oxide, my dear sir, or rust," of the weapon which had dealt such a blow to all the previous hypotheses of Science.

Mr Fleg was playing Golf when he received a telegram informing him that the relic, restored so far as might be to its first form, was that day being despatched again by special messenger from London—to speak exactly, Mr Fleg was in a bunker. In an instant all the familiar horrors of that situation were dissipated. He gave up the hole to Colonel Burscough, with whom he was playing, and felt scarcely a pang of regret. He neglected his methodical grasp of the driver, he forgot about the wooden foot-framework, which lay idle in his caddie's hand, while Colonel Burs-

cough with immense joy won from him hole after
hole. At the end of the round he paid to the
Colonel their statutory wager of half-a-crown
without his usual harmless necessary joke, " Look
upon it, my dear sir, I would beg you, in the
light simply of a loan," and hurried the Colonel
greatly in his preparations for leaving the Golf
Club and walking back to Pebblecombe.

On the walk Mr Fleg was silent and abstracted.
At the door of his house he was trembling with an
overpowering nervousness. " My friend," he said
to the Colonel, as the latter was about to leave
him (it was the preface to some very momentous
statement when Mr Fleg abandoned his usual style
of address, as "my dear sir," for the yet more
impressive cordiality of "my friend"), "my friend,
I would beg of you a favour. I would beg of you
to come in with me and be present with me on
this, which is immensely the greatest moment of
my life. There will be awaiting me, as I conceive,
within this little villa, a treasure which shall alter
the reading of nearly all the history of the world's
creation—an iron weapon coeval with the cave-
dweller. Will you be with me, my friend, at
this great moment of my life, when I shall see
my treasure trove in something approaching its
original shape?"

" Why, yes, of course, Fleg; jammed interesting, you know. Great privilege, I mean to say. Assure you I feel it so."

The *savant* grasped his friend's hand with grateful pressure, and the two entered the house together. The servant told Mr Fleg that a young man from London had delivered a parcel, with careful instructions for its safety and welfare. Mr Fleg led the way into his study, and there beneath the approving figures of the giant skeletons rested, in an ordinary deal box, on an ordinary mahogany table, the iron weapon of the cave-man. Then Mr Fleg rang the bell for hammer and chisel. His nervousness was something pitiable to see. He could not sit still while the tools were brought. His hand trembled so that he could not use them to any effect when they came.

"Here, let me!"

Colonel Burscough took them from him and began to work and hammer on the box in angry vigour. Mr Fleg seated himself in an armchair at the other end of the room, and burying his face in his hands rocked himself back and forward in the agony of his suspense. He could not bear to look.

There was a sound of crashing wood and rending metal. Then there was comparative silence while the Colonel rummaged in the shavings and

paper with which the box was stuffed. Mr Fleg
no longer groaned. His suspense had become
too intense for any expression, and he remained motionless, without a sound, awaiting
Colonel Burscough's word that the relic was
revealed.

The waiting seemed very long. Mr Fleg
grasped an arm of his chair with either hand,
and in a semi-catalepsy of the muscles fastened
his eyes rigidly upon Colonel Burscough's face
to read the feelings evoked by the first sight of
the wondrous relic.

For the Colonel's expression had undergone a
singular change.

The silence grew deeper and more painful, and
to Mr Fleg it began to seem that Colonel Burscough, the room, the relic, everything, were far,
far away. He was mocked by a sense of dream-
like unreality.

And the change on Colonel Burscough's face
responded likewise to a vision of things far away
—far distant both in time and place. He felt
himself transported back to a certain day a
twelvemonth since, and to a painful scene of
his humiliation upon the Pebblecombe links—
the day on which he had first suffered defeat
at the learned hands of Mr Fleg. The whole
scene was before him. The day was a particu-

larly warm and sunny one. The bees hummed over the wild flowers, the sand-flies buzzed in the bunkers. Warmth and flies are fearful aggravations to the wrath of an angry man. And Colonel Burscough, on this particularly beautiful summer's day, saw himself a very angry man indeed—angry so much beyond his wont that his anger found no expression ; it was at silent white heat. He took his clubs from his caddie with an unusual gentleness that had meaning. He handled them with the caressant ferocity of a cat playing with a mouse. He strode over the great ridge of pebbles which keeps back the sea at Pebblecombe and down on to the sands. It was low tide. No one was in the immediate neighbourhood ; but he well knew that in ambush on the top of the pebble ridge, peering over, were all the members there present of the Royal Pebblecombe Golf Club, and all the club-makers, caddies, ground-men, and all who were in any capacity whatsoever associated with the royal and ancient game in the vicinity. And each looked over with all his two eyes, as carefully as though he had been stalking a tiger, and gazed at the Colonel, who had seated himself on the foot of the ridge.

The Colonel took off his boots. And though none of the watchers might know what this be-

tokened, they held a collective silence and looked
with all their eyes.

The Colonel took off his clothes—that is to say,
very nearly all—retaining only such as a per-
functory regard for decency forbade him to part
with. Then he walked out, carrying his clubs
over the sand.

And all the while he was conscious of the
watchers, who watched him in silence as he
walked, walking with the deliberate purpose of
a man whose mind is firmly fixed. He did not
pause an instant when he reached the sea. He
went straight in, and presently the breakers were
dashing now over his hips, now over his shoulders.
If he went deeper he would have to swim. Once
he stumbled badly, but contrived to recover himself; then he drew himself to his full height in the
water and raised his right hand high out of it.
And in his right hand was a golf club. He
whirled this golf club once round his head, as a
cowboy twirls his lasso—then launched it out,
far as ever he could throw it, into the sea.

Then he reached down for another, under his
left arm — even as an archer reaches for the
arrows in his quiver—and hurled that one after
the first.

Again and yet again, and again he did this—
until the whole set of nine clubs had been hurled

beyond the furthest breaker. Then he turned and strode back out of the surf, the blackness of his mood a trifle tempered by the completeness of the sacrifice. And thus was consummated the third and last of the great ordeals—the Ordeal by Water.

Such was the vision that passed before the Colonel's dreamy eyes while he gazed upon Mr Fleg's wondrous relic, and while Mr Fleg grasped convulsively the two arms of his chair.

At length to Mr Fleg's expectancy the very silence grew full of menacant voices. He could endure no longer.

" Well ? " he gasped.

Then Colonel Burscough roused himself from his abstraction, and he too said " Well ! "—but without the interrogation.

Then he paused again ; but after a moment he resumed, speaking very solemnly—" Fleg, do you remember that day on which you first beat me in a golf match ? "

Did he remember it ? Would he ever forget it ? Mr Fleg thought the Colonel was about to draw some fruitful comparison between that great red letter day in the professorial life and this. " Indeed, my friend, I remember it well," Mr Fleg gasped from the chair.

" And on that day, Fleg, I waded far out into

the sea. I threw my golf clubs from me—for
ever, as I thought—into the Atlantic."

"I know, I know, my friend," said Mr Fleg
moved, in this the day of his brightest triumph,
to deepest sympathy for that, the blackest day of
defeat, for his friend.

"I slipped," the Colonel continued. "For a
moment I thought I was drowned——"

"I remember," Mr Fleg murmured, with yet
warmer sympathy.

"But I recovered myself by sticking one of my
clubs down through the sea upon the treacherous
mud on which I slipped. I recovered myself, but
the club broke short off at the head."

"Ah!" said Mr Fleg vaguely.

"It was the niblick, Fleg—and I had thought
never to see that niblick-head again. But here—
steel yourself, Fleg, I fear this may be a blow to
you—it is no cave-man's weapon, this, Fleg ; only
a bunker-man's—this iron weapon of your Stone
Age is that very niblick. Here is the inscrip-
tion, legible on it still—*James Wilson, Maker,
St Andrews.*"

PRINTED BY
TURNBULL AND SPEARS,
EDINBURGH

A CATALOGUE OF BOOKS AND ANNOUNCEMENTS OF METHUEN AND COMPANY PUBLISHERS : LONDON 36 ESSEX STREET W.C.

CONTENTS

APRIL 1898

MESSRS. METHUEN'S
ANNOUNCEMENTS

Poetry

THE POEMS OF WILLIAM SHAKESPEARE. Edited with an Introduction and Notes by GEORGE WYNDHAM, M.P. *Demy 8vo. Buckram, gilt top.* 10s. 6d.

This edition contains the 'Venus,' 'Lucrece' and Sonnets, and is prefaced with an elaborate introduction of over 140 pp. The text is founded on the first quartos, with an endeavour to retain the original reading. A set of notes deals with the problems of Date, The Rival Poets, Typography, and Punctuation; and the editor has commented on obscure passages in the light of contemporary works. The publishers believe that no such complete edition has ever been published.

Travel and Adventure

THREE YEARS IN SAVAGE AFRICA. By LIONEL DECLE. With an Introduction by H. M. STANLEY, M.P. With 100 Illustrations and 5 Maps. *Demy 8vo.* 21s.

Few Europeans have had the same opportunity of studying the barbarous parts of Africa as Mr. Decle. Starting from the Cape, he visited in succession Bechuanaland, the Zambesi, Matabeleland and Mashonaland, the Portuguese settlement on the Zambesi, Nyasaland, Ujiji, the headquarters of the Arabs, German East Africa, Uganda (where he saw fighting in company with the late Major 'Roddy' Owen), and British East Africa. In his book he relates his experiences, his minute observations of native habits and customs, and his views as to the work done in Africa by the various European Governments, whose operations he was able to study. The whole journey extended over 7000 miles, and occupied exactly three years.

EXPLORATION AND HUNTING IN CENTRAL AFRICA. By Major A. ST. H. GIBBONS, F.R.G.S. With 8 full-page Illustrations by C. WHYMPER, photographs and Map. *Demy 8vo.* 15s.

This is an account of travel and adventure among the Marotse and contiguous tribes, with a description of their customs, characteristics, and history, together with the author's experiences in hunting big game. The illustrations are by Mr. Charles Whymper, and from photographs. There is a map by the author of the hitherto unexplored regions lying between the Zambezi and Kafukwi rivers and from 18° to 15° S. lat.

WITH THE MOUNTED INFANTRY AND MASHONA-LAND FIELD FORCE, 1896. By Lieut.-Colonel ALDERSON. With numerous Illustrations and Plans. *Demy 8vo.* 10s. 6d.

This is an account of the military operations in Mashonaland by the officer who commanded the troops in that district during the late rebellion. Besides its interest as a story of warfare, it will have a peculiar value as an account of the services of mounted infantry by one of the chief authorities on the subject.

CAMPAIGNING ON THE UPPER NILE AND NIGER. By Lieut. SEYMOUR VANDELEUR. With an Introduction by Sir G. GOLDIE. With four Maps, Illustrations and Plans. *Large Cr. 8vo.* 10s. 6d.

A narrative of service (1) in the Equatorial Lakes and on the Upper Nile in 1895 and 1896 ; and (2) under Sir George Goldie in the Niger campaign of January 1897, describing the capture of Bida and Ilorin, and the French occupation of Boussa. The book thus deals with the two districts of Africa where now the French and English stand face to face.

THE NIGER SOURCES. By Colonel J. TROTTER, R.A. With a Map and Illustrations. *Crown 8vo.* 5s.

A book which at the present time should be of considerable interest, being an account of a Commission appointed for frontier delimitation.

LIFE AND PROGRESS IN AUSTRALASIA. By MICHAEL DAVITT, M.P. With two Maps. *Crown 8vo.* 6s.

This book, the outcome of a recent journey through the seven Australasian colonies, is an attempt to give to English readers a more intimate knowledge of a continent colonised by their own race. The author sketches the general life, resources, politics, parties, progress, prospects, and scenery of each colony. He made a careful examination of the West Australian goldfields, and he has paid special attention to the development of practical politics in the colonies. The book is full of anecdotes and picturesque description.

History and Biography

A HISTORY OF THE ART OF WAR. By C. W. OMAN, M.A., Fellow of All Souls', Oxford. Vol. II. MEDIÆVAL WAR-FARE. *Demy 8vo Illustrated.* 21s.

Mr. Oman is engaged on a History of the Art of War, of which the above, though covering the middle period from the fall of the Roman Empire to the general use of gunpowder in Western Europe, is the first instalment. The first battle dealt with will be Adrianople (378) and the last Navarette (1367). There will appear later a volume dealing with the Art of War among the Ancients, and another covering the 15th, 16th, and 17th centuries.
The book will deal mainly with tactics and strategy, fortifications and siegecraft, but subsidiary chapters will give some account of the development of arms and armour, and of the various forms of military organization known to the Middle Ages.

RELIGION AND CONSCIENCE IN ANCIENT EGYPT. By W. M. FLINDERS PETRIE, D.C.L., LL.D. *Fully Illustrated. Crown 8vo.* 2s. 6d.

This volume deals mainly with the historical growth of the Egyptian religion, and the arrangement of all the moral sayings into something like a handbook. But far larger interests are also discussed as the origin of intolerance, the fusion of religions, the nature of conscience, and the experimental illustration of British conscience.

SYRIA AND EGYPT FROM THE TELL EL AMARNA TABLETS. By W. M. FLINDERS PETRIE, D.C.L., LL.D. *Crown 8vo.* 2s. 6d.

This book describes the results of recent researches and discoveries and the light thereby thrown on Egyptian history.

THE DECLINE AND FALL OF THE ROMAN EMPIRE.
By EDWARD GIBBON.   A New Edition, edited with Notes,
Appendices, and Maps by J. B. BURY, M.A., Fellow of Trinity
College, Dublin.   *In Seven Volumes.   Demy 8vo, gilt top.   8s. 6d.
each.   Crown 8vo.   6s. each.   Vol. V.*

THE EASTERN QUESTION IN THE EIGHTEENTH
CENTURY.   By ALBERT SOREL of the French Academy.   Translated by F. C. BRAMWELL, M.A., with an Introduction by R. C. L.
FLETCHER, Fellow of Magdalen College, Oxford.   With a Map.
Crown 8vo.   4s. 6d.
This book is a study of the political conditions which led up to and governed the
first partition of Poland, and the Russo-Turkish war of 1768-1774.   It is
probably the best existing examination of Eastern European politics in the
eighteenth century, and is an early work of one of the ablest of living historians.

THE LETTERS OF VICTOR HUGO.   Translated from the
French by F. CLARKE, M.A.   *In Two Volumes.   Demy 8vo.
10s. 6d. each.   Vol. II.   1815-35.*

A HISTORY OF THE GREAT NORTHERN RAILWAY,
1845-95.   By C. H. GRINLING.   With Maps and many Illustrations.
Demy 8vo.   10s. 6d.
A record of Railway enterprise and development in Northern England, containing
much matter hitherto unpublished.   It appeals both to the general reader and to
those specially interested in railway construction and management.

ANARCHISM.   By E. V. ZENKER.   *Demy 8vo.   7s. 6d.*
A critical study and history, as well as trenchant criticism of the Anarchist movement
in Europe.   The book has aroused considerable attention on the Continent.

THOMAS CRANMER.   By A. J. MASON, D.D., Canon of Canterbury.   With a Portrait.   *Crown 8vo.   3s. 6d.*
[*Leaders of Religion.*

Theology

THE MINISTRY OF DEACONESSES.   By CECILIA ROBIN-
SON, Deaconess.   With an Introduction by the LORD BISHOP OF
WINCHESTER, and an Appendix by Professor ARMITAGE ROBINSON.
Crown 8vo.   3s. 6d.
This book is a review of the history and theory of the office and work of a Deaconess
and it may be regarded as authoritative.

DISCIPLINE AND LAW.   By H. HENSLEY HENSON, B.D.,
Fellow of All Soul's, Oxford ; Incumbent of St. Mary's Hospital,
Ilford ; Chaplain to the Bishop of St. Albans.   *Fcap. 8vo.   2s. 6d.*
This volume of devotional addresses, suitable for Lent, is concerned with the value,
method, and reward of Discipline ; and with Law—family, social and individual.

REASONABLE CHRISTIANITY.   By HASTINGS RASHDALL,
M.A., Fellow and Tutor of New College, Oxford.   *Crown 8vo.   6s.*
This volume consists of twenty sermons, preached chiefly before the University of
Oxford.   They are an attempt to translate into the language of modern thought
some of the leading ideas of Christian theology and ethics.

THE HOLY SACRIFICE. By F. WESTON, M.A., Curate of St. Matthew's, Westminster. *Pott 8vo. 6d. net.*

A small volume of devotions at the Holy Communion, especially adapted to the needs of servers and of those who do not communicate.

The Churchman's Library.

Edited by J. H. BURN, B.D.

A series of books by competent scholars on Church History, Institutions, and Doctrine, for the use of clerical and lay readers.

THE BEGINNINGS OF ENGLISH CHRISTIANITY. By W. E. COLLINS, M.A., Professor of Ecclesiastical History at King's College, London. With Map. *Crown 8vo. 3s. 6d.*

An investigation in detail, based upon original authorities, of the beginnings of the English Church, with a careful account of earlier Celtic Christianity. The larger aspects of the continental movement are described, and some very full appendices treat of a number of special subjects.

SOME NEW TESTAMENT PROBLEMS. By ARTHUR WRIGHT, Fellow and Tutor of Queen's College, Cambridge. *Crown 8vo. 6s.*

This book deals with a number of important problems from the standpoint of the 'Higher Criticism,' and is written in the hope of advancing the historico-critical study of the Synoptic Gospels and of the Acts.

The Library of Devotion.

Messrs. METHUEN have arranged to publish under the above title a number of the older masterpieces of devotional literature. It is their intention to entrust each volume of the series to an editor who will not only attempt to bring out the spiritual importance of the book, but who will lavish such scholarly care upon it as is generally expended only on editions of the ancient classics.

The books will be furnished with such Introductions and Notes as may be necessary to explain the standpoint of the author, and to comment on such difficulties as the ordinary reader may find, without unnecessary intrusion between the author and reader.

Mr. Laurence Housman has designed a title-page and a cover design. *Pott 8vo. 2s.; leather 3s.*

THE CONFESSIONS OF ST. AUGUSTINE. Newly Translated, with an Introduction and Notes, by C. BIGG, D.D., late Student of Christ Church.

This volume contains the nine books of the 'Confessions' which are suitable for devotional purposes.

THE CHRISTIAN YEAR. By JOHN KEBLE. With Introduction and Notes, by WALTER LOCK, D.D., Warden of Keble College, Ireland Professor at Oxford.

THE IMITATION OF CHRIST. A Revised Translation with an Introduction, by C. BIGG, D.D., late Student of Christ Church.

Dr. Bigg has made a practically new translation of this book, which the reader will have, almost for the first time, exactly in the shape in which it left the hands of the author.

A BOOK OF DEVOTIONS. By J. W. STANBRIDGE, M.A., Rector of Bainton, Canon of York, and sometime Fellow of St. John's College, Oxford. *Pott 8vo.*

This book contains devotions, Eucharistic, daily and occasional, for the use of members of the English Church, sufficiently diversified for those who possess other works of the kind. It is intended to be a companion in private and public worship, and is in harmony with the thoughts of the best Devotional writers.

General Literature

THE GOLFING PILGRIM. By HORACE G. HUTCHINSON. *Crown 8vo.* 6s.

This book, by a famous golfer, contains the following sketches lightly and humorously written :—The Prologue—The Pilgrim at the Shrine—Mecca out of Season—The Pilgrim at Home—The Pilgrim Abroad—The Life of the Links—A Tragedy by the Way—Scraps from the Scrip—The Golfer in Art—Early Pilgrims in the West —An Interesting Relic.

WORKHOUSES AND PAUPERISM. By LOUISA TWINING. *Crown 8vo.* 2s. 6d. [*Social Questions Series.*

Educational

THE ODES AND EPODES OF HORACE. Translated by A. D. GODLEY, M.A., Fellow of Magdalen College, Oxford. *Crown 8vo.* 2s. [*Classical Translations.*

PASSAGES FOR UNSEEN TRANSLATION. By E. C. MARCHANT, M.A., Fellow of Peterhouse, Cambridge; and A. M. COOK, M.A., late Scholar of Wadham College, Oxford: Assistant Masters at St. Paul's School. *Crown 8vo.* 3s. 6d.

This book contains Two Hundred Latin and Two Hundred Greek Passages, and has been very carefully compiled to meet the wants of V. and VI. Form Boys at Public Schools. It is also well adapted for the use of Honour men at the Universities.

EASY LATIN EXERCISES ON THE SYNTAX OF THE SHORTER AND REVISED LATIN PRIMER. By A. M. M. STEDMAN, M.A. With Vocabulary. *Seventh and Cheaper Edition. Crown 8vo.* 1s. 6d. Issued with the consent of Dr. Kennedy.

A new and cheaper edition, thoroughly revised by Mr. C. G. Botting, of St. Paul's School.

TEST CARDS IN EUCLID AND ALGEBRA. By D. S. CALDERWOOD, Headmaster of the Normal School, Edinburgh. In a Packet of 40, with Answers. 1s.

A set of cards for advanced pupils in elementary schools.

Byzantine Texts

Edited by J. B. BURY, M.A., Professor of Modern History at
Trinity College, Dublin.

EVAGRIUS. Edited by PROFESSOR LÉON PARMENTIER of
Liége and M. BIDEZ of Gand. *Demy 8vo.*

PSELLUS (HISTORIA). Edited by C. SATHAS. *Demy 8vo.*

Fiction

THE STANDARDBEARER. By S. R. CROCKETT, Author
of 'The Raiders,' Lochinvar,' etc. *Large crown 8vo. 6s.*

SIMON DALE. By ANTHONY HOPE. Illustrated by W. ST. J.
HARPER. *Crown 8vo. 6s.*
A romance of the reign of Charles II., and Mr. Anthony Hope's first historical novel.

TRAITS AND CONFIDENCES. By The Hon. EMILY LAW-
LESS, Author of 'Hurrish,' 'Maelcho,' etc. *Crown 8vo. 6s.*

THE VINTAGE. By E. F. BENSON, Author of 'Dodo.' Illustrated by G. P. JACOMB-HOOD. *Crown 8vo. 6s.*
A romance of the Greek War of Independence.

A VOYAGE OF CONSOLATION. By SARA JEANETTE
DUNCAN. Author of 'An American Girl in London.' Illustrated by
ROBERT SAUBER. *Crown 8vo. 6s.*
The adventures of an American girl in Europe.

THE CROOK OF THE BOUGH. By MÉNIE MURIEL DOWIE,
Author of 'Gallia.' *Crown 8vo. 6s.*

ACROSS THE SALT SEAS. By J. BLOUNDELLE-BURTON.
Crown 8vo. 6s.

SONS OF ADVERSITY. By L. COPE CORNFORD, Author of
'Captain Jacobus.' *Crown 8vo. 6s.*
A romance of Queen Elizabeth's time.

MISS ERIN. By M. E. FRANCIS, Author of 'In a Northern
Village.' *Crown 8vo. 6s.*

WILLOWBRAKE. By R. MURRAY GILCHRIST. *Crown 8vo. 6s.*

THE KLOOF BRIDE. By ERNEST GLANVILLE, Author of
'The Fossicker.' Illustrated. *Crown 8vo. 3s. 6d.*
A story of South African Adventure.

BIJLI THE DANCER. By JAMES BLYTHE PATTON. Illustrated. *Crown 8vo. 6s.*
A Romance of India.

JOSIAH'S WIFE. By NORMA LORIMER. *Crown 8vo. 6s.*

BETWEEN SUN AND SAND. By W. C. SCULLY, Author
of 'The White Hecatomb.' *Crown 8vo. 6s.*

CROSS TRAILS. By VICTOR WAITE. Illustrated. *Crown
8vo. 6s.*
A romance of adventure in America and Australia.

THE PHILANTHROPIST. By LUCY MAYNARD. *Crown
8vo. 6s.*

VAUSSORE. By FRANCIS BRUNE. *Crown 8vo. 6s.*

A LIST OF
MESSRS. METHUEN'S
PUBLICATIONS

———◆———

Poetry

RUDYARD KIPLING'S NEW POEMS

Rudyard Kipling. THE SEVEN SEAS. By RUDYARD KIPLING. *Third Edition. Crown 8vo. Buckram, gilt top.* 6s.

'The new poems of Mr. Rudyard Kipling have all the spirit and swing of their predecessors. Patriotism is the solid concrete foundation on which Mr. Kipling has built the whole of his work.'—*Times.*

'The Empire has found a singer; it is no depreciation of the songs to say that statesmen may have, one way or other, to take account of them.'—*Manchester Guardian.*

'Animated through and through with indubitable genius.'—*Daily Telegraph.*

'Packed with inspiration, with humour, with pathos.'—*Daily Chronicle.*

'All the pride of empire, all the intoxication of power, all the ardour, the energy, the masterful strength and the wonderful endurance and death-scorning pluck which are the very bone and fibre and marrow of the British character are here.'—*Daily Mail.*

Rudyard Kipling. BARRACK-ROOM BALLADS. By RUDYARD KIPLING. *Thirteenth Edition. Crown 8vo.* 6s.

'Mr. Kipling's verse is strong, vivid, full of character. . . . Unmistakable genius rings in every line.'—*Times.*

'The ballads teem with imagination, they palpitate with emotion. We read them with laughter and tears; the metres throb in our pulses, the cunningly ordered words tingle with life; and if this be not poetry, what is?'—*Pall Mall Gazette.*

'Q." POEMS AND BALLADS. By "Q." *Crown 8vo.* 3s. 6d.

'This work has just the faint, ineffable touch and glow that make poetry.'—*Speaker.*

"Q." GREEN BAYS: Verses and Parodies. By "Q.," Author of 'Dead Man's Rock,' etc. *Second Edition. Crown 8vo.* 3s. 6d.

E. Mackay. A SONG OF THE SEA. By ERIC MACKAY, *Second Edition. Fcap. 8vo.* 5s.

'Everywhere Mr. Mackay displays himself the master of a style marked by all the characteristics of the best rhetoric.'—*Globe.*

Ibsen. BRAND. A Drama by HENRIK IBSEN. Translated by WILLIAM WILSON. *Second Edition. Crown 8vo.* 3s. 6d.

'The greatest world-poem of the nineteenth century next to "Faust." It is in the same set with "Agamemnon," with "Lear," with the literature that we now instinctively regard as high and holy.'—*Daily Chronicle.*

"A. G." VERSES TO ORDER. By "A. G." *Cr. 8vo.* 2s. 6d.
net.

A capital specimen of light academic poetry. These verses are very bright and engaging, easy and sufficiently witty.'—*St. James's Gazette.*

Cordery. THE ODYSSEY OF HOMER. A Translation by J. G. CORDERY. *Crown 8vo.* 7s. 6d.

'This new version of the Odyssey fairly deserves a place of honour among its many rivals. Perhaps there is none from which a more accurate knowledge of the original can be gathered with greater pleasure, at least of those that are in metre.' —*Manchester Guardian.*

Belles Lettres, Anthologies, etc.

R. L. Stevenson. VAILIMA LETTERS. By ROBERT LOUIS STEVENSON. With an Etched Portrait by WILLIAM STRANG, and other Illustrations. *Second Edition. Crown 8vo. Buckram.* 7s. 6d.

'Few publications have in our time been more eagerly awaited than these "Vailima Letters," giving the first fruits of the correspondence of Robert Louis Stevenson. But, high as the tide of expectation has run, no reader can possibly be disappointed in the result.'—*St. James's Gazette.*

Henley. ENGLISH LYRICS. Selected and Edited by W. E. HENLEY. *Crown 8vo. Buckram gilt top.* 6s.

'It is a body of choice and lovely poetry.'—*Birmingham Gazette.*
'Mr. Henley's notes, in their brevity and their fulness, their information and their suggestiveness, seem to us a model of what notes should be.'—*Manchester Guardian.*

Henley and Whibley. A BOOK OF ENGLISH PROSE. Collected by W. E. HENLEY and CHARLES WHIBLEY. *Crown 8vo. Buckram gilt top.* 6s.

'A unique volume of extracts—an art gallery of early prose.'—*Birmingham Post.*
'An admirable companion to Mr. Henley's "Lyra Heroica."'—*Saturday Review.*
'Quite delightful. A greater treat for those not well acquainted with pre-Restoration prose could not be imagined.'—*Athenæum.*

H. C. Beeching. LYRA SACRA : An Anthology of Sacred Verse. Edited by H. C. BEECHING, M.A. *Crown 8vo. Buckram.* 6s.

'A charming selection, which maintains a lofty standard of excellence.'—*Times.*

"Q." THE GOLDEN POMP : A Procession of English Lyrics from Surrey to Shirley, arranged by A. T. QUILLER COUCH. *Crown 8vo. Buckram.* 6s.

'A delightful volume : a really golden "Pomp."'—*Spectator.*

W. B. Yeats. AN ANTHOLOGY OF IRISH VERSE. Edited by W. B. YEATS. *Crown 8vo.* 3s. 6d.

'An attractive and catholic selection.'—*Times.*

A 2

G. W. Steevens. MONOLOGUES OF THE DEAD. By
G. W. Steevens. *Foolscap 8vo.* 3s. 6d.

A series of Soliloquies in which famous men of antiquity—Julius Cæsar, Nero,
Alcibiades, etc., attempt to express themselves in the modes of thought and
language of to-day.

'The effect is sometimes splendid, sometimes bizarre, but always amazingly clever.
—*Pall Mall Gazette.*

Victor Hugo. THE LETTERS OF VICTOR HUGO.
Translated from the French by F. CLARKE, M.A. *In Two Volumes.*
Demy 8vo. 10s. 6d. each. *Vol. I.* 1815-35.

C. H. Pearson. ESSAYS AND CRITICAL REVIEWS. By
C. H. PEARSON, M.A., Author of 'National Life and Character.'
With a Portrait. *Demy 8vo.* 10s. 6d.

W. M. Dixon. A PRIMER OF TENNYSON. By W. M.
DIXON, M.A., Professor of English Literature at Mason College.
Crown 8vo. 2s. 6d.

'Much sound and well-expressed criticism and acute literary judgments. The biblio-
graphy is a boon.'—*Speaker.*

W. A. Craigie. A PRIMER OF BURNS. By W. A. CRAIGIE.
Crown 8vo. 2s. 6d.

'A valuable addition to the literature of the poet.'—*Times.*
'An admirable introduction.'—*Globe.*

Magnus. A PRIMER OF WORDSWORTH. By LAURIE
MAGNUS. *Crown 8vo.* 2s. 6d.

'A valuable contribution to Wordsworthian literature.'—*Literature.*
'A well-made primer, thoughtful and informing.'—*Manchester Guardian.*

Sterne. THE LIFE AND OPINIONS OF TRISTRAM
SHANDY. By LAWRENCE STERNE. With an Introduction by
CHARLES WHIBLEY, and a Portrait. 2 *vols.* 7s.

'Very dainty volumes are these; the paper, type, and light-green binding are all
very agreeable to the eye. *Simplex munditiis* is the phrase that might be applied
to them.'—*Globe.*

Congreve. THE COMEDIES OF WILLIAM CONGREVE.
With an Introduction by G. S. STREET, and a Portrait. 2 *vols.* 7s.

Morier. THE ADVENTURES OF HAJJI BABA OF
ISPAHAN. By JAMES MORIER. With an Introduction by E. G.
BROWNE, M.A., and a Portrait. 2 *vols.* 7s.

Walton. THE LIVES OF DONNE, WOTTON, HOOKER,
HERBERT, AND SANDERSON. By IZAAK WALTON. With
an Introduction by VERNON BLACKBURN, and a Portrait. 3s. 6d.

Johnson. THE LIVES OF THE ENGLISH POETS. By
SAMUEL JOHNSON, LL.D. With an Introduction by J. H. MILLAR,
and a Portrait. 3 *vols.* 10s. 6d.

Burns. THE POEMS OF ROBERT BURNS. Edited by ANDREW LANG and W. A. CRAIGIE. With Portrait. *Demy 8vo, gilt top.* 6s.

This edition contains a carefully collated Text, numerous Notes, critical and textual, a critical and biographical Introduction, and a Glossary.

'Among the editions in one volume, Mr. Andrew Lang's will take the place of authority.'—*Times.*

F. Langbridge. BALLADS OF THE BRAVE : Poems of Chivalry, Enterprise, Courage, and Constancy. Edited by Rev. F. LANGBRIDGE. *Crown 8vo.* 3s. 6d. *School Edition.* 2s. 6d.

'A very happy conception happily carried out. These "Ballads of the Brave" are intended to suit the real tastes of boys, and will suit the taste of the great majority.' —*Spectator.*   'The book is full of splendid things.'—*World.*

Illustrated Books

Bedford. NURSERY RHYMES. With many Coloured Pictures. By F. D. BEDFORD. *Super Royal 8vo.* 5s.

An excellent selection of the best known rhymes, with beautifully coloured pictures exquisitely printed.'—*Pall Mall Gazette.*

'The art is of the newest, with well harmonised colouring.'—*Spectator.*

S. Baring Gould. A BOOK OF FAIRY TALES retold by S. BARING GOULD. With numerous illustrations and initial letters by ARTHUR J. GASKIN. *Second Edition. Crown 8vo. Buckram.* 6s.

'Mr. Baring Gould is deserving of gratitude, in re-writing in honest, simple style the old stories that delighted the childhood of "our fathers and grandfathers."'— *Saturday Review.*

S. Baring Gould. OLD ENGLISH FAIRY TALES. Collected and edited by S. BARING GOULD. With Numerous Illustrations by F. D. BEDFORD. *Second Edition. Crown 8vo. Buckram.* 6s.

'A charming volume. The stories have been selected with great ingenuity from various old ballads and folk-tales, and now stand forth, clothed in Mr. Baring Gould's delightful English, to enchant youthful readers.'—*Guardian.*

S. Baring Gould. A BOOK OF NURSERY SONGS AND RHYMES. Edited by S. BARING GOULD, and Illustrated by the Birmingham Art School. *Buckram, gilt top. Crown 8vo.* 6s.

'The volume is very complete in its way, as it contains nursery songs to the number of 77, game-rhymes, and jingles. To the student we commend the sensible introduction, and the explanatory notes.'—*Birmingham Gazette.*

H. C. Beeching. A BOOK OF CHRISTMAS VERSE. Edited by H. C. BEECHING, M.A., and Illustrated by WALTER CRANE. *Crown 8vo, gilt top.* 5s.

A collection of the best verse inspired by the birth of Christ from the Middle Ages to the present day.

'An anthology which, from its unity of aim and high poetic excellence, has a better right to exist than most of its fellows.'—*Guardian.*

History

Gibbon. THE DECLINE AND FALL OF THE ROMAN EMPIRE. By EDWARD GIBBON. A New Edition, Edited with Notes, Appendices, and Maps, by J. B. BURY, M.A., Fellow of Trinity College, Dublin. *In Seven Volumes. Demy 8vo. Gilt top. os. 6d. each. Also crown 8vo. 6s. each. Vols. I., II., III., and IV.*

'The time has certainly arrived for a new edition of Gibbon's great work. . . . Professor Bury is the right man to undertake this task. His learning is amazing, both in extent and accuracy. The book is issued in a handy form, and at a moderate price, and it is admirably printed.'—*Times.*

'This edition, so far as one may judge from the first instalment, is a marvel of erudition and critical skill, and it is the very minimum of praise to predict that the seven volumes of it will supersede Dean Milman's as the standard edition of our great historical classic.'—*Glasgow Herald.*

'The beau-ideal Gibbon has arrived at last.'—*Sketch.*

'At last there is an adequate modern edition of Gibbon. . . . The best edition the nineteenth century could produce.'—*Manchester Guardian.*

Flinders Petrie. A HISTORY OF EGYPT, FROM THE EARLIEST TIMES TO THE PRESENT DAY. Edited by W. M. FLINDERS PETRIE, D.C.L., LL.D., Professor of Egyptology at University College. *Fully Illustrated. In Six Volumes. Crown 8vo. 6s. each.*

Vol. I. PREHISTORIC TIMES TO XVITH. DYNASTY. W. M. F. Petrie. *Third Edition.*

Vol. II. THE XVIITH AND XVIIITH DYNASTIES. W. M. F. Petrie. *Second Edition.*

'A history written in the spirit of scientific precision so worthily represented by Dr. Petrie and his school cannot but promote sound and accurate study, and supply a vacant place in the English literature of Egyptology.'—*Times.*

Flinders Petrie. EGYPTIAN TALES. Edited by W. M. FLINDERS PETRIE. Illustrated by TRISTRAM ELLIS. *In Two Volumes. Crown 8vo. 3s. 6d. each.*

'A valuable addition to the literature of comparative folk-lore. The drawings are really illustrations in the literal sense of the word.'—*Globe.*

'It has a scientific value to the student of history and archæology. —*Scotsman.*

'Invaluable as a picture of life in Palestine and Egypt.'—*Daily News.*

Flinders Petrie. EGYPTIAN DECORATIVE ART. By W. M. FLINDERS PETRIE. With 120 Illustrations. *Cr. 8vo. 3s. 6d.*

'Professor Flinders Petrie is not only a profound Egyptologist, but an accomplished student of comparative archæology. In these lectures he displays both qualifications with rare skill in elucidating the development of decorative art in Egypt, and in tracing its influence on the art of other countries.'—*Times.*

S. Baring Gould. THE TRAGEDY OF THE CÆSARS. With numerous Illustrations from Busts, Gems, Cameos, etc. By S. BARING GOULD. *Fourth Edition. Royal 8vo. 15s.*

'A most splendid and fascinating book on a subject of undying interest. The great feature of the book is the use the author has made of the existing portraits of the Caesars, and the admirable critical subtlety he has exhibited in dealing with this line of research. It is brilliantly written, and the illustrations are supplied on a scale of profuse magnificence.'—*Daily Chronicle.*

H. de B. Gibbins. INDUSTRY IN ENGLAND : HISTORI-
CAL OUTLINES. By H. DE B. GIBBINS, M.A., D.Litt. With
5 Maps. *Second Edition. Demy 8vo.* 10s. 6d.

This book is written with the view of affording a clear view of the main facts of
English Social and Industrial History placed in due perspective.

H. E. Egerton. A HISTORY OF BRITISH COLONIAL
POLICY. By H. E. EGERTON, M.A. *Demy 8vo.* 12s. 6d.

This book deals with British Colonial policy historically from the beginnings of
English colonisation down to the present day. The subject has been treated by
itself, and it has thus been possible within a reasonable compass to deal with a
mass of authority which must otherwise be sought in the State papers. The
volume is divided into five parts :—(1) The Period of Beginnings, 1497-1650;
(2) Trade Ascendancy, 1651-1830 ; (3) The Granting of Responsible Government,
1831-1860 ; (4) *Laissez Aller*, 1861-1885 ; (5) Greater Britain.

'The whole story of the growth and administration of our colonial empire is comprehensive and well arranged, and is set forth with marked ability.'—*Daily Mail.*
'It is a good book, distinguished by accuracy in detail, clear arrangement of facts,
and a broad grasp of principles '—*Manchester Guardian.*
'Able, impartial, clear. . . . A most valuable volume.'—*Athenæum.*

A. Clark. THE COLLEGES OF OXFORD : Their History
and their Traditions. By Members of the University. Edited by A.
CLARK, M.A., Fellow and Tutor of Lincoln College. 8vo. 12s. 6d.

'A work which will certainly be appealed to for many years as the standard book on
the Colleges of Oxford.'—*Athenæum.*

Perrens. THE HISTORY OF FLORENCE FROM 1434
TO 1492. By F. T. PERRENS. 8vo. 12s. 6d.

A history of Florence under the domination of Cosimo, Piero, and Lorenzo de
Medicis.

J. Wells. A SHORT HISTORY OF ROME. By J. WELLS,
M.A., Fellow and Tutor of Wadham Coll., Oxford. With 4 Maps.
Crown 8vo. 3s. 6d.

This book is intended for the Middle and Upper Forms of Public Schools and for
Pass Students at the Universities. It contains copious Tables, etc.
'An original work written on an original plan, and with uncommon freshness and
vigour.'—*Speaker.*

O. Browning. A SHORT HISTORY OF MEDIÆVAL ITALY,
A.D. 1250-1530. By OSCAR BROWNING, Fellow and Tutor of King's
College, Cambridge. *Second Edition. In Two Volumes. Crown
8vo.* 5s. *each.*

VOL. I. 1250-1409.—Guelphs and Ghibellines.
VOL. II. 1409-1530.—The Age of the Condottieri.

'Mr. Browning is to be congratulated on the production of a work of immense
labour and learning.'—*Westminster Gazette.*

O'Grady. THE STORY OF IRELAND. By STANDISH
O'GRADY, Author of 'Finn and his Companions.' *Cr. 8vo.* 2s. 6d.

Most delightful, most stimulating. Its racy humour, its original imaginings,
make it one of the freshest, breeziest volumes.'—*Methodist Times.*

Biography

S. Baring Gould. THE LIFE OF NAPOLEON BONA-
PARTE. By S. BARING GOULD. With over 450 Illustrations in
the Text and 12 Photogravure Plates. *Large quarto. Gilt top.* 36s.

'The best biography of Napoleon in our tongue, nor have the French as good a
biographer of their hero. A book very nearly as good as Southey's "Life of
Nelson."'—*Manchester Guardian.*
'The main feature of this gorgeous volume is its great wealth of beautiful photo-
gravures and finely-executed wood engravings, constituting a complete pictorial
chronicle of Napoleon I.'s personal history from the days of his early childhood
at Ajaccio to the date of his second interment under the dome of the Invalides in
Paris.'—*Daily Telegraph.*
'Particular notice is due to the vast collection of contemporary illustrations.'—
Guardian.
'Nearly all the illustrations are real contributions to history.'—*Westminster Gazette.*

Morris Fuller. THE LIFE AND WRITINGS OF JOHN
DAVENANT, D.D. (1571-1641), Bishop of Salisbury. By MORRIS
FULLER, B.D. *Demy 8vo.* 10s. 6d.
'A valuable contribution to ecclesiastical history.'—*Birmingham Gazette.*

J. M. Rigg. ST. ANSELM OF CANTERBURY: A CHAPTER
IN THE HISTORY OF RELIGION. By J. M. RIGG. *Demy 8vo.* 7s. 6d.
'Mr. Rigg has told the story of the great Primate's life with scholarly ability, and
has thereby contributed an interesting chapter to the history of the Norman period.'
—*Daily Chronicle.*

F. W. Joyce. THE LIFE OF SIR FREDERICK GORE
OUSELEY. By F. W. JOYCE, M.A. With Portraits and Illustrations. *Crown 8vo.* 7s. 6d.
'This book has been undertaken in quite the right spirit, and written with sympathy,
insight, and considerable literary skill.'—*Times.*

W. G. Collingwood. THE LIFE OF JOHN RUSKIN. By
W. G. COLLINGWOOD, M.A. With Portraits, and 13 Drawings by
Mr. Ruskin. *Second Edition.* 2 vols. *8vo.* 32s.
'No more magnificent volumes have been published for a long time.'—*Times.*
'It is long since we had a biography with such delights of substance and of form.
Such a book is a pleasure for the day, and a joy for ever.'—*Daily Chronicle.*

C. Waldstein. JOHN RUSKIN: a Study. By CHARLES
WALDSTEIN, M.A., Fellow of King's College, Cambridge. With a
Photogravure Portrait after Professor HERKOMER. *Post 8vo.* 5s.
A thoughtful, impartial, well-written criticism of Ruskin's teaching, intended to
separate what the author regards as valuable and permanent from what is transient
and erroneous in the great master's writing.'—*Daily Chronicle.*

Darmesteter. THE LIFE OF ERNEST RENAN. By MADAME DARMESTETER. With Portrait. *Second Edition. Cr. 8vo. 6s.*

A biography of Renan by one of his most intimate friends.

'A polished gem of biography, superior in its kind to any attempt that has been made of recent years in England. Madame Darmesteter has indeed written for English readers "*The Life of Ernest Renan*."'—*Athenæum.*

'It is a fascinating and biographical and critical study, and an admirably finished work of literary art.'—*Scotsman.*

'It is interpenetrated with the dignity and charm, the mild, bright, classical grace of form and treatment that Renan himself so loved ; and it fulfils to the uttermost the delicate and difficult achievement it sets out to accomplish.'—*Academy.*

W. H. Hutton. THE LIFE OF SIR THOMAS MORE. By W. II. HUTTON, M.A. *With Portraits. Crown 8vo. 5s.*

'The book lays good claim to high rank among our biographies. It is excellently, even lovingly, written.'—*Scotsman.*   'An excellent monograph.'—*Times.*

Travel, Adventure and Topography

Johnston. BRITISH CENTRAL AFRICA. By Sir H. H. JOHNSTON, K.C.B. With nearly Two Hundred Illustrations, and Six Maps. *Second Edition. Crown 4to. 30s. net.*

'A fascinating book, written with equal skill and charm—the work at once of a literary artist and of a man of action who is singularly wise, brave, and experienced. It abounds in admirable sketches from pencil.'—*Westminster Gazette.*

'A delightful book . . . collecting within the covers of a single volume all that is known of this part of our African domains. The voluminous appendices are of extreme value.'—*Manchester Guardian.*

'The book takes front rank as a standard work by the one man competent to write it.'—*Daily Chronicle.*

'The book is crowded with important information, and written in a most attractive style ; it is worthy, in short, of the author's established reputation.'—*Standard.*

Prince Henri of Orleans. FROM TONKIN TO INDIA. By PRINCE HENRI OF ORLEANS. Translated by HAMLEY BENT, M.A. With 100 Illustrations and a Map. *Second Edition. Crown 4to, gilt top. 25s.*

The travels of Prince Henri in 1895 from China to the valley of the Bramaputra covered a distance of 2100 miles, of which 1600 was through absolutely unexplored country. No fewer than seventeen ranges of mountains were crossed at altitudes of from 11,000 to 13,000 feet. The journey was made memorable by the discovery of the sources of the Irrawaddy.

'A welcome contribution to our knowledge. The narrative is full and interesting, and the appendices give the work a substantial value.'—*Times.*

'The Prince's travels are of real importance . . . his services to geography have been considerable. The volume is beautifully illustrated.'—*Athenæum.*

'The story is instructive and fascinating, and will certainly make one of the books of 1898. The book attracts by its delightful print and fine illustrations. A nearly model book of travel.'—*Pall Mall Gazette.*

'An entertaining record of pluck and travel in important regions.'—*Daily Chronicle.*

'The illustrations are admirable and quite beyond praise.'—*Glasgow Herald.*

'The Prince's story is charmingly told, and presented with an attractiveness which will make it, in more than one sense, an outstanding book of the season.'—*Birmingham Post.*

'An attractive book which will prove of considerable interest and no little value. A narrative of a remarkable journey.'—*Literature.*

'China is the country of the hour. All eyes are turned towards her, and Messrs. Methuen have opportunely selected the moment to launch Prince Henri's work.'—*Liverpool Daily Post.*

R. S. S. Baden-Powell. THE DOWNFALL OF PREMPEH. A Diary of Life in Ashanti, 1895. By Colonel BADEN-POWELL. With 21 Illustrations and a Map. *Demy 8vo.* 10s. 6d.

'A compact, faithful, most readable record of the campaign.'—*Daily News.*

R. S. S. Baden-Powell. THE MATABELE CAMPAIGN 1896. By Colonel BADEN-POWELL. With nearly 100 Illustrations. *Second Edition. Demy 8vo.* 15s.

'As a straightforward account of a great deal of plucky work unpretentiously done, this book is well worth reading. The simplicity of the narrative is all in its favour, and accords in a peculiarly English fashion with the nature of the subject.' *Times.*

Captain Hinde. THE FALL OF THE CONGO ARABS. By L. HINDE. With Plans, etc. *Demy 8vo.* 12s. 6d.

The book is full of good things, and of sustained interest.'—*St. James's Gazette.*

'A graphic sketch of one of the most exciting and important episodes in the struggle for supremacy in Central Africa between the Arabs and their European rivals. Apart from the story of the campaign, Captain Hinde's book is mainly remarkable for the fulness with which he discusses the question of cannibalism. It is, indeed, the only connected narrative—in English, at any rate—which has been published of this particular episode in African history.'—*Times.*

W. Crooke. THE NORTH-WESTERN PROVINCES OF INDIA : THEIR ETHNOLOGY AND ADMINISTRATION. By W. CROOKE. With Maps and Illustrations. *Demy 8vo.* 10s. 6d.

'A carefully and well-written account of one of the most important provinces of the Empire. In seven chapters Mr. Crooke deals successively with the land in its physical aspect, the province under Hindoo and Mussulman rule, the province under British rule, the ethnology and sociology of the province, the religious and social life of the people, the land and its settlement, and the native peasant in his relation to the land. The illustrations are good and well selected, and the map is excellent.'—*Manchester Guardian.*

A. Boisragon. THE BENIN MASSACRE. By CAPTAIN BOISRAGON. With Portrait and Map. *Second Edition. Crown 8vo.* 3s. 6d.

'If the story had been written four hundred years ago it would be read to-day as an English classic.'—*Scotsman.*

'If anything could enhance the horror and the pathos of this remarkable book it is the simple style of the author, who writes as he would talk, unconscious of his own heroism, with an artlessness which is the highest art.'—*Pall Mall Gazette.*

H. S. Cowper. THE HILL OF THE GRACES : OR, THE GREAT STONE TEMPLES OF TRIPOLI. By H. S. COWPER, F.S.A. With Maps, Plans, and 75 Illustrations. *Demy 8vo.* 10s. 6d.

'The book has the interest of all first-hand work, directed by an intelligent man towards a worthy object, and it forms a valuable chapter of what has now become quite a large and important branch of antiquarian research.'—*Times.*

Kinnaird Rose. WITH THE GREEKS IN THESSALY. By W. KINNAIRD ROSE, Reuter's Correspondent. With Plans and 23 Illustrations. *Crown 8vo.* 6s.

W. B. Worsfold. SOUTH AFRICA. By W. B. WORSFOLD, M.A. *With a Map. Second Edition. Crown 8vo.* 6s.

'A monumental work compressed into a very moderate compass.'—*World.*

Naval and Military

G. W. Steevens. NAVAL POLICY : By. G. W. STEEVENS. *Demy 8vo.* 6s.

This book is a description of the British and other more important navies of the world, with a sketch of the lines on which our naval policy might possibly be developed.
'An extremely able and interesting work.'—*Daily Chronicle.*

D. Hannay. A SHORT HISTORY OF THE ROYAL NAVY, FROM EARLY TIMES TO THE PRESENT DAY. By DAVID HANNAY. Illustrated. *2 Vols. Demy 8vo.* 7s. 6d. each. Vol. I., 1200-1688.

'We read it from cover to cover at a sitting, and those who go to it for a lively and brisk picture of the past, with all its faults and its grandeur, will not be disappointed. The historian is competent, and he is endowed with literary skill and style.'—*Standard.*
'We can warmly recommend Mr. Hannay's volume to any intelligent student of naval history. Great as is the merit of Mr. Hannay's historical narrative, the merit of his strategic exposition is even greater.'—*Times.*
'His book is brisk and pleasant reading, for he is gifted with a most agreeable style. His reflections are philosophical, and he has seized and emphasised just those points which are of interest.'—*Graphic.*

Cooper King. THE STORY OF THE BRITISH ARMY. By Lieut.-Colonel COOPER KING, of the Staff College, Camberley. Illustrated. *Demy 8vo.* 7s. 6d.

An authoritative and accurate story of England's military progress.'—*Daily Mail.*
'This handy volume contains, in a compendious form, a brief but adequate sketch of the story of the British army.'—*Daily News.*

R. Southey. ENGLISH SEAMEN (Howard, Clifford, Hawkins, Drake, Cavendish). By ROBERT SOUTHEY. Edited, with an Introduction, by DAVID HANNAY. *Second Edition. Crown 8vo.* 6s.

'Admirable and well-told stories of our naval history.'—*Army and Navy Gazette.*
'A brave, inspiriting book.'—*Black and White.*

W. Clark Russell. THE LIFE OF ADMIRAL LORD COLLINGWOOD. By W. CLARK RUSSELL, With Illustrations by F. BRANGWYN. *Third Edition. Crown 8vo.* 6s.

'A book which we should like to see in the hands of every boy in the country.'—*St. James's Gazette.*   'A really good book.'—*Saturday Review.*

E. L. S. Horsburgh. THE CAMPAIGN OF WATERLOO. By E. L. S. HORSBURGH, B.A. *With Plans. Crown 8vo.* 5s.

'A brilliant essay—simple, sound, and thorough.'—*Daily Chronicle.*

H. B. George. BATTLES OF ENGLISH HISTORY. By H. B. GEORGE, M.A., Fellow of New College, Oxford. *With numerous Plans. Third Edition. Crown 8vo.* 6s.

'Mr. George has undertaken a very useful task—that of making military affairs intelligible and instructive to non-military readers—and has executed it with laudable intelligence and industry, and with a large measure of success.'—*Times.*

General Literature

S. Baring Gould. OLD COUNTRY LIFE. By S. BARING GOULD. With Sixty-seven Illustrations. *Large Crown 8vo. Fifth Edition.* 6s.

'"Old Country Life," as healthy wholesome reading, full of breezy life and movement, full of quaint stories vigorously told, will not be excelled by any book to be published throughout the year. Sound, hearty, and English to the core.'—*World.*

S. Baring Gould. HISTORIC ODDITIES AND STRANGE EVENTS. By S. BARING GOULD. *Fourth Edition. Crown 8vo.* 6s.

'A collection of exciting and entertaining chapters. The whole volume is delightful reading.'—*Times.*

S. Baring Gould. FREAKS OF FANATICISM. By S. BARING GOULD. *Third Edition. Crown 8vo.* 6s.

'Mr. Baring Gould has a keen eye for colour and effect, and the subjects he has chosen give ample scope to his descriptive and analytic faculties. A perfectly fascinating book.'—*Scottish Leader.*

S. Baring Gould. A GARLAND OF COUNTRY SONG: English Folk Songs with their Traditional Melodies. Collected and arranged by S. BARING GOULD and H. F. SHEPPARD. *Demy 4to.* 6s.

S. Baring Gould. SONGS OF THE WEST: Traditional Ballads and Songs of the West of England, with their Traditional Melodies. Collected by S. BARING GOULD, M.A., and H. F. SHEPPARD, M.A. Arranged for Voice and Piano. In 4 Parts *Parts I., II., III.,* 3s. *each. Part IV.,* 5s. *In one Vol., French morocco,* 15s.

'A rich collection of humour, pathos, grace, and poetic fancy.'—*Saturday Review.*

S. Baring Gould. YORKSHIRE ODDITIES AND STRANGE EVENTS. *Fourth Edition. Crown 8vo.* 6s.

S. Baring Gould. STRANGE SURVIVALS AND SUPERSTITIONS. With Illustrations. By S. BARING GOULD. *Crown 8vo. Second Edition.* 6s.

S. Baring Gould. THE DESERTS OF SOUTHERN FRANCE. By S. BARING GOULD. *2 vols. Demy 8vo.* 32s.

Cotton Minchin. OLD HARROW DAYS. By J. G. COTTON MINCHIN. *Crown 8vo. Second Edition.* 5s.

'This book is an admirable record.'—*Daily Chronicle.*

'Mr. Cotton Minchin's bright and breezy reminiscences of 'Old Harrow Days' will delight all Harrovians, old and young, and may go far to explain the abiding enthusiasm of old Harrovians for their school to readers who have not been privileged to be their schoolfellows.'—*Times.*

W. E. Gladstone. THE SPEECHES OF THE RT. HON. W. E. GLADSTONE, M.P. Edited by A. W. HUTTON, M.A., and H. J. COHEN, M.A. With Portraits. *8vo. Vols. IX. and X.* 12s. 6d. *each.*

J. Wells. OXFORD AND OXFORD LIFE. By Members of the University. Edited by J. WELLS, M.A., Fellow and Tutor of Wadham College. *Crown 8vo.* 3*s.* 6*d.*

'We congratulate Mr. Wells on the production of a readable and intelligent account of Oxford as it is at the present time, written by persons who are possessed of a close acquaintance with the system and life of the University.'—*Athenæum.*

J. Wells. OXFORD AND ITS COLLEGES. By J. WELLS, M.A., Fellow and Tutor of Wadham College. Illustrated by E. H. NEW. *Second Edition. Fcap. 8vo.* 3*s.* *Leather.* 4*s.*

This is a guide—chiefly historical—to the Colleges of Oxford. It contains numerous illustrations.

'An admirable and accurate little treatise, attractively illustrated.'—*World.*
'A luminous and tasteful little volume.'—*Daily Chronicle.*
'Exactly what the intelligent visitor wants.'—*Glasgow Herald.*

C. G. Robertson. VOCES ACADEMICÆ. By C. GRANT ROBERTSON, M.A., Fellow of All Souls', Oxford. *With a Frontispiece. Pott. 8vo.* 3*s.* 6*d.*

'Decidedly clever and amusing.'—*Athenæum.*
'The dialogues are abundantly smart and amusing.'—*Glasgow Herald.*
'A clever and entertaining little book.'—*Pall Mall Gazette.*

L. Whibley. GREEK OLIGARCHIES : THEIR ORGANISA-TION AND CHARACTER. By L. WHIBLEY, M.A., Fellow of Pembroke College, Cambridge. *Crown 8vo.* 6*s.*

'An exceedingly useful handbook : a careful and well-arranged study.'—*Times.*

L. L. Price. ECONOMIC SCIENCE AND PRACTICE. By L. L. PRICE, M.A., Fellow of Oriel College, Oxford. *Crown 8vo.* 6*s.*

'The book is well written, giving evidence of considerable literary ability, and clear mental grasp of the subject under consideration.'—*Western Morning News.*

J. S. Shedlock. THE PIANOFORTE SONATA : Its Origin and Development. By J. S. SHEDLOCK. *Crown 8vo.* 5*s.*

'This work should be in the possession of every musician and amateur. A concise and lucid history of the origin of one of the most important forms of musical composition. A very valuable work for reference.'—*Athenæum.*

E. M. Bowden. THE EXAMPLE OF BUDDHA: Being Quota-tions from Buddhist Literature for each Day in the Year. Compiled by E. M. BOWDEN. *Third Edition.* 16*mo.* 2*s.* 6*d.*

Morgan-Browne. SPORTING AND ATHLETIC RECORDS. By H. MORGAN-BROWNE. *Crown 8vo.* 1*s.* *paper* ; 2*s.* *cloth.*

Should meet a very wide demand.'—*Daily Mail.*
'A very careful collection, and the first one of its kind.'—*Manchester Guardian.*
'Certainly the most valuable of all books of its kind.'—*Birmingham Gazette.*

Science

Freudenreich. DAIRY BACTERIOLOGY. A Short Manual for the Use of Students. By Dr. ED. VON FREUDENREICH. Translated by J. R. AINSWORTH DAVIS, B.A. *Crown 8vo.* 2*s.* 6*d.*

Chalmers Mitchell. OUTLINES OF BIOLOGY. By P. CHALMERS MITCHELL, M.A., *Illustrated. Crown 8vo. 6s.*

A text-book designed to cover the new Schedule issued by the Royal College of Physicians and Surgeons.

G. Massee. A MONOGRAPH OF THE MYXOGASTRES. By GEORGE MASSEE. With 12 Coloured Plates. *Royal 8vo. 18s. net.*

'A work much in advance of any book in the language treating of this group of organisms. Indispensable to every student of the Myxogastres.'—*Nature.*

Technology

Stephenson and Suddards. ORNAMENTAL DESIGN FOR WOVEN FABRICS. By C. STEPHENSON, of The Technical College, Bradford, and F. SUDDARDS, of The Yorkshire College, Leeds. With 65 full-page plates, and numerous designs and diagrams in the text. *Demy 8vo. 7s. 6d.*

'The book is very ably done, displaying an intimate knowledge of principles, good taste, and the faculty of clear exposition.'—*Yorkshire Post.*

HANDBOOKS OF TECHNOLOGY.

Edited by PROFESSORS GARNETT and WERTHEIMER.

HOW TO MAKE A DRESS. By J. A. E. WOOD. *Illustrated. Crown 8vo. 1s. 6d.*

A text-book for students preparing for the City and Guilds examination, based on the syllabus. The diagrams are numerous.
'Though primarily intended for students, Miss Wood's dainty little manual may be consulted with advantage by any girls who want to make their own frocks. The directions are simple and clear, and the diagrams very helpful.'—*Literature.*
'A splendid little book.'—*Evening News.*

Philosophy

L. T. Hobhouse. THE THEORY OF KNOWLEDGE. By L. T. HOBHOUSE, Fellow of C.C.C, Oxford. *Demy 8vo. 21s.*

'The most important contribution to English philosophy since the publication of Mr. Bradley's "Appearance and Reality." Full of brilliant criticism and of positive theories which are models of lucid statement.'—*Glasgow Herald.*
'A brilliantly written volume.'—*Times.*

W. H. Fairbrother. THE PHILOSOPHY OF T. H. GREEN. By W. H. FAIRBROTHER, M.A. *Crown 8vo. 3s. 6d.*

'In every way an admirable book.'—*Glasgow Herald.*

F. W. Bussell. THE SCHOOL OF PLATO: its Origin and its Revival under the Roman Empire. By F. W. BUSSELL, D.D., Fellow and Tutor of Brasenose College, Oxford. *Demy 8vo. 10s. 6d.*

'A highly valuable contribution to the history of ancient thought.'—*Glasgow Herald.*
'A clever and stimulating book, provocative of thought and deserving careful reading.' —*Manchester Guardian.*

F. S. Granger. THE WORSHIP OF THE ROMANS. By
F. S. GRANGER, M.A., Litt.D., Professor of Philosophy at University College, Nottingham. *Crown 8vo. 6s.*
'A scholarly analysis of the religious ceremonies, beliefs, and superstitions of ancient Rome, conducted in the new light of comparative anthropology.'—*Times.*

Theology

HANDBOOKS OF THEOLOGY.

General Editor, A. ROBERTSON, D.D., Principal of King's College,
London.

THE XXXIX. ARTICLES OF THE CHURCH OF ENGLAND. Edited with an Introduction by E. C. S. GIBSON, D.D.,
Vicar of Leeds, late Principal of Wells Theological College. *Second
and Cheaper Edition in One Volume. Demy 8vo. 12s. 6d.*
'Dr. Gibson is a master of clear and orderly exposition, and he has enlisted in his service all the mechanism of variety of type which so greatly helps to elucidate a complicated subject. And he has in a high degree a quality very necessary, but rarely found, in commentators on this topic, that of absolute fairness. His book is pre-eminently honest.'—*Times.*
'After a survey of the whole book, we can bear witness to the transparent honesty of purpose, evident industry, and clearness of style which mark its contents. They maintain throughout a very high level of doctrine and tone.'—*Guardian.*
'An elaborate and learned book, excellently adapted to its purpose.'—*Speaker.*
'The most convenient and most acceptable commentary.'—*Expository Times.*

AN INTRODUCTION TO THE HISTORY OF RELIGION.
By F. B. JEVONS, M.A., Litt.D., Principal of Bishop Hatfield's
Hall. *Demy 8vo. 10s. 6d.*
'Dr. Jevons has written a notable work, which we can strongly recommend to the serious attention of theologians and anthropologists.'—*Manchester Guardian.*
'The merit of this book lies in the penetration, the singular acuteness and force of the author's judgment. He is at once critical and luminous, at once just and suggestive. A comprehensive and thorough book.'—*Birmingham Post.*

THE DOCTRINE OF THE INCARNATION. By R. L.
OTTLEY, M.A., late fellow of Magdalen College, Oxon., and Principal of Pusey House. *In Two Volumes. Demy 8vo. 15s.*
'Learned and reverent : lucid and well arranged.'—*Record.*
'Accurate, well ordered, and judicious.'—*National Observer.*
'A clear and remarkably full account of the main currents of speculation. Scholarly precision . . . genuine tolerance . . . intense interest in his subject—are Mr. Ottley's merits.'—*Guardian.*

C. F. Andrews. CHRISTIANITY AND THE LABOUR
QUESTION. By C. F. ANDREWS, B.A. *Crown 8vo. 2s. 6d.*

S. R. Driver. SERMONS ON SUBJECTS CONNECTED
WITH THE OLD TESTAMENT. By S. R. DRIVER, D.D.,
Canon of Christ Church, Regius Professor of Hebrew in the University of Oxford. *Crown 8vo. 6s.*
'A welcome companion to the author's famous 'Introduction.' No man can read these discourses without feeling that Dr. Driver is fully alive to the deeper teaching of the Old Testament.'—*Guardian.*

T. K. Cheyne. FOUNDERS OF OLD TESTAMENT CRITI-
CISM　y T. K. CHEYNE, D.D., Oriel Professor at Oxford.
Large crown 8vo.　7s. 6d.

> This book is a historical sketch of O. T. Criticism in the form of biographical studies
> from the days of Eichhorn to those of Driver and Robertson Smith.
> 'A very learned and instructive work.'—*Times.*

H. H. Henson. LIGHT AND LEAVEN : HISTORICAL AND
SOCIAL SERMONS.　By the Rev. H. HENSLEY HENSON, M.A.,
Fellow of All Souls', Incumbent of St. Mary's Hospital, Ilford.
Crown 8vo.　6s.

> 'They are always reasonable as well as vigorous, and they are none the less impres-
> sive because they regard the needs of a life on this side of a hereafter.'—
> *Scotsman.*

W. H. Bennett. A PRIMER OF THE BIBLE. By Prof.
W. H. BENNETT. *Second Edition.　Crown 8vo.　2s. 6d.*

> 'The work of an honest, fearless, and sound critic, and an excellent guide in a small
> compass to the books of the Bible.'—*Manchester Guardian,*
> 'A unique primer.　Mr. Bennett has collected and condensed a very extensive and
> diversified amount of material, and no one can consult his pages and fail to
> acknowledge indebtedness to his undertaking.'—*English Churchman.*

C. H. Prior. CAMBRIDGE SERMONS. Edited by C. H. PRIOR,
M.A., Fellow and Tutor of Pembroke College.　*Crown 8vo.　6s.*

> A volume of sermons preached before the University of Cambridge by various
> preachers, including the late Archbishop of Canterbury and Bishop Westcott.

E. B. Layard.　RELIGION IN BOYHOOD.　Notes on the
Religious Training of Boys　By E. B. LAYARD, M.A.　18mo.　1s.

W. Yorke Faussett.　THE *DE CATECHIZANDIS
RUDIBUS* OF ST. AUGUSTINE.　Edited, with Introduction,
Notes, etc., by W. YORKE FAUSSETT. M.A., late Scholar of Balliol
Coll.　*Crown 8vo.　3s. 6d.*

> An edition of a Treatise on the Essentials of Christian Doctrine, and the best
> methods of impressing them on candidates for baptism.

À Kempis.　THE IMITATION OF CHRIST.　By THOMAS A
KEMPIS.　With an Introduction by DEAN FARRAR.　Illustrated by
C. M. GERE, and printed in black and red.　*Second Edition.　Fcap.
8vo.　Buckram.　3s. 6d.　Padded morocco, 5s.*

> 'Amongst all the innumerable English editions of the "Imitation," there can have
> been few which were prettier than this one, printed in strong and handsome type,
> with all the glory of red initials.'—*Glasgow Herald.*

J. Keble. THE CHRISTIAN YEAR. By JOHN KEBLE. With an
Introduction and Notes by W. LOCK, D.D., Warden of Keble College,
Ireland Professor at Oxford.　Illustrated by R. ANNING BELL.
Second Edition.　Fcap. 8vo.　Buckram.　3s. 6d.　Padded morocco, 5s.

> 'The present edition is annotated with all the care and insight to be expected from
> Mr. Lock.　The progress and circumstances of its composition are detailed in the
> Introduction.　There is an interesting Appendix on the MSS. of the "Christian
> Year," and another giving the order in which the poems were written.　A "Short
> Analysis of the Thought" is prefixed to each, and any difficulty in the text is ex-
> plained in a note.'—*Guardian.*

Leaders of Religion

Edited by H. C. BEECHING, M.A.   *With Portraits, crown 8vo.*

A series of short biographies of the most prominent leaders of religious life and thought of all ages and countries.

The following are ready—

CARDINAL NEWMAN. By R. H. HUTTON.
JOHN WESLEY. By J. H. OVERTON, M.A.
BISHOP WILBERFORCE. By G. W. DANIEL, M.A.
CARDINAL MANNING. By A. W. HUTTON, M.A.
CHARLES SIMEON. By H. C. G. MOULE, M.A.
JOHN KEBLE. By WALTER LOCK, D.D.
THOMAS CHALMERS. By Mrs. OLIPHANT.
LANCELOT ANDREWES. By R. L. OTTLEY, M.A.
AUGUSTINE OF CANTERBURY. By E. L. CUTTS, D.D.
WILLIAM LAUD. By W. H. HUTTON, B.D.
JOHN KNOX. By F. M'CUNN.
JOHN HOWE. By R. F. HORTON, D.D.
BISHOP KEN. By F. A. CLARKE, M.A.
GEORGE FOX, THE QUAKER. By T. HODGKIN, D.C.L.
JOHN DONNE. By AUGUSTUS JESSOPP, D.D.

Other volumes will be announced in due course.

Fiction

SIX SHILLING NOVELS

Marie Corelli's Novels

Crown 8vo. 6s. each.

A ROMANCE OF TWO WORLDS. *Seventeenth Edition.*
VENDETTA. *Thirteenth Edition.*
THELMA. *Eighteenth Edition.*
ARDATH. *Eleventh Edition.*
THE SOUL OF LILITH *Ninth Edition.*
WORMWOOD. *Eighth Edition.*
BARABBAS: A DREAM OF THE WORLD'S TRAGEDY. *Thirty-first Edition.*

'The tender reverence of the treatment and the imaginative beauty of the writing have reconciled us to the daring of the conception, and the conviction is forced on us that even so exalted a subject cannot be made too familiar to us, provided it be presented in the true spirit of Christian faith. The amplifications of the Scripture narrative are often conceived with high poetic insight, and this "Dream of the World's Tragedy" is, despite some trifling incongruities, a lofty and not inadequate paraphrase of the supreme climax of the inspired narrative.'—*Dublin Review.*

THE SORROWS OF SATAN. *Thirty-seventh Edition.*

'A very powerful piece of work. . . . The conception is magnificent, and is likely to win an abiding place within the memory of man. . . . The author has immense command of language, and a limitless audacity. . . . This interesting and remarkable romance will live long after much of the ephemeral literature of the day is forgotten. . . . A literary phenomenon . . . novel, and even sublime.'—W. T. STEAD in the *Review of Reviews.*

Anthony Hope's Novels
Crown 8vo. 6s. each.

THE GOD IN THE CAR. *Seventh Edition.*

'A very remarkable book, deserving of critical analysis impossible within our limit; brilliant, but not superficial; well considered, but not elaborated; constructed with the proverbial art that conceals, but yet allows itself to be enjoyed by readers to whom fine literary method is a keen pleasure.'—*The World.*

A CHANGE OF AIR. *Fourth Edition.*

'A graceful, vivacious comedy, true to human nature. The characters are traced with a masterly hand.'—*Times.*

A MAN OF MARK. *Fourth Edition.*

'Of all Mr. Hope's books, "A Man of Mark" is the one which best compares with "The Prisoner of Zenda."'—*National Observer.*

THE CHRONICLES OF COUNT ANTONIO. *Third Edition.*

'It is a perfectly enchanting story of love and chivalry, and pure romance. The Count is the most constant, desperate, and modest and tender of lovers, a peerless gentleman, an intrepid fighter, a faithful friend, and a magnanimous foe.'—*Guardian.*

PHROSO. Illustrated by H. R. MILLAR. *Third Edition.*

'The tale is thoroughly fresh, quick with vitality, stirring the blood, and humorously, dashingly told.'—*St. James's Gazette.*
'A story of adventure, every page of which is palpitating with action.'—*Speaker.*
'From cover to cover "Phroso" not only engages the attention, but carries the reader in little whirls of delight from adventure to adventure.'—*Academy.*

S. Baring Gould's Novels
Crown 8vo. 6s. each.

'To say that a book is by the author of "Mehalah" is to imply that it contains a story cast on strong lines, containing dramatic possibilities, vivid and sympathetic descriptions of Nature, and a wealth of ingenious imagery.'—*Speaker.*
'That whatever Mr. Baring Gould writes is well worth reading, is a conclusion that may be very generally accepted. His views of life are fresh and vigorous, his language pointed and characteristic, the incidents of which he makes use are striking and original, his characters are life-like, and though somewhat exceptional people, are drawn and coloured with artistic force. Add to this that his descriptions of scenes and scenery are painted with the loving eyes and skilled hands of a master of his art, that he is always fresh and never dull, and under such conditions it is no wonder that readers have gained confidence both in his power of amusing and satisfying them, and that year by year his popularity widens.'—*Court Circular.*

ARMINELL : A Social Romance. *Fourth Edition.*

URITH : A Story of Dartmoor. *Fifth Edition*

'The author is at his best.'—*Times.*

IN THE ROAR OF THE SEA   *Sixth Edition.*
'One of the best imagined and most enthralling stories the author has produced.'
—*Saturday Review.*

MRS. CURGENVEN OF CURGENVEN.   *Fourth Edition.*
' The swing of the narrative is splendid.'—*Sussex Daily News.*

CHEAP JACK ZITA.   *Fourth Edition.*
' A powerful drama of human passion.'—*Westminster Gazette.*
' A story worthy the author.'—*National Observer.*

THE QUEEN OF LOVE.   *Fourth Edition.*
' Can be heartily recommended to all who care for cleanly, energetic, and interesting fiction.'—*Sussex Daily News.*

KITTY ALONE.   *Fourth Edition.*
' A strong and original story, teeming with graphic description, stirring incident, and, above all, with vivid and enthralling human interest.'—*Daily Telegraph.*

NOÉMI: A Romance of the Cave-Dwellers.   Illustrated by R. CATON WOODVILLE.   *Third Edition.*
' A powerful story, full of strong lights and shadows.'—*Standard.*

THE BROOM-SQUIRE.   Illustrated by FRANK DADD.   *Fourth Edition.*
' A strain of tenderness is woven through the web of his tragic tale, and its atmosphere is sweetened by the nobility and sweetness of the heroine's character.'—*Daily News.*

THE PENNYCOMEQUICKS.   *Third Edition.*

DARTMOOR IDYLLS.
' A book to read, and keep and read again; for the genuine fun and pathos of it will not early lose their effect.'—*Vanity Fair.*

GUAVAS THE TINNER.   Illustrated by FRANK DADD.   *Second Edition.*
' There is a kind of flavour about this book which alone elevates it above the ordinary novel. The story itself has a grandeur in harmony with the wild and rugged scenery which is its setting.'—*Athenæum.*

BLADYS.   *Second Edition.*
' A story of thrilling interest.'—*Scotsman.*
' A sombre but powerful story.'—*Daily Mail.*

Gilbert Parker's Novels
Crown 8vo.   6s. each.

PIERRE AND HIS PEOPLE.   *Fourth Edition.*
'Stories happily conceived and finely executed. There is strength and genius in Mr. Parker's style.'—*Daily Telegraph.*

MRS. FALCHION.   *Fourth Edition.*
' A splendid study of character.'—*Athenæum.*
' But little behind anything that has been done by any writer of our time.'—*Pall Mall Gazette.*   ' A very striking and admirable novel.'—*St. James's Gazette.*

THE TRANSLATION OF A SAVAGE.
' The plot is original and one difficult to work out; but Mr. Parker has done it with great skill and delicacy. The reader who is not interested in this original, fresh, and well-told tale must be a dull person indeed.'—*Daily Chronicle.*

THE TRAIL OF THE SWORD. *Fifth Edition. Illustrated.*

'A rousing and dramatic tale. A book like this, in which swords flash, great surprises are undertaken, and daring deeds done, in which men and women live and love in the old passionate way, is a joy inexpressible .'—*Daily Chronicle.*

WHEN VALMOND CAME TO PONTIAC: The Story of a Lost Napoleon. *Fourth Edition.*

'Here we find romance—real, breathing, living romance. The character of Valmond is drawn unerringly. The book must be read, we may say re-read, for any one thoroughly to appreciate Mr. Parker's delicate touch and innate sympathy with humanity.'—*Pall Mall Gazette.*

AN ADVENTURER OF THE NORTH: The Last Adventures of 'Pretty Pierre.' *Second Edition.*

'The present book is full of fine and moving stories of the great North, and it will add to Mr. Parker's already high reputation.'—*Glasgow Herald.*

THE SEATS OF THE MIGHTY. *Illustrated. Ninth Edition.*

'The best thing he has done; one of the best things that any one has done lately.'—*St. James's Gazette.*

'Mr. Parker seems to become stronger and easier with every serious novel that he attempts. He shows the matured power which his former novels have led us to expect, and has produced a really fine historical novel. The finest novel he has yet written.'—*Athenæum.*

'A great book.'—*Black and White.*

'One of the strongest stories of historical interest and adventure that we have read for many a day. . . . A notable and successful book.'—*Speaker.*

THE POMP OF THE LAVILETTES. *Second Edition.* 3s. 6d.

'Living, breathing romance, genuine and unforced pathos, and a deeper and more subtle knowledge of human nature than Mr. Parker has ever displayed before. It is, in a word, the work of a true artist.'—*Pall Mall Gazette.*

Conan Doyle. ROUND THE RED LAMP. By A. CONAN DOYLE, Author of 'The White Company,' 'The Adventures of Sherlock Holmes,' etc. *Fifth Edition. Crown 8vo. 6s.*

'The book is, indeed, composed of leaves from life, and is far and away the best view that has been vouchsafed us behind the scenes of the consulting-room. It is very superior to "The Diary of a late Physician."'—*Illustrated London News.*

Stanley Weyman. UNDER THE RED ROBE. By STANLEY WEYMAN, Author of 'A Gentleman of France.' With Twelve Illustrations by R. Caton Woodville. *Twelfth Edition. Crown 8vo. 6s.*

'A book of which we have read every word for the sheer pleasure of reading, and which we put down with a pang that we cannot forget it all and start again.'—*Westminster Gazette.*

'Every one who reads books at all must read this thrilling romance, from the first page of which to the last the breathless reader is haled along. An inspiration of manliness and courage.'—*Daily Chronicle.*

Lucas Malet. THE WAGES OF SIN. By LUCAS MALET. *Thirteenth Edition. Crown 8vo. 6s.*

Lucas Malet. THE CARISSIMA. By LUCAS MALET, Author of 'The Wages of Sin,' etc. *Third Edition. Crown 8vo. 6s.*

S. R. Crockett. LOCHINVAR. By S. R. CROCKETT, Author of 'The Raiders,' etc. Illustrated. *Second Edition. Crown 8vo. 6s.*

'Full of gallantry and pathos, of the clash of arms, and brightened by episodes of humour and love. . . . Mr. Crockett has never written a stronger or better book. An engrossing and fascinating story. The love story alone is enough to make the book delightful.'—*Westminster Gazette.*

Arthur Morrison. TALES OF MEAN STREETS. By ARTHUR MORRISON. *Fourth Edition. Crown 8vo. 6s.*

'Told with consummate art and extraordinary detail. In the true humanity of the book lies its justification, the permanence of its interest, and its indubitable triumph.'—*Athenæum.*

'A great book. The author's method is amazingly effective, and produces a thrilling sense of reality. The writer lays upon us a master hand. The book is simply, appalling and irresistible in its interest. It is humorous also; without humou it would not make the mark it is certain to make.'—*World.*

Arthur Morrison. A CHILD OF THE JAGO. By ARTHUR MORRISON. *Third Edition. Crown 8vo. 6s.*

'The book is a masterpiece.'—*Pall Mall Gazette.*
'Told with great vigour and powerful simplicity.'—*Athenæum.*

Mrs. Clifford. A FLASH OF SUMMER. By Mrs. W. K. CLIFFORD, Author of 'Aunt Anne,' etc. *Second Edition. Crown 8vo. 6s.*

'The story is a very sad and a very beautiful one, exquisitely told, and enriched with many subtle touches of wise and tender insight.'—*Speaker.*

Emily Lawless. HURRISH. By the Honble. EMILY LAWLESS, Author of 'Maelcho,' etc. *Fifth Edition. Crown 8vo. 6s.*

A reissue of Miss Lawless' most popular novel, uniform with 'Maelcho.'

Emily Lawless. MAELCHO: a Sixteenth Century Romance. By the Honble. EMILY LAWLESS. *Second Edition. Crown 8vo. 6s.*

'A really great book.'—*Spectator.*
'There is no keener pleasure in life than the recognition of genius. A piece of work of the first order, which we do not hesitate to describe as one of the most remarkable literary achievements of this generation.'—*Manchester Guardian.*

Jane Barlow. A CREEL OF IRISH STORIES. By JANE BARLOW, Author of 'Irish Idylls.' *Second Edition. Crown 8vo. 6s.*

'Vivid and singularly real.'—*Scotsman.*
'Genuinely and naturally Irish.'—*Scotsman.*
'The sincerity of her sentiments, the distinction of her style, and the freshness of her themes, combine to lift her work far above the average level of contemporary fiction.'—*Manchester Guardian.*

J. H. Findlater. THE GREEN GRAVES OF BALGOWRIE. By JANE II. FINDLATER. *Fourth Edition. Crown 8vo. 6s.*

'A powerful and vivid story.'—*Standard.*
'A beautiful story, sad and strange as truth itself.'—*Vanity Fair.*
'A work of remarkable interest and originality.'—*National Observer.*
'A very charming and pathetic tale.'—*Pall Mall Gazette.*
'A singularly original, clever, and beautiful story.'—*Guardian.*
'Reveals to us a new writer of undoubted faculty and reserve force.'—*Spectator.*
'An exquisite idyll, delicate, affecting, and beautiful.'—*Black and White.*

J. H. Findlater. A DAUGHTER OF STRIFE. By JANE HELEN FINDLATER, Author of 'The Green Graves of Balgowrie.' *Crown 8vo.* 6s.

'A story of strong human interest.'—*Scotsman.*
'It has a sweet flavour of olden days delicately conveyed.'—*Manchester Guardian.*
'Her thought has solidity and maturity.'—*Daily Mail.*

Mary Findlater. OVER THE HILLS. By MARY FINDLATER. *Second Edition. Crown 8vo.* 6s.

'A strong and fascinating piece of work.'—*Scotsman.*
'A charming romance, and full of incident. The book is fresh and strong.'—*Speaker.*
'There is quiet force and beautiful simplicity in this book which will make the author's name loved in many a household.'—*Literary World.*
'Admirably fresh and broad in treatment. The novel is markedly original and excellently written.'—*Daily Chronicle.*
'A strong and wise book of deep insight and unflinching truth.'—*Birmingham Post.*
'Miss Mary Findlater combines originality with strength.'—*Daily Mail.*

H. G. Wells. THE STOLEN BACILLUS, and other Stories. By H. G. WELLS. *Second Edition. Crown 8vo.* 6s.

'The ordinary reader of fiction may be glad to know that these stories are eminently readable from one cover to the other, but they are more than that ; they are the impressions of a very striking imagination, which, it would seem, has a great deal within its reach.'—*Saturday Review.*

H. G. Wells. THE PLATTNER STORY AND OTHERS. By H. G. WELLS. *Second Edition. Crown 8vo.* 6s.

'Weird and mysterious, they seem to hold the reader as by a magic spell.'—*Scotsman.*
'No volume has appeared for a long time so likely to give equal pleasure to the simplest reader and to the most fastidious critic.'—*Academy.*

E. F. Benson. DODO : A DETAIL OF THE DAY. By E. F. BENSON. *Sixteenth Edition. Crown 8vo.* 6s.

'A delightfully witty sketch of society.'—*Spectator.*
'A perpetual feast of epigram and paradox.'—*Speaker.*

E. F. Benson. THE RUBICON. By E. F. BENSON, Author of 'Dodo.' *Fifth Edition. Crown 8vo.* 6s.

Mrs. Oliphant. SIR ROBERT'S FORTUNE. By MRS. OLIPHANT. *Crown 8vo.* 6s.

'Full of her own peculiar charm of style and simple, subtle character-painting comes her new gift, the delightful story.'—*Pall Mall Gazette.*

Mrs. Oliphant. THE TWO MARYS. By MRS. OLIPHANT. *Second Edition. Crown 8vo.* 6s.

Mrs. Oliphant. THE LADY'S WALK. By Mrs. OLIPHANT. *Second Edition. Crown 8vo.* 6s.

'A story of exquisite tenderness, of most delicate fancy.'—*Pall Mall Gazette.*
'It contains many of the finer characteristics of her best work.'—*Scotsman.*
'It is little short of sacrilege on the part of a reviewer to attempt to sketch its outlines or analyse its peculiar charm.'—*Spectator.*

W. E. Norris. MATTHEW AUSTIN. By W. E. NORRIS, Author of 'Mademoiselle de Mersac,' etc. *Fourth Edition. Crown 8vo. 6s.*

"An intellectually satisfactory and morally bracing novel.'—*Daily Telegraph.*

W. E. Norris. HIS GRACE. By W. E NORRIS. *Third Edition. Crown 8vo. 6s.*

'Mr. Norris has drawn a really fine character in the Duke of Hurstbourne, at once unconventional and very true to the conventionalities of life.'—*Athenæum.*

W. E. Norris. THE DESPOTIC LADY AND OTHERS. By W. E. NORRIS. *Crown 8vo. 6s.*

'A budget of good fiction of which no one will tire.'—*Scotsman.*

W. E. Norris. CLARISSA FURIOSA. By W. E. NORRIS. *Crown 8vo. 6s.*

'As a story it is admirable, as a *jeu d'esprit* it is capital, as a lay sermon studded with gems of wit and wisdom it is a model.'—*The World.*

W. Clark Russell. MY DANISH SWEETHEART. By W. CLARK RUSSELL, Author of 'The Wreck of the Grosvenor,' etc. *Illustrated. Fourth Edition. Crown 8vo. 6s.*

Robert Barr. THE MUTABLE MANY. By ROBERT BARR, Author of 'In the Midst of Alarms,' 'A Woman Intervenes,' etc. *Second Edition. Crown 8vo. 6s.*

'Very much the best novel that Mr. Barr has yet given us. There is much insight in it, much acute and delicate appreciation of the finer shades of character and much excellent humour.'—*Daily Chronicle.*
'An excellent story. It contains several excellently studied characters, and is filled with lifelike pictures of modern life.'—*Glasgow Herald.*

Robert Barr. IN THE MIDST OF ALARMS. By ROBERT BARR. *Third Edition. Crown 8vo. 6s.*

'A book which has abundantly satisfied us by its capital humour. —*Daily Chronicle.*
'Mr. Barr has achieved a triumph whereof he has every reason to be proud.'—*Pall Mall Gazette.*

J. Maclaren Cobban. THE KING OF ANDAMAN: A Saviour of Society. By J. MACLAREN COBBAN. *Crown 8vo. 6s.*

'An unquestionably interesting book. It contains one character, at least, who has in him the root of immortality, and the book itself is ever exhaling the sweet savour of the unexpected.'—*Pall Mall Gazette.*

J. Maclaren Cobban. WILT THOU HAVE THIS WOMAN? By J. M. COBBAN, Author of 'The King of Andaman.' *Crown 8vo. 6s.*

Robert Hichens. BYEWAYS. By ROBERT HICHENS. Author of 'Flames,' etc. *Crown 8vo.* 6s.

'A very high artistic instinct and striking command of language raise Mr. Hichens' work far above the ruck.'—*Pall Mall Gazette.*
'The work is undeniably that of a man of striking imagination and no less striking powers of expression.'—*Daily News.*

Percy White. A PASSIONATE PILGRIM. By PERCY WHITE, Author of 'Mr. Bailey-Martin.' *Crown 8vo.* 6s.

'A work which it is not hyperbole to describe as of rare excellence.'—*Pall Mall Gazette.*
'The clever book of a shrewd and clever author.'—*Athenæum.*
'Mr. Percy White's strong point is analysis, and he has shown himself, before now, capable of building up a good book upon that foundation.'—*Standard.*

W. Pett Ridge. SECRETARY TO BAYNE, M.P. By W. PETT RIDGE. *Crown 8vo.* 6s.

'Sparkling, vivacious, adventurous.—*St. James's Gazette.*
'Ingenious, amusing, and especially smart.'—*World.*
'The dialogue is invariably alert and highly diverting.'—*Spectator.*

J. S. Fletcher. THE BUILDERS. By J. S. FLETCHER, Author of 'When Charles I. was King.' *Second Edition. Crown 8vo.* 6s.

'Replete with delightful descriptions.'—*Vanity Fair.*
'The background of country life has never, perhaps, been sketched more realistically.'—*World.*

Andrew Balfour. BY STROKE OF SWORD. By ANDREW BALFOUR. Illustrated by W. CUBITT COOKE. *Fourth Edition. Crown 8vo.* 6s.

'A banquet of good things.'—*Academy.*
'A recital of thrilling interest, told with unflagging vigour.'—*Globe*
'An unusually excellent example of a semi-historic romance.'—*World.*
'Manly, healthy, and patriotic.'—*Glasgow Herald.*

I. Hooper. THE SINGER OF MARLY. By I. HOOPER. Illustrated by W. CUBITT COOKE. *Crown 8vo.* 6s.
'Its scenes are drawn in vivid colours, and the characters are all picturesque.'—*Scotsman.*
'A novel as vigorous as it is charming.'—*Literary World.*

M. C. Balfour. THE FALL OF THE SPARROW. By M. C. BALFOUR. *Crown 8vo.* 6s.
'A powerful novel.'—*Daily Telegraph.*
'It is unusually powerful, and the characterization is uncommonly good.'—*World.*
'It is a well-knit, carefully-wrought story.'—*Academy.*

H. Morrah. A SERIOUS COMEDY. By HERBERT MORRAH. *Crown 8vo.* 6s.

H. Morrah. THE FAITHFUL CITY. By HERBERT MORRAH, Author of 'A Serious Comedy.' *Crown 8vo.* 6s.

L. B. Walford. SUCCESSORS TO THE TITLE. By Mrs. WALFORD, Author of 'Mr. Smith,' etc. *Second Edition. Crown 8vo.* 6s.

Mary Gaunt.   KIRKHAM'S FIND.   By MARY GAUNT, Author of ' The Moving Finger.'   *Crown 8vo.*   6s.

' A really charming novel.'—*Standard.*
' A capital book, in which will be found lively humour, penetrating insight, and the sweet savour of a thoroughly healthy moral.'—*Speaker.*

M. M. Dowie.   GALLIA.   By MÉNIE MURIEL DOWIE, Author of ' A Girl in the Carpathians.'   *Third Edition.   Crown 8vo.*   6s.

'The style is generally admirable, the dialogue not seldom brilliant, the situations surprising in their freshness and originality, while the characters live and move, and the story itself is readable from title-page to colophon.'—*Saturday Review.*

J. A. Barry.   IN THE GREAT DEEP.   BY J. A. BARRY. Author of ' Steve Brown's Bunyip.'   *Crown 8vo.*   6s.

' A collection of really admirable short stories of the sea, very simply told, and placed before the reader in pithy and telling English.'—*Westminster Gazette.*

J. B. Burton.   IN THE DAY OF ADVERSITY.   By J. BLOUN-DELLE-BURTON.'   *Second Edition.   Crown 8vo.*   6s.

' Unusually interesting and full of highly dramatic situations. —*Guardian.*

J. B. Burton.   DENOUNCED.   By J. BLOUNDELLE-BURTON. *Second Edition.   Crown 8vo.*   6s.

'The plot is an original one, and the local colouring is laid on with a delicacy and an accuracy of detail which denote the true artist.'—*Broad Arrow.*

J. B. Burton.   THE CLASH OF ARMS.   By J. BLOUNDELLE-BURTON, Author of ' In the Day of Adversity.'   *Second Edition. Crown 8vo.*   6s.

A brave story—brave in deed, brave in word, brave in thought.'—*St. James's Gazette.*
' A fine, manly, spirited piece of work.'—*World.*

W. C. Scully.   THE WHITE HECATOMB.   By W. C. SCULLY, Author of ' Kafir Stories.'   *Crown 8vo.*   6s.

' It reveals a marvellously intimate understanding of the Kaffir mind, allied with literary gifts of no mean order.'—*African Critic.*

Julian Corbett.   A BUSINESS IN GREAT WATERS.   By JULIAN CORBETT.   *Second Edition.   Crown 8vo.*   6s.

' Mr. Corbett writes with immense spirit. The salt of the ocean is in it, and the right heroic ring resounds through its gallant adventures.'—*Speaker.*

L. Cope Cornford.   CAPTAIN JACOBUS: A ROMANCE OF THE ROAD.   By L. COPE CORNFORD.   Illustrated.   *Crown 8vo.*   6s.

' An exceptionally good story of adventure and character.'—*World.*

L. Daintrey.   THE KING OF ALBERIA.   A Romance of the Balkans.   By LAURA DAINTREY.   *Crown 8vo.*   6s.

M. A. Owen.   THE DAUGHTER OF ALOUETTE.   By MARY A. OWEN.   *Crown 8vo.*   6s.

Mrs. Pinsent. CHILDREN OF THIS WORLD. By ELLEN F. PINSENT, Author of 'Jenny's Case.' *Crown 8vo.* 6s.

G. Manville Fenn. AN ELECTRIC SPARK. By G. MANVILLE FENN, Author of 'The Vicar's Wife,' 'A Double Knot,' etc. *Second Edition. Crown 8vo.* 6s.

L. S. McChesney. UNDER SHADOW OF THE MISSION. By L. S. McCHESNEY. *Crown 8vo.* 6s.

'Those whose minds are open to the finer issues of life, who can appreciate graceful thought and refined expression of it, from them this volume will receive a welcome as enthusiastic as it will be based on critical knowledge.'—*Church Times.*

J. F. Brewer. THE SPECULATORS. By J. F. BREWER. *Second Edition. Crown 8vo.* 6s.

Ronald Ross. THE SPIRIT OF STORM. By RONALD ROSS, Author of 'The Child of Ocean.' *Crown 8vo.* 6s.

C. F. Wolley. THE QUEENSBERRY CUP. A Tale of Adventure. By CLIVE P. WOLLEY. *Illustrated. Crown 8vo.* 6s.

T. L. Paton. A HOME IN INVERESK. By T. L. PATON. *Crown 8vo.* 6s.

John Davidson. MISS ARMSTRONG'S AND OTHER CIR-CUMSTANCES. By JOHN DAVIDSON. *Crown 8vo.* 6s.

H. Johnston. DR. CONGALTON'S LEGACY. By HENRY JOHNSTON. *Crown 8vo.* 6s.

R. Pryce. TIME AND THE WOMAN. By RICHARD PRYCE. *Second Edition. Crown 8vo.* 6s.

Mrs. Watson. THIS MAN'S DOMINION. By the Author of 'A High Little World.' *Second Edition. Crown 8vo.* 6s.

Marriott Watson. DIOGENES OF LONDON. By H. B. MARRIOTT WATSON. *Crown 8vo. Buckram.* 6s.

M. Gilchrist. THE STONE DRAGON. By MURRAY GIL-CHRIST. *Crown 8vo. Buckram.* 6s.

E. Dickinson. A VICAR'S WIFE. By EVELYN DICKINSON. *Crown 8vo.* 6s.

E. M. Gray. ELSA. By E. M'QUEEN GRAY. *Crown 8vo.* 6s.

THREE-AND-SIXPENNY NOVELS
Crown 8vo.

DERRICK VAUGHAN, NOVELIST. By Edna Lyall.
MARGERY OF QUETHER. By S. Baring Gould.
JACQUETTA. By S. Baring Gould.
SUBJECT TO VANITY. By Margaret Benson.
THE SIGN OF THE SPIDER. By Bertram Mitford.
THE MOVING FINGER. By Mary Gaunt.
JACO TRELOAR. By J. H. Pearce.
THE DANCE OF THE HOURS. By 'Vera.'
A WOMAN OF FORTY. By Esmé Stuart.
A CUMBERER OF THE GROUND. By Constance Smith.
THE SIN OF ANGELS. By Evelyn Dickinson.
AUT DIABOLUS AUT NIHIL. By X. L.
THE COMING OF CUCULAIN. By Standish O'Grady.
THE GODS GIVE MY DONKEY WINGS. By Angus Evan Abbott.
THE STAR GAZERS. By G. Manville Fenn.
THE POISON OF ASPS. By R. Orton Prowse.
THE QUIET MRS. FLEMING. By R. Pryce.
DISENCHANTMENT. By F. Mabel Robinson.
THE SQUIRE OF WANDALES. By A. Shield.
A REVEREND GENTLEMAN. By J. M. Cobban.
A DEPLORABLE AFFAIR. By W. E. Norris.
A CAVALIER'S LADYE. By Mrs. Dicker.
THE PRODIGALS. By Mrs. Oliphant.
THE SUPPLANTER. By P. Neumann.
A MAN WITH BLACK EYELASHES. By H. A. Kennedy.
A HANDFUL OF EXOTICS. By S. Gordon.
AN ODD EXPERIMENT. By Hannah Lynch.
SCOTTISH BORDER LIFE. By James C. Dibdin.

HALF-CROWN NOVELS
A Series of Novels by popular Authors.

HOVENDEN, V.C. By F. Mabel Robinson.
THE PLAN OF CAMPAIGN. By F. Mabel Robinson.
MR. BUTLER'S WARD. By F. Mabel Robinson.
ELI'S CHILDREN. By G. Manville Fenn.
A DOUBLE KNOT. By G. Manville Fenn.
DISARMED. By M. Betham Edwards.
A MARRIAGE AT SEA. By W. Clark Russell.
IN TENT AND BUNGALOW. By the Author of 'Indian Idylls.'

MY STEWARDSHIP. By E. M'QUEEN GRAY.
JACK'S FATHER. By W. E. NORRIS.
JIM B.
A LOST ILLUSION. By LESLIE KEITH.

Lynn Linton. THE TRUE HISTORY OF JOSHUA DAVID-SON, Christian and Communist. By E. LYNN LINTON. *Eleventh Edition. Post 8vo.* 1s.

Books for Boys and Girls

A Series of Books by well-known Authors, well illustrated.

THREE-AND-SIXPENCE EACH

THE ICELANDER'S SWORD. By S. BARING GOULD.
TWO LITTLE CHILDREN AND CHING. By EDITH E. CUTHELL.
TODDLEBEN'S HERO. By M. M. BLAKE.
ONLY A GUARD-ROOM DOG. By EDITH E. CUTHELL.
THE DOCTOR OF THE JULIET. By HARRY COLLING-WOOD.
MASTER ROCKAFELLAR'S VOYAGE. By W. CLARK RUSSELL.
SYD BELTON: Or, The Boy who would not go to Sea. By G. MANVILLE FENN.
THE WALLYPUG IN LONDON. By G. E. FARROW.

The Peacock Library

A Series of Books for Girls by well-known Authors, handsomely bound in blue and silver, and well illustrated.

THREE-AND-SIXPENCE EACH

A PINCH OF EXPERIENCE. By L. B. WALFORD.
THE RED GRANGE. By Mrs. MOLESWORTH.
THE SECRET OF MADAME DE MONLUC. By the Author of 'Mdle Mori.'
DUMPS. By Mrs. PARR, Author of 'Adam and Eve.'
OUT OF THE FASHION. By L. T. MEADE.
A GIRL OF THE PEOPLE. By L. T. MEADE.
HEPSY GIPSY. By L. T. MEADE. 2s. 6d.
THE HONOURABLE MISS. By L. T. MEADE.
MY LAND OF BEULAH. By Mrs. LEITH ADAMS.

University Extension Series

A series of books on historical, literary, and scientific subjects, suitable for extension students and home-reading circles. Each volume is complete in itself, and the subjects are treated by competent writers in a broad and philosophic spirit.

Edited by J. E. SYMES, M.A.,
Principal of University College, Nottingham.

Crown 8vo. Price (with some exceptions) 2s. 6d.

The following volumes are ready :—

THE INDUSTRIAL HISTORY OF ENGLAND. By H. DE B. GIBBINS, D.Litt., M.A., late Scholar of Wadham College, Oxon., Cobden Prizeman. *Fifth Edition, Revised. With Maps and Plans.* 3s.

'A compact and clear story of our industrial development. A study of this concise but luminous book cannot fail to give the reader a clear insight into the principal phenomena of our industrial history. The editor and publishers are to be congratulated on this first volume of their venture, and we shall look with expectant interest for the succeeding volumes of the series.'—*University Extension Journal.*

A HISTORY OF ENGLISH POLITICAL ECONOMY. By L. L. PRICE, M.A., Fellow of Oriel College, Oxon. *Second Edition.*

PROBLEMS OF POVERTY: An Inquiry into the Industrial Conditions of the Poor. By J. A. HOBSON, M.A. *Third Edition.*

VICTORIAN POETS. By A. SHARP.

THE FRENCH REVOLUTION. By J. E. SYMES, M.A.

PSYCHOLOGY. By F. S. GRANGER, M.A. *Second Edition.*

THE EVOLUTION OF PLANT LIFE: Lower Forms. By G. MASSEE. *With Illustrations.*

AIR AND WATER. By V. B. LEWES, M.A. *Illustrated.*

THE CHEMISTRY OF LIFE AND HEALTH. By C. W. KIMMINS, M.A. *Illustrated.*

THE MECHANICS OF DAILY LIFE. By V. P. SELLS, M.A. *Illustrated.*

ENGLISH SOCIAL REFORMERS. By H. DE B. GIBBINS, D.Litt., M.A.

ENGLISH TRADE AND FINANCE IN THE SEVENTEENTH CENTURY. By W. A. S. HEWINS, B.A.

THE CHEMISTRY OF FIRE. The Elementary Principles of Chemistry. By M. M. PATTISON MUIR, M.A. *Illustrated.*

A TEXT-BOOK OF AGRICULTURAL BOTANY. By M. C. POTTER, M.A., F.L.S. *Illustrated.* 3s. 6d.

THE VAULT OF HEAVEN. A Popular Introduction to Astronomy. By R. A. GREGORY. *With numerous Illustrations.*

METEOROLOGY. The Elements of Weather and Climate. By H. N. DICKSON, F.R.S.E., F.R. Met. Soc. *Illustrated.*

A MANUAL OF ELECTRICAL SCIENCE. By GEORGE J. BURCH, M.A. *With numerous Illustrations.* 3s.

THE EARTH. An Introduction to Physiography. By EVAN SMALL, M.A. *Illustrated.*

INSECT LIFE. By F. W. THEOBALD, M.A. *Illustrated.*

ENGLISH POETRY FROM BLAKE TO BROWNING. By W. M. DIXON, M.A.

ENGLISH LOCAL GOVERNMENT. By E. JENKS, M.A., Professor of Law at University College, Liverpool.

THE GREEK VIEW OF LIFE. By G. L. DICKINSON, Fellow of King's College, Cambridge. *Second Edition.*

Social Questions of To-day

Edited by H. DE B. GIBBINS, D.Litt., M.A.

Crown 8vo. 2s. 6d.

A series of volumes upon those topics of social, economic, and industrial interest that are at the present moment foremost in the public mind. Each volume of the series is written by an author who is an acknowledged authority upon the subject with which he deals.

The following Volumes of the Series are ready :—

TRADE UNIONISM—NEW AND OLD. By G. HOWELL. *Second Edition.*

THE CO-OPERATIVE MOVEMENT TO-DAY. By G. J. HOLYOAKE, *Second Edition.*

MUTUAL THRIFT. By Rev. J. FROME WILKINSON, M.A.

PROBLEMS OF POVERTY. By J. A. HOBSON, M.A. *Third Edition.*

THE COMMERCE OF NATIONS. By C. F. BASTABLE, M.A., Professor of Economics at Trinity College, Dublin.

THE ALIEN INVASION. By W. H. WILKINS, B.A.

THE RURAL EXODUS. By P. ANDERSON GRAHAM.

LAND NATIONALIZATION. By HAROLD COX, B.A.

A SHORTER WORKING DAY. By H. DE B. GIBBINS, D.Litt., M.A., and R. A. HADFIELD, of the Hecla Works, Sheffield.

BACK TO THE LAND: An Inquiry into the Cure for Rural Depopulation By H. E. MOORE.

TRUSTS, POOLS AND CORNERS. By J. STEPHEN JEANS.

THE FACTORY SYSTEM. By R. W. COOKE-TAYLOR.

THE STATE AND ITS CHILDREN. By GERTRUDE TUCKWELL.

WOMEN'S WORK. By LADY DILKE, Miss BULLEY, and Miss WHITLEY.

MUNICIPALITIES AT WORK. The Municipal Policy of Six Great Towns, and its Influence on their Social Welfare. By FREDERICK DOLMAN.

SOCIALISM AND MODERN THOUGHT. By M. KAUFMANN.

THE HOUSING OF THE WORKING CLASSES. By E. BOWMAKER.

MODERN CIVILIZATION IN SOME OF ITS ECONOMIC ASPECTS. By W. CUNNINGHAM, D.D., Fellow of Trinity College, Cambridge.

THE PROBLEM OF THE UNEMPLOYED. By J. A. HOBSON, B.A.,

LIFE IN WEST LONDON. By ARTHUR SHERWELL, M.A. *Second Edition.*

RAILWAY NATIONALIZATION. By CLEMENT EDWARDS.

Classical Translations

Edited by H. F. FOX, M.A., Fellow and Tutor of Brasenose College, Oxford.

ÆSCHYLUS—Agamemnon, Chöephoroe, Eumenides. Translated by LEWIS CAMPBELL, LL.D., late Professor of Greek at St. Andrews, 5s.

CICERO—De Oratore I. Translated by E. N. P. MOOR, M.A. 3s. 6d.

CICERO — Select Orations (Pro Milone, Pro Murena, Philippic II., In Catilinam). Translated by H. E. D. BLAKISTON, M.A., Fellow and Tutor of Trinity College, Oxford. 5s.

CICERO—De Natura Deorum. Translated by F. BROOKS, M.A., late Scholar of Balliol College, Oxford. 3s. 6d.

LUCIAN—Six Dialogues (Nigrinus, Icaro-Menippus, The Cock, The Ship, The Parasite, The Lover of Falsehood). Translated by S. T. IRWIN, M.A., Assistant Master at Clifton; late Scholar of Exeter College, Oxford. 3s. 6d.

SOPHOCLES—Electra and Ajax. Translated by E. D. A. MORSHEAD, M.A., Assistant Master at Winchester. 2s. 6d.

TACITUS—Agricola and Germania. Translated by R. B. TOWNSHEND, late Scholar of Trinity College, Cambridge. 2s. 6d.

Educational Books

CLASSICAL

PLAUTI BACCHIDES. Edited with Introduction, Commentary, and Critical Notes by J. M'COSH, M.A. *Fcap. 4to.* 12s. 6d.
'The notes are copious, and contain a great deal of information that is good and useful.'—*Classical Review.*

TACITI AGRICOLI. With Introduction, Notes, Map, etc. By R. F. DAVIS, M.A., Assistant Master at Weymouth College. *Crown 8vo.* 2s.

TACITI GERMANIA. By the same Editor. *Crown 8vo.* 2s.

HERODOTUS: EASY SELECTIONS. With Vocabulary. By A. C. LIDDELL, M.A. *Fcap. 8vo.* 1s. 6d.

SELECTIONS FROM THE ODYSSEY. By E. D. STONE, M.A., late Assistant Master at Eton. *Fcap. 8vo. 1s. 6d.*

PLAUTUS: THE CAPTIVI. Adapted for Lower Forms by J. H. FRESSE, M.A., late Fellow of St. John's, Cambridge. *1s. 6d.*

DEMOSTHENES AGAINST CONON AND CALLICLES. Edited with Notes and Vocabulary, by F. DARWIN SWIFT, M.A., formerly Scholar of Queen's College, Oxford. *Fcap. 8vo. 2s.*

EXERCISES ON LATIN ACCIDENCE. By S. E. WINBOLT, Assistant Master at Christ's Hospital. *Crown 8vo. 1s. 6d.*

An elementary book adapted for Lower Forms to accompany the shorter Latin primer.
'Skilfully arranged.'—*Glasgow Herald.*
'Accurate and well arranged.'—*Athenæum.*

NOTES ON GREEK AND LATIN SYNTAX. By G. BUCKLAND GREEN, M.A., Assistant Master at Edinburgh Academy, late Fellow of St. John's College, Oxon. *Crown 8vo. 3s. 6d.*

Notes and explanations on the chief difficulties of Greek and Latin Syntax, with numerous passages for exercise.
'Supplies a gap in educational literature.'—*Glasgow Herald.*

GERMAN

A COMPANION GERMAN GRAMMAR. By H. DE B. GIBBINS, D.Litt., M.A., Assistant Master at Nottingham High School. *Crown 8vo. 1s. 6d.*

GERMAN PASSAGES FOR UNSEEN TRANSLATION. By E. M'QUEEN GRAY. *Crown 8vo. 2s. 6d.*

SCIENCE

THE WORLD OF SCIENCE. Including Chemistry, Heat, Light, Sound, Magnetism, Electricity, Botany, Zoology, Physiology, Astronomy, and Geology. By R. ELLIOTT STEEL, M.A., F.C.S. 147 Illustrations. *Second Edition. Crown 8vo. 2s. 6d.*

ELEMENTARY LIGHT. By R. E. STEEL. With numerous Illustrations. *Crown 8vo. 4s. 6d.*

ENGLISH

ENGLISH RECORDS. A Companion to the History of England. By H. E. MALDEN, M.A. *Crown 8vo. 3s. 6d.*

A book which aims at concentrating information upon dates, genealogy, officials, constitutional documents, etc., which is usually found scattered in different volumes.

THE ENGLISH CITIZEN: HIS RIGHTS AND DUTIES. By H. E. MALDEN, M.A. *1s. 6d.*

A DIGEST OF DEDUCTIVE LOGIC. By JOHNSON BARKER, B.A. *Crown 8vo. 2s. 6d.*

METHUEN'S COMMERCIAL SERIES

Edited by H. DE B. GIBBINS, D.Litt., M.A.

BRITISH COMMERCE AND COLONIES FROM ELIZABETH TO VICTORIA. By H. DE B. GIBBINS, D.Litt., M.A. 2s. *Second Edition.*

COMMERCIAL EXAMINATION PAPERS. By H. DE B. GIBBINS, D.Litt., M.A., 1s. 6d.

THE ECONOMICS OF COMMERCE. By H. DE B. GIBBINS, D.Litt., M.A. 1s. 6d.

FRENCH COMMERCIAL CORRESPONDENCE. By S. E. BALLY, Modern Language Master at the Manchester Grammar School. 2s. *Second Edition.*

GERMAN COMMERCIAL CORRESPONDENCE. By S. E. BALLY, 2s. 6d.

A FRENCH COMMERCIAL READER. By S. E. BALLY. 2s.

COMMERCIAL GEOGRAPHY, with special reference to the British Empire. By L. W. LYDE, M.A., of the Academy, Glasgow. 2s. *Second Edition.*

A PRIMER OF BUSINESS. By S. JACKSON, M.A. 1s. 6d.

COMMERCIAL ARITHMETIC. By F. G. TAYLOR, M.A. 1s. 6d.

PRÉCIS WRITING AND OFFICE CORRESPONDENCE. By E. E. WHITFIELD, M.A. 2s.

WORKS BY A. M. M. STEDMAN, M.A.

INITIA LATINA: Easy Lessons on Elementary Accidence. *Second Edition.* Fcap. 8vo. 1s.

FIRST LATIN LESSONS. *Fourth Edition. Crown 8vo.* 2s.

FIRST LATIN READER. With Notes adapted to the Shorter Latin Primer and Vocabulary. *Fourth Edition revised.* 18mo. 1s. 6d.

EASY SELECTIONS FROM CAESAR. Part I. The Helvetian War. 18mo. 1s.

EASY SELECTIONS FROM LIVY. Part I. The Kings of Rome. 18mo. 1s. 6d.

EASY LATIN PASSAGES FOR UNSEEN TRANSLATION. *Fifth Edition.* Fcap. 8vo. 1s. 6d.

EXEMPLA LATINA. First Lessons in Latin Accidence. With Vocabulary. Crown 8vo. 1s.

EASY LATIN EXERCISES ON THE SYNTAX OF THE SHORTER AND REVISED LATIN PRIMER. With Vocabulary. *Seventh and cheaper Edition re-written. Crown 8vo.* 1s. 6d. Issued with the consent of Dr. Kennedy.

THE LATIN COMPOUND SENTENCE: Rules and Exercises. *Crown 8vo.* 1s. 6d. With Vocabulary. 2s.

NOTANDA QUAEDAM: Miscellaneous Latin Exercises on Common Rules and Idioms. *Third Edition. Fcap. 8vo.* 1s. 6d. With Vocabulary. 2s.

LATIN VOCABULARIES FOR REPETITION: Arranged according to Subjects. *Sixth Edition. Fcap. 8vo.* 1s. 6d.

A VOCABULARY OF LATIN IDIOMS AND PHRASES. 18mo. *Second Edition.* 1s.

STEPS TO GREEK. 18mo. 1s.

EASY GREEK PASSAGES FOR UNSEEN TRANSLATION. *Second Edition.* Fcap. 8vo. 1s. 6d.

GREEK VOCABULARIES FOR REPETITION. Arranged according to Subjects. *Second Edition.* Fcap. 8vo. 1s. 6d.

GREEK TESTAMENT SELECTIONS. For the use of Schools. *Third Edition.* With Introduction, Notes, and Vocabulary. Fcap. 8vo. 2s. 6d.

STEPS TO FRENCH. *Second Edition.* 18mo. 8d.

FIRST FRENCH LESSONS. *Second Edition.* Crown 8vo. 1s.

EASY FRENCH PASSAGES FOR UNSEEN TRANSLATION. *Third Edition revised.* Fcap. 8vo. 1s. 6d.

EASY FRENCH EXERCISES ON ELEMENTARY SYNTAX. With Vocabulary. *Second Edition.* Crown 8vo. 2s. 6d.

FRENCH VOCABULARIES FOR REPETITION : Arranged according to Subjects. *Sixth Edition.* Fcap. 8vo. 1s.

SCHOOL EXAMINATION SERIES

EDITED BY A. M. M. STEDMAN, M.A. *Crown 8vo.* 2s. 6d.

FRENCH EXAMINATION PAPERS IN MISCELLANEOUS GRAMMAR AND IDIOMS. By A. M. M. STEDMAN, M.A. *Ninth Edition.* A KEY, issued to Tutors and Private Students only, to be had on application to the Publishers. *Fourth Edition.* Crown 8vo. 6s. net.

LATIN EXAMINATION PAPERS IN MISCELLANEOUS GRAMMAR AND IDIOMS. By A. M. M. STEDMAN, M.A. *Eighth Edition.* KEY (*Third Edition*) issued as above. 6s. net.

GREEK EXAMINATION PAPERS IN MISCELLANEOUS GRAMMAR AND IDIOMS. By A. M. M. STEDMAN, M.A. *Fifth Edition.* KEY (*Second Edition*) issued as above. 6s. net.

GERMAN EXAMINATION PAPERS IN MISCELLANEOUS GRAMMAR AND IDIOMS. By R. J. MORICH, Manchester. *Fifth Edition.* KEY (*Second Edition*) issued as above. 6s. net.

HISTORY AND GEOGRAPHY EXAMINATION PAPERS. By C. H. SPENCE, M.A., Clifton College. *Second Edition.*

SCIENCE EXAMINATION PAPERS. By R. E. STEEL, M.A., F.C.S., Chief Natural Science Master, Bradford Grammar School. *In two vols.* Part I. Chemistry ; Part II. Physics.

GENERAL KNOWLEDGE EXAMINATION PAPERS. By A. M. M. STEDMAN, M.A. *Third Edition.* KEY (*Second Edition*) issued as above. 7s. net.

www.ingramcontent.com/pod-product-compliance
Lightning Source LLC
Chambersburg PA
CBHW030921050726
47498CB00003BA/841